# THE PUBLICAN

# AND

# THE PASTORALIST

PETER & LEONORE MORTON

Front Cover Image: Bronco Panel at Mount Leonard Station.
Photo: Peter Morton

Back Cover Image: Royal Hotel and former Australian Inland Mission Hospital
at Birdsville
Heritage branch staff, CC BY 3.0
<https://creativecommons.org/licenses/by/3.0>, via Wikimedia Commons

# DEDICATION

To Phillip and Christine Stain, great friends of ours since we were children as individuals and as a couple for the last forty years. We have enjoyed the many trips we have made together, especially the two to Mount Leonard Station, both memorable but for different reasons.

This book is dedicated to you both.

You have faced many tough challenges and now both of you have to do it again. Thanks for the memories and we hope there will be many more.

# TUCKER FAMILY TREE

William Albert Goodson TUCKER
B: 1859 Ballarat
D: 1890 Birdsville

M: 1886 Birdsville

Susana Josephine HONAN
B: 1858 Country Clare, Ireland
D: 1915 Jamestown

---

May TUCKER
B: 1887 Birdsville
D: 1973 Sydney
(Sister Dolorosa)

Frederick Leslie TUCKER
B: 1888 Ballarat
D: 1918 Hindenberg Line

Alberta Jessamine TUCKER
B: 1894 Birdsville
D: 1956 Glen Osmond

M: 1915 Windorah

John James SCOTT
B: 1882 Kersbrook
D: 1928 Diamantina River

---

Leonard
B: 1914 Adelaide
D: 1944 Ambon

Mary
B: 1915 Adelaide
D: 1987 Adelaide

Jean
B: 1916 Mount Leonard
D: 1996 Adelaide
M: 1942 Michael SULLIVAN

Clare
B: 1918 Adelaide
D: 2001 Adelaide

Frederick
B: 1920 Long Reach
D: 1974 Adelaide

---

Susan
B: 1943
D: 2008

Leonore
B: 1946

Tim
B: 1948
D: 2006

Jacqueline
B: 1950

Michael Jnr
B: 1951

John
B: 1953

Simon
B: 1956

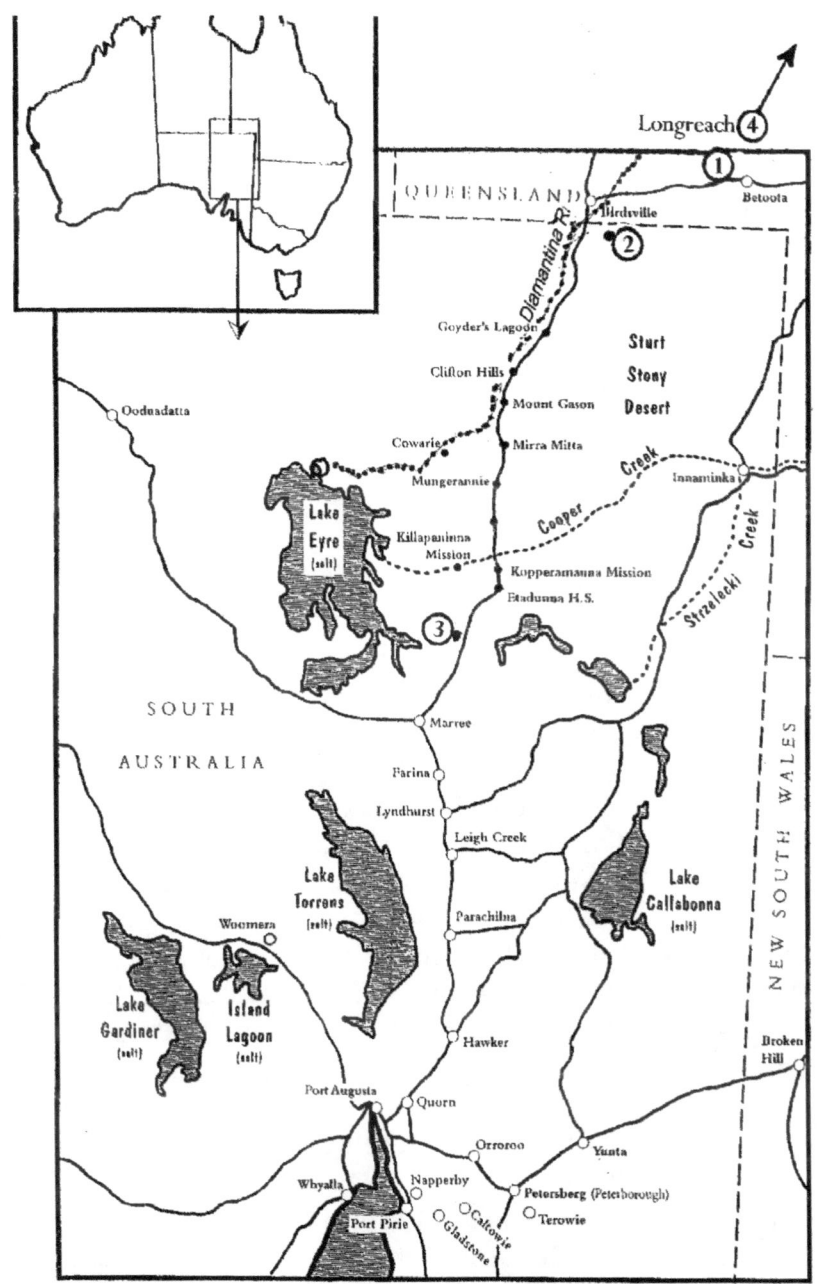

① Mount Leonard ② Miranda ③ Dulkaninna ④ Longreach

# CONTENTS

# FOREWORD

This historical novel is about Leonore's great grandmother Susana Honan born in 1858 in Co Clare, Ireland. Amidst the chaos, fear, despair and uncertainty of post famine Ireland, she emigrated to Australia in 1877, arriving in Brisbane in 1878 on the steel clipper *Gauntlet.* She made her way to Birdsville where she married William Tucker in 1886. It is also about her daughter Alberta, Leonore's well-remembered Nana, who married the manager and part owner of Mount Leonard Station.

Susana's husband built, owned, and ran The Royal Hotel in Birdsville from 1884-1886 only 20 or so years after the Burke and Wills expedition and later managed Tattersalls Hotel where he died in 1890. Susana managed Tattersalls on and off until 1912, helped in the latter years by Alberta. They both suffered immeasurable tragedies in their lives but survived. It likely reflects the life stories of many women of the Australian outback in those times.

This is not a research paper. Rather it is a work of historical fiction. Hopefully, it reminds readers of who and what went before us and how lucky we are.

## FURTHER READING

For those interested in further reading I recommend:

*Sand Hills and Channel Country Carolyn Nolan. Published by the Diamantina Shire Council.*

*The Great Shame. Thomas Keneally. Random House Australia.* This was invaluable for the section on Irish Life.

*Tin Mosques and Ghan towns. Christine Stevens. Oxford University Press* The seminal work on the Afghan Camel drivers in Australia.

*Marree and the tracks beyond in black and white. Lois Litchfield Box 343 Quorn SA 5433. Digital Print Australia.*

*KidmanThe Forgotten King. Jill Bowen Angus and Robertson.* This is a fantastic book and showed multiple facets of his life and businesses that have not been published before. For anyone with an interest in this man it is a 'must read'.

*Mr Stuart's Track. John Bailey Picador.* The Channel Country rush and Birdsville rush would not have happened when it did had Stuart not paved the way for the telegraph the railway followed.

*Life in the Country. Australia in the Victorian Age 2. Michael Cannon. Nelson.* A scholarly work of great interest for the Warwick section. Rolf Boldrewood is cited ten times commenting about contentious issues at various times.

### IMPERIAL WEIGHTS AND MEASURES

As this is an historical novel about people and events that occurred when the imperial system of weights and measures was in use, I have included some relevant metric equivalents below.

One mile is approximately 1.64 kilometres.
One pound is approximately 0.45 kilograms.
100 points, or one inch of rain, is approximately 25ml.

# BOOK 1

# FROM

# IRELAND

# TO AUSTRALIA

*Susana Honan*

# 1

# Susana Honan

# – Childhood

I was born in 1858 in Kildysart, County Clare, Ireland. My father was John Honan born in 1821 and mother Deliah Walsh born in 1823. I had a sister, Catherine, five years older than me.

My parents owned an acre of land with a hotel and a cottage on the northern side of the River Shannon estuary. Our property was large enough to grow vegetables for ourselves, the hotel patrons and sometimes others. We also had chickens and a cow. The chickens were for scratching around and eating insects, for eggs and a rare treat to eat at Christmas and the cow for milk. The animals also gave us manure to mix with seaweed for the vegetables. Catherine and I spent hours as children helping Da in the garden and learned to milk early in life.

We helped Ma with washing, ironing, cleaning, collecting wood, peat and gorse, cooking, mending clothes, feeding animals at home and cooking and cleaning in the hotel.

Our family attended church on Sundays and walked home through meadows that, at the right time of the year, were awash with the smell and colour of flowers. This made me happy and feel close to God. Sometimes we walked along the estuary or the banks of the river for pleasure and always took our warmest clothes because the winds off the North Atlantic would freeze a gull in flight as my grand da used to say.

My da told me that, as a boy, he used to think the winds kept Kildysart free of plant and human disease but a tear or two ran down his cheeks as if life had taught him different. This puzzled me but Da was often given to quiet, thoughtful and sad moods. I was a curious child and asked Ma and Da endless questions about the countryside, nature and our world and they always answered me as best they could. I was much loved and had a happy, well-fed childhood.

Ireland had long been called the Land of Saints and Scholars and my family respected and followed this tradition. In 1835 the National Education Scheme was introduced and Catherine and I attended the National School in Kildysart from the ages of six to twelve. At school and in Church I heard about the English overlords, plague and famine in the bible and in Ireland and the sufferings of saints. I didn't want to think about these horrible things as my life was so nice but I soon found appalling truths there as well.

One day, when we were about ten, my friend Mary and I were exploring near our house and found mounds of earth marked with wooden crosses. That night, by the fire I asked Da about the graves. For the first time he told Catherine and me, in some detail, about the Great Irish Famine and the damage it had done to the fabric and people of Ireland. He was almost twenty when the loss of people from starvation, disease and fleeing Ireland forever to save the lives of themselves and their children was noticeable.

I was to learn that it was hard to find anyone in Ireland who had not lost a family member, a loved one, a close friend or all three. Da looked into the fire and then at Catherine and me and told us, almost choking on the words, that the graves were those of our neighbours.

The parents, dying of famine fever, in desperation, had sent their oldest child and his only surviving sister on a long walk to where they might get some food. Da found him walking along the road carrying a bag containing her little body and not knowing what to do or where to go as he had been turned away from a church. Da took him home and later he and his da buried the dead. They looked after the little boy until they found a relative willing to care for him.

Da was a gentle and kind man but burned with anger when he told us this ghastly story. He almost keened his grief and anger. 'If you had money you had the church behind you; lived well and died well, if not you lived a pauper's life and had a pauper's grave.'

Da said, 'It was abhorrent. It was repulsive. Quarries were summarily consecrated as burial places and bodies were thrown in and covered with lime. Only about half of the hundreds of thousands who died had a proper burial.'

One family he had known had to sell their donkey to buy food. Then they had to pull their cart of turf they cut for a living with an obvious end sooner or later.

Da described, 'A land full of nothing. No love. No food. No kindness. The best that people could hope for was a quick exit. To paradise, if lucky.'

Da said that his and Ma's families had suffered but not to the extent others did by any means although he did wonder whether only having two live children from four pregnancies may have been the cross they had to bear from the Famine.

We were very fortunate with the food we grew or were allowed to gather like collected seaweed, blown or washed onto the beaches, by the westerly winds off the Atlantic Ocean as it was very good fertiliser for potatoes. A handful of seaweed and one seed potato in one hole was the ancient Celtic custom we followed.

3

The sea and river were good for the soul and for the body. Mussels, periwinkles, cockles and eels could be gathered or caught and were very nutritious. Peppery watercress grew in the streams with other edible bulbs and fleshy leaves and there was Irish moss, a seaweed, Da said, 'Was a miracle from God.' It was sad that people had to eat it, but the goodness it provided, particularly after being soaked in cider vinegar, saved countless lives during the Great Famine and other tough times. We ate it every New Year's Day in gratitude for its powers and in hope for the year to come.

The conversation that evening changed the way I thought about life in general and mine forever. I learned much about the past and became even more confused, at times, about the history of Ireland and the English. The fighting and hatred seemed to have gone on forever. It was like peeling an onion as there was always another layer. I read books and pestered my parents, friends, school and church to help me find some meaning from the chaos. I became so enthusiastic in this task that Da called me 'Herring Gull', the local pest that bothered everyone searching here and there for scraps. I was cross but did smile at the comment.

In my last year at school we learned that the Irish troubles began when an army led by the deposed King of England, James the second and his Irish Catholic followers suffered a terrible defeat by the Protestant army of William of Orange, James's son-in-law, at the Battle of Boyne River in 1690.

In an attempt to ensure that Catholics did not rise again penal laws were legislated to keep 'Irish natives, powerless, poor and stupid' and there was religious persecution until the cancelled priesthood was legalised in 1782. Catholics could not hold legal, government or military positions or live in walled cities. That effectively stopped children going to school until emancipation in

1829.

Unsurprisingly, secret societies of young men grew to prevent land being taken away from tenants, often themselves, and other injustices. There were the Whiteboys, Rockites, Ribbon Societies and undoubtedly more. Many members of these societies were caught, imprisoned, transported or even hanged, sometimes in front of their very family. Some of those transported were recognised as political prisoners and later released in Australia and treated as 'ticket of leave' prisoners.

Ireland loved anti-heroes and people like convicted felon and prison escapee Lawrence Kavanagh from Waterford County who was transported to Australia in 1838 and ultimately hanged at Norfolk Island. He, with Martin Cash from Wrexford, like so many, 'graduated' to become a highwayman, known as a bushranger, in Australia. After many years in prison Cash was said to have been the only bushranger to die in his bed and one of the few to dictate his life story and have it published. The best known of the Convict Outlaws was 'Bold' Jack Donohoe, who arrived in Botany Bay, from Dublin, in 1825. He was a 'Robin Hood', literally robbing the rich to give to the poor. He was shot by the police as he screamed abuse and died a loved and admired man when he was twenty three. He was known as 'The Wild Colonial Boy' and a song of that name was written and sung in Ireland and Australia. I was very excited to find out about this man because I had heard the song in our hotel. These men lived and died long before I was born. Most bushrangers were cruel, hard and merciless and lived short brutal lives often betrayed by their fellows. There was little honour amongst these thieves.

Some people suggested that England so feared the common man who wanted political influence and freedom of thought, that minor criminals and political rebels were treated very harshly.

Capital punishment was common, as was transportation to Australia, a cruel and degrading punishment. For the great majority it meant that the return journey to their family and home would be impossible. Writers even described England's harsh policies and practices as being at war with their own people in response to fears that revolutions would occur in Great Britain and Ireland as in the United States of America and France.

Transportation to Tasmania and New South Wales started in 1788 and stopped in those colonies in 1853 and in Western Australia in 1868. This was widely and joyously publicised in Ireland. My uncle gave me a pretty little notebook with a bright green shamrock on the cover for my tenth birthday where he had recorded the end of transportation to Australia. It was so special.

The next exodus to Australia was during the Great Irish Famine from 1841-45 and following it, another in response to the gold rushes in the 1850s in New South Wales and then Victoria. The reasons for the Irish going to Australia had changed from 1788 to 1858 when I was born, and I soon found out they would change again in my lifetime.

# 2
# Susana Honan
# – Growing Up

I enjoyed school, making new friends, the play and games, the challenge of learning to read and write and the history and traditions of our land. I learned to play the piano and tin whistle, joined the choir and proudly sang in church. My teachers and our priest were pleased with me. I had learned to read and write and I was often asked to help other children who were ill, miserable, or not coping with school. I enjoyed and was proud to do this particularly when the parents thanked me and even gave me a little present or a card sometimes.

I was excited about leaving school when I was twelve to prepare for my life as a woman in an Irish world and knew about my duties at home, in the community, church and helping Da, Ma and Catherine. My family, church, relatives and community were an inseparable whole. I was pleased that I did not have to leave home because there was a baby taking my bed as happened in many homes in Ireland. I might have had to go to a convent, find a position in a big house, be a dairy maid or something else. I was so lucky.

Like all Irish girls I learned where babies came from, how they got there and what happened when they were born, both good and bad. I was very close to Ma and Catherine and grateful that my questions about my body changing were answered frankly. When I was fourteen, I had my first monthly bleeding and celebrated with my parents and sister. I had an uninformed friend who was terrified when it happened to her and ran screaming to her mother. She was given some cloths and told to keep away from boys.

After that happened Ma explained more about the role of women in Irish society. All parents had to provide food, drink, shelter for children but to the mothers fell the task of providing comfort and reassurance to sick, injured or frightened children, neighbours and even strangers. I began to understand the glue that held our world together, what it meant to be Irish and an Irish woman at that. My grandma had passed Irish lore to my ma who now passed this tradition to me. Nothing was more important than the care of the family in the narrow and broad sense.

Once a week Ma, often with us girls, would call on friends, relatives, fellow parishioners and sometimes strangers. She would take food, flowers, read to people or just chat. If they were ill, Ma would have some herbs or medicine. I soon realised that the hotel and garden provided herbs and food that others did not have and was always thankful in my private prayers and at Mass that we could help others.

We Irish girls and women were well prepared when medicines were needed. There were herbs such as parsley, sage, rosemary, thyme and lavender. Friar's Balsam, lemon, vinegar, honey and borax were used as drinks, gargles, inhalations and embrocation. Extracts were made from willow tree bark and used for pain and fever, from the foxglove for the treatment of dropsy and the leaves of comfrey as a compress for injuries and as a medicine for colds and fevers. One of the many names for comfrey was 'knit-bone' a testament to its benefits. It was necessary to lance boils, dress wounds and prepare salves for burns and skin complaints including persistent warts, help with constipation, the opposite and many other complaints. A distant relative, Mary Sullivan, was wise in these matters. Perhaps the most important thing she told us was that peeling potatoes was throwing away goodness. Our family followed her rules for life.

I was indoctrinated to keep the kitchen table free and clean because if men were hurt that was where they would be treated; a frightening, daunting and common occurrence. Ma gave me that responsibility and I always cleared and cleaned the table after it was used for meals, sewing, writing or any other activity.

Some women developed great skill in the healing arts and travelled far and wide. People 'took the waters' particularly those with a holy connotation, either by themselves or with a healer. Some healers made little caves with rocks, peat and grass and treated people for a variety of muscle and joint troubles. They did this by heating rocks and putting them either on another rock or in a pail of water to provide dry or moist heat. Massage was also used as were bandages and splints.

Women were expected to look after their families and friends with care, kindness and physical help such as warmth and cooling and herbal remedies. Travelling healers had advanced knowledge and skill and put great store in touching, kindness and love, not only their nostrums and physical treatments. I was learning.

We were superstitious about fairies, the best known being Leprechauns but there were Banshees whose screams warned of impending death, Pookas took the form of horses or goblins and frightened farmers so much that a share of the crop was left for them. There was Dullahan, the headless horseman and many others. They were a far cry from the delicate little girl creatures that babies laughed with and lavender attracted.

Our family were Christians and rejected these beliefs but it was easy to fear these spirits on a cold and foggy night. The most powerful and harmful belief was the concept of changelings. People believed that fairies had babies in a human form but often, if those babies were sick or deformed, the fairies swapped them for human babies.

This had a twofold affect. Irish mothers were fiercely protective of their own children but it was not uncommon for a mentally or physically ill or deformed child to be left outside for the fairies to take him or her back.

I happened to write to a friend in Australia and mentioned that a changeling had been left to die nearby. Her reply was: 'They don't go for that nasty fairy stuff over here.' I remembered that because, deep down in the primitive part of my being, I was afraid of fairies and the inference that fairies did not live in Australia was something I tucked away in my memory box.

Catherine helped in the house and hotel but also worked part time in the local school. Catherine loved parties, dressing up and meeting people. One day she met a Sinan McInerney at a race meeting. He was a handsome man with a personality that glowed and very soon they were seeing more of each other.

Sinan worked for the company that operated the little ships that travelled from Limerick to Kildysart and he wore his splendid uniform with self-assurance. Catherine was smitten despite him being in his late twenties. They spent every spare minute together, but this pleasure was interrupted when he was transferred from Kildysart to Limerick with the same company but with added responsibility for the fast spreading railways.

He still made trips to Kildysart and soon they became engaged and married at an appropriate time when family and church requirements were met. Catherine was 18 and Sinan 29. Their wedding was held at our parents' hotel and in typical Irish fashion celebrated long and late. The next day they departed for their new life in Limerick.

I had known Sinan's brother, Seamus for years but our friendship blossomed along with Catherine and Sinan's. Soon he was the only boy for me and vice versa. I was sixteen with auburn hair, clear fair skin, slim but strong and about five feet four inches tall and eight stone in weight. Seamus was five feet six inches and nine stone with blue black hair and lovely skin. We were not betrothed but soon both our families had an understanding that we would marry when I was twenty.

I knew some things about sexual activities and their variations between girls and boys, but they were not something I wished to explore particularly with the abrupt, insensitive, coarse and unromantic lot I knew. Seamus was different; never a robust lad he liked music, reading, walks in the countryside and quiet moments. We went to the same church, enjoyed family picnics, collected shell fish, watched birds, sang in the choir and played the piano together.

Love is said to be blind and although Seamus had told me that he had suffered 'the rheumatics' as a child and was left with bad joints and a damaged heart I accepted this as being part of him and enjoyed his company so much I could not bear to dwell on what might be because I knew children who had died from that complaint.

We had a fine friendship not full of fiery passion, but a relationship rooted in respect, simple pleasures and the company of each other. We became closer as the years passed and were inseparable from when I was seventeen.

I often felt I lived in a strange and inconsistent world. Most Irish teenagers knew the smell, sight and sounds of sexual activity.

Fornication though, was frowned upon and virginity expected of a bride and yet there were hundreds of highly emotional poems and songs that stretched the sexual tensions that existed in us young people, often to breaking point. Some of these were 'The Foggy, Foggy Dew,' 'She Lay Naked on Her Bed,' and 'A Young Man's Dream.' All known and sung by my friends and sometimes even me. My solace was the realisation that it was the way we were.

Da being a publican, like many in Ireland, often acted as an undertaker. This was common as there was no room in most houses to store bodies and hotels could also provide the liquor, food and facilities for the wake, so vital in Irish culture. Seamus and I and our parents were sober folk, but for many, a wake was a major social event and some turned into nothing less than debauchery. Seamus and I attended and helped at many funerals and were distressed by that sort of behaviour. It was said that 'Those who wanted to mourn could do so behind the screen hiding the body but, for everyone else, wakes were about drinking and courting'. This meant gross, visible and unseemly behaviour, by married and single people together and in groups at times. Once I saw a girl at the funeral of a person she did not know and asked her why she was there. She looked up at me, smiled knowingly and said 'Well me good friend the wake be for the drinkin' and the courtin' y'know,' and added, with a wink, 'but I ain't thirsty.'

Seamus and I, as would be expected, had sexual feeling for each other and shared pleasant interludes learning about each other in a patient, gentle and caring way. One beautiful, warm, soft summer evening we were alone on the bank of the Shannon River after church and I was feeling very different towards Seamus who had removed his shirt to wash some beetroot stains and then hung it on a bush to dry. I was wearing a light blouse.

We warmly embraced. I was breathing fast; my heart was

racing, and my face flushed. I had not felt like this before and softly kissed him. Seamus had a beautiful look on his face and breathed a little faster. I rested my head on his bare, thin chest for the first time and heard something that struck fear into my very marrow and I would remember forever. His heart sounded like a galloping horse and was making a whooshing noise as it beat. When he drew breath, it sounded like it was through water.

I lay there for a long time and remembered things I had noticed but never discussed with him. He had become short of breath more often and reluctant and slow to climb hills. On walks he removed and replaced his boots when we stopped for a rest. I realised now that his feet had been swollen. And he was thinner.

I then had the worst feeling in my life. A Banshee tore into my head and mind, and screamed three words, 'HE HAS DROPSY,' was silent and then, with a wail left me. It was all so obvious. I had been staring at it for months hiding in plain sight. I knew many people with that complaint from the community rounds and at church. To seal my suspicions, I also recalled that he frequently sipped from a bottle of foxglove essence, a treatment for that complaint. I had seen Ma make and give it to people countless times. It meant a heart was worn out and literally 'broken' and death did not long delay its claim on a sufferer. We cried, begged, prayed and cursed God, until we fell, exhausted, into each other's arms and slept.

We were late arriving home and Da and had stern words to Seamus that he accepted, apologised and left. The next day Seamus delivered a letter to Da. He wrote; 'Sir, not only did I not do anything improper, with or to Susana, but I cannot. Please forgive me but there is no future for us, my bad heart is failing and I fear the worst.' He was a kind, decent, lovely, gentle man. I thought and felt that my soul had been torn from my body by sadness, loss and guilt.

A month later, on his death bed, Seamus removed his mother's wedding ring he always wore and placed it on my right ring finger. In his impish way and giving the crooked smile, I so loved, he said, 'With the ring on that finger you will not scare away a suitor.' Holding that hand, he added 'God be with you. Travel well and love someone as I love you.' Soon, after he drew breath, he whispered 'I am so tired' and gently breathed his last. He was twenty three and I was nearly eighteen.

He was laid to rest covered with the scented blossoms of the whitethorn bush and other sweet summer flowers he lovedthat I had gathered through a veil of tears.

# 3
# Emigration Calls

I had long loved and was proud of the Ireland of my birth but with the death of Seamus and the fog of forgotten and remembered lost souls that still hung over the land from the Famine, evictions, politics and sectarian violence sorely troubled me, as did the fairies more than I liked to admit. Emigration had always been a negative thing to Irish people, but attitudes had rapidly changed. For many years it was a chance of life to leave but death to stay.

By the time I went to school, communications with Australia had improved in leaps and bounds. The telegraph allowed main news items to get to London almost instantly and to be distributed further in the same way, or by newspapers carried by trains, or even small ships, in our area from Limerick. Letters took two months between the two countries, a huge difference to the six months 50 years before.

There had been great interest in Kildysart parish and across Ireland about individuals and happenings in Australia as so many Irish people had been transported as convicts, left Ireland in the time of the famine or during the gold rushes. Many convicts who were granted tickets of leave worked at the goldfields at honest toil, but many plied their criminal talents as bushrangers making the roads to and from the goldfields dangerous. There was also a political element simmering at the diggings in that miners, often known as diggers, had to hold a special licence to prospect and mine, keep it on their person and present it when asked by the police. Inability to do this resulted in a fine and or imprisonment. It was perceived by the Irish to be an imposition directed at them by a government that favoured the upper classes.

Unsurprisingly the diggers, led by an Irishman Peter Lalor, protested by burning their licences and erecting a fortification, the Eureka Stockade, where they sought refuge. Twenty-two diggers and six soldiers were killed and many more injured when the police and soldiers attacked on 3rd December 1854. Da kept a newspaper cutting he later gave to me. It read: 'At the Eureka Stockade the battle for Constitutional recognition, democratic process and equality of opportunity in the transportation of the Scottish Chartists, the Tolpuddle unionists, the Irish revolutionists and the diaspora of the unwanted English criminal poor was lost but the war was eventually won.' There were far reaching consequences indeed in this new land of freedom.

Another spectacular news-worthy figure was Ned Kelly, born in Australia, but Catholic, Irish and loyal to his family to the core of his being. He was born in 1854 and went to gaol from 1871-1874 for horse stealing. He became a murderer, thief, great publicist, clever writer and one of the most talked about people in Australian history, hated and loved with equal passion.

I knew of both Lalor and Kelly and their deeds and could not help but muse at the sheer Irishness of the situation. One an outlaw, the other a Member of Parliament for 30 years. Strangely this bizarre situation made me feel comfortable that Australia would a good place for an Irish girl to make her home. Someone told me that 'Eureka' meant 'I have found it' and was supposedly first used by Archimedes when he learned to purify gold. When I was told that I stood in wonder shaking my head. This was yet another call and I tucked 'Eureka' into my box of thoughts.

Both parents encouraged my interest in Australia literally half a world away. By the time I was eighteen or nineteen the gold rushes were well and truly over, the bushrangers caught and the Famine receding from memories. Australia had only been settled by Europeans 70 years before I was born, a short time indeed compared to the centuries of culture, life and religion in Ireland and Europe It was still a place of intrigue, mystery, interest, promise and a journey there was not without some anxiety.

I knew that Irish farm hands and domestic workers were wanted and welcomed in Australia and that free or subsidised passage was available but, in the later part of the century, the majority of emigrants were voluntary and self-funded. My confidence grew as I read the countless positive references to Australian letters and newspaper reports. One letter I read in a newspaper and copied in my book was from a Michael Normile from County Clare to his father when he was 20.

He wrote:

*My dear father*

*I am to inform you that I received you welcomed letter on the 15th March dated January 15 which gave me and my sister an ocean of consolation to hear that you my Stepmother, Brothers and Sisters are in good health thank God. As for my uncles and Aunts {erased: you never mentioned a word about them but} I hope they are in good health too-at the same time, this leaves us in a perfect State of health thanks to our Blessed Redeemer for his goodness towards us.*

This was written before I was born, and he came from a part of County Clare that was sorely damaged by the famine. I read it when I was the same age as Michael at the time of writing and I was deeply moved by his courage and the importance he attached to his connection with home. I knew the letter was twenty years old and that cheered me because I knew there were many more

Irish people in Australia in the 1870s than then and the tidings were better year after year.

Soon after reading this letter I attended a farewell service and party to say goodbye to some neighbours who had been offered assisted passages and jobs as farmhands and domestic help in Queensland. They showed sketches that friends had drawn of the beaches and other scenery in Queensland to show how pleasant the weather was compared to Ireland and I knew well-paid jobs were available.

I walked home deep in thought. I was loved, cared for and enjoyed our home and helping in the hotel where I was gaining some skills in book-keeping and handling money but thought there could be more to life. When home I looked around through different eyes. There was a bedroom where the four of us had slept. Catherine furthest from the door, then me, Ma and Da with any visitors or relatives nearest the door. I reminded Da that the Vikings did not raid anymore since Brian Boru chased them off and they became Christian so they really did not need to continue this practice. He just smiled.

Our family was luckier than most with shutters on the windows and a fireplace with a chimney all built by Da. An Irishman's hearth was his castle where he and his family could be safe from the fear and suffering outside. The house was comfortable and with a chimney and windows there was warmth and fresh air and we were not half suffocated with peat smoke. The house was stone and there were straw mattresses and some night attire and blankets. The other room was the kitchen with a large fireplace with a tripod for pots and pans where gorse, peat or driftwood were burnt for cooking, heating and light.

There was a bath for washing people and anything else and chamber pots or pails that were tipped into a cesspit outside.

Whale oil was used in lamps instead of smelly and inefficient tallow 'slush' lamps and there was a degree of privacy at most times. This was home, but it was crowded and cold. Seamus's spirit was all pervading and the emptiness and sadness outside seeped through the walls and made me shiver, not only from the cold. All I could hope for was more of the same. I could not stop my thoughts turning to the sun, light and freedom of Queensland.

Next day I shared my thoughts and feelings with my family and they were both pleased and sad, as was I. Realistically this would separate us forever, a huge and frightening thing to consider. I also discussed this with my parish priest, Father Michael McMahon and a teacher I respected, Jane Moloney. They both welcomed and encouraged my decision as they had many positive letters from their parishioners and ex-pupils in Australia. Father McMahon confirmed that the Queensland government still made assisted or free travel available to emigrants who had trades or were men familiar with farm work or women with domestic work.

Father McMahon advised me to contact the Queensland agent in Dublin, gave me the address and kindly wrote a letter mentioning my fine character, morality and loyalty to family and the church at which I blushed crimson. As he closed the envelope he smiled and reminded me that County Clare, of all the Irish Counties, had provided the most emigrants to Australia so I would likely find a kindred group. Jane Moloney was also warm, friendly and helpful and offered me some extra tuition in bookkeeping and letter construction and suggested that I brush up on arithmetic and hand writing. I sat down there and then and wrote to the agent in Dublin asking how to go about this momentous change in my life and was very pleased that the letter needed no correcting.

My teacher told me she had always thought me mature for my years and remembered me questioning and bewailing the lack of opportunity and diminution of women in Irish society. Any money a married woman earned belonged to her husband and I had complained in class about the way that birth notices were presented in the local newspaper. These were, Patrick O'Brien announces birth of baby boy, Bill Nolan's lady has a baby or sometimes Mr and Mrs Williams have a son. Any Irish girl knew much about babies and where they came from, how they got there, how they come out and how mothers can be injured, or worse, and had by far, the lion's share in the making and raising of a baby, but received little recognition.

Jane Moloney took a special interest in me and invited me to her home many times and she emphasised how things had changed in her lifetime. It was the height of the industrial revolution. Men could still earn a living by their strength, but machines were taking over. Farming was declining and people moving to the cities or emigrating to Australia, USA and Canada and even to Devon and Wiltshire in England.

Women also worked as labourers called domestic servants. Jane said 'Susana, change is here and will increase. Old jobs and our way of life are disappearing, and this is likely to increase rather than decrease in a new and young society. Women will need and want to play a bigger role in the future and skills in money management and other business matters will become more and more important for women themselves to survive and to help their families. You have the skills and qualities to make more of your life than churning out babies, cooking and cleaning.'

Finally, she reminded me that when I was fourteen or fifteen I had asked about a Caroline Chisholm, who had done extraordinary things for young women and others in India, Australia and Ireland and we talked about her deeds, courage and determination. She then gave me a small book about that very person and said it was an inspiring story and very relevant to where I was going to live and how I would get there. I thanked her and she gave me a bunch of flowers, a hug and kiss on the cheek, held my hands in hers and with, I fancy, tears in her eyes that I could not see clearly, said 'Goodbye Susana, Godspeed and be true to yourself.'

I walked home, my mind racing, and then, when settled, I opened the book and soon had the distinct feeling that my eyes were standing out on stalks.

In summary it read: *'Chisholm was born in 1808 of well-to-do parents near Northampton and was 'Raised in the tradition of Evangelical philanthropy.' She married a Catholic army officer and later converted to his religion. They were posted to Madras in 1832, where, appalled by the apparently discarded young women who were the detritus of the British Army, she established the Female School of Industry for the Daughters of European Soldiers.*

*She and her husband then took leave in Australia where the situation for young woman enraged her again. She met immigrants from ships, found them accommodation, sometimes in her own home and helped find them jobs. She fought politicians and protesters and eventually convinced Governor Gipps to allocate her an unused immigration barracks in 1841 where up to 100 young women were safe, sheltered and fed by her philanthropy and that of others. She then, literally riding a white charger, travelled throughout New South Wales finding jobs, accommodation and shelter for those in need under her care. She was so effective that the barracks were closed in 1842.*

*Her husband retired and they returned to the United Kingdom to promote reforms and her own colonisation schemes to improve the lot of immigrants. She stablished the successful Family Colonisation Loan Society in 1849 to enable families to join emancipated convicts in Australia. Supported by Earl Grey, the Prime Minister and other luminaries including Charles Dickens, she addressed the House of Lords on colonisation from Ireland and in 1852 she reported on the poor shipboard conditions for emigrants that were later improved by the resulting Passenger Act of 1852 to the extent that the journey was more an adventure than something to fear'.*

My teacher understood my admiration and the sense of security about my future journey that Caroline Chisholm had given me and had included, in the book, a beautiful hand-written note she had copied from an unknown writer.

It read. *'Russet-haired, tall and sweet - voiced, her serene face lit by grey eyes, Caroline Chisholm began her work accepting established conventions, but when she encountered the obstruction and indifference of officialdom, her attitude began to harden and she became an uncompromising radical, expounding her belief in universal suffrage, vote by ballot and payment of members of parliament. Herself a devoted wife and mother, she helped to give dignity to women and families in a harsh colonial society. Her achievement was made possible by her idealism and courage allied to her executive ability and personal charm and the unwavering support of her husband.'*

I added 'She was a woman from my past, her deeds vital to my present and her dreams a guiding light for my future' to the note, folded it and put it in my journal and referred to it often in the days, months and years to come.

# 4

# Journey to Australia
# – Preparation

I had always pictured my life being in Ireland with my family and later with Seamus at my side. We did talk about what Australia might offer us, but the sad reality was that it was an illusion. Australia was never going to be for him. I believed that his last words meant for me to do what made me happy. Yes, he had died, but deep inside I knew that he was smiling down on me. Sad though it was, this comforted me.

It was clear from letters, conversation and newspapers that many of the old prejudices about convicts and the Irish were waning. The majority of settlers in the late nineteenth century were voluntary and paid their way. Many were capitalists, some with the eight to ten thousand pounds necessary to establish a large rural enterprise in an environment of fluctuating prices, high costs, flooding rains and choking droughts. Some were the second sons of families or had had relatives who needed someone to look after their land so far away. Others yearned to leave the institutions of the old world and were looking for freedom and respect in a new society.

I was still the Herring Gull, always looking for bits and pieces of information about Australia and somewhere I heard about a man called Quinn. He was a doctor and the new Bishop of

Queensland and made a speech quoted in a newspaper where he stressed that, *'Australia was not looking for flotsam and jetsam but quality people.'* He went on to say, *'On the way to Australia people had written journals of self- discovery. Not about an oppressed and restricted old self in Ireland but a new self in dynamic Australian society and taking advantage of the prospects of a better life.'* I was in a dreamy state, as I often was when I read, but I soon awoke and copied it into my book. Everything had crystallised and I saw my destiny.

It was also an uncanny reminder about the conversation I had with another teacher, Timothy O'Reilly about my dreams and doubts. He opened Shakespeare's *Julius Caesar,* searched the pages briefly to where Brutus reflects on opportunities taken or lost in life and passed the book to me. As I read what he had pointed out I felt a shiver all over my body and wanted to laugh, cry and scream 'Eureka' all at once. Those words crashed and thundered and took over my whole being. They were:

*There is a tide in the affairs of man*
*Which taken at the flood leads on to fortune*
*Omitted, all the voyages of their life*
*Is bound in shallows and miseries*

It was a sudden and great revelation for me. Brutus's and Quinn's words were my epiphany. Seamus's passing still hurt, as did the idea of leaving home, but my doubts and fears were fading, and my soul was starting to heal. This voyage was my destiny.

I soon had an answer from Dublin with forms to complete and documents to read. I needed my parents' permission to emigrate and another reference to go with my priest's that my teacher and friend Jane Moloney gladly provided. I completed the formalities and returned the papers to the agent and later received tickets to travel on the steam packet from Kildysart to Limerick and then by train to Dublin for two night's accommodation. I had a little map and found my way from the station to the agent's office.

Da, with me doing the sanding and oiling, made a box for my journey from lovely golden oak he had kept for years. It was about three feet long, two feet wide and eighteen inches high, with leather straps for handles and a steel clasp with a lock. It was the exact size the agent recommended. The care of passengers that Caroline Chisholm introduced was evident in the questions I was asked about my health, fitness and clothing. If I did not have the right things for warmth, hygiene and comfort in cold and hot weather I could not board.

I kept a record of the clothes I took with me. Like my friends I did not wear shoes in the summer but had a pair of lace up brogues I kept soft and clean by rubbing fat into the leather, for the winter. Ma knitted me some socks, a skull cap and some heavier socks I could wear on the ship without shoes if I wished and made me little slippers of canvas to wear when it was hot. I had to get an extra pair of boots for the journey. Women needed six linen undergarments that were long shirts called chemises that were topped by a woollen skirt or linen dress or worn as a night gown. Six pairs of stockings, two flannel petticoats, two lighter petticoats were also required as were a light and heavy dress. My other undergarments were cotton, with a vertical slit on each side held by horizontal loops and buttons above both hips. Last but not least were items for cold and hot weather. An ancient Irish hooded cloak and shawl that had both belonged to my grandma were warm to wear or to use as an extra blanket. At the other extreme a friend had made me a light bonnet for the hot days ahead from local reeds and straw. The bright green band she had embroidered with a shamrock, a lovely touch.

I was even more assured about the level of care on the ship

when I found out that any company operating an Emigrant Ship was fined 1000 pounds for a death that was proven to be due to negligence, or was foreseeable, or caused by preventable hazards, such as contaminated food or water. I was told that the Captain and the Doctor likely shared a large part of such a fine.

I had hair ribbons, pencils and paper, a book about bookkeeping, other books, needles and cotton, buttons and other knick-knacks that girls need in another little box Da also made.

Ma had made me a dear little embroidered calico bag about a foot square with some handmade cloths with my name embroidered on them and a little coin purse that I could wear around my neck. This made me burst into tears. It held a St. Christopher medal blessed by Father McMahon and a sovereign, a coin I had not seen before. I always kept that coin bag and medal around my neck. My Bible, with loving words written by my family on the inside, and my journal also went into the bag as did the many papers essential for the journey.

# 5

## Susana's Journey
## – From Home to London

My friends, relatives, neighbours, priest, teachers and parents had already said their goodbyes at our home or church but on October 1st 1877 many still came to the little jetty at Kildysart to wave goodbye. I stood on deck of the steam packet waving and crying as it gathered speed steaming for Limerick and the train I would catch to Dublin. I remembered little of the journey on the boat or the train other than my sister Catherine meeting me with a parcel of lovely cake and other nice food and taking me to the Dublin train. I was tired, sick with worry and self-doubt, guilty at leaving my parents and overwhelmingly sad at leaving what had been a happy life.

Mr O'Sullivan, the Queensland Government Agent and his wife met me at the Dublin Station. I was sobbing when they arrived but my natural curiosity soon overcame that. Mr O'Sullivan did not make a fuss and put my luggage in his trap, pulled by a prancing black horse. We drove to a beautiful stone building and he showed me where to put my things. He said that there would be about sixty girls on the ship to Australia but there were only two leaving from Dublin, me and another other girl who would arrive later and share my bedroom. Her Uncle and Aunty had business in Dublin and wanted her to have a good night's rest and would meet her at the ship in the morning as they were also emmigrating.

They waited until I had a wash and combed my hair and then asked me to have supper with them, an offer I gladly accepted. The three of us went to a hotel and ate a lovely stew, the first meal I had ever eaten not cooked by family or friends. There were two other things I remembered about that meal. The first was my first cup of coffee. I preferred tea. The second was that Mr and Mrs O' Sullivan lifted my spirits when they told me that their two daughters had emmigrated to Australia, one with her husband and the other who married an Australian. They spoke for an hour or more about how happy they were in their new land, earning good wages, saving money and enjoying the land, the climate and the freedom.

After the meal he told me that the other girl and I would be sailing directly to Brisbane from London and he thought that positions had been arranged for us at or near Warwick, about 100 miles south west of Brisbane and connected by rail since 1871. He added that Queensland was twenty times bigger than Ireland and nearly six times bigger than Great Britain and Ireland together. I had talked to people, read books and looked at atlases and knew it was a big place but when I heard that my jaw just dropped and my brain felt numb and totally unable to think how big the whole of Australia might be.

Their kindness, the food and the story of their daughters pleased me but what was to follow, later that night, was beyond anything I could ever have dreamed or believed and shook my numb brain back into a fast whirl. When we arrived back at the O'Sullivan's we, the ladies, got out of the trap at the front door. Mr O'Sullivan then took the horse to the groom to settle him into the barn for a feed of oats, a drink and a brush.

Mrs O'Sullivan rang the bell and the door was opened by the

maid who, after saying good evening, said, 'The other young gel has come in Ma'am and 'ad some suppa and a cuppa tea and a wash an' has just gone to 'er bed.' Mrs O'Sullivan and I went to the quarters and knocked on the bedroom door. It was opened by a very tired, thin and sad looking girl about thirteen or fourteen.

I was puzzled by the look on Mrs O'Sullivan's face and her theatrical manner. She asked the other girl about her journey to the point where she sat on her bed and looked like she was going to cry or fall asleep or both. Then I had to tell my story.

Finally, she said 'Oh my goodness gracious I have not introduced you both. I do beg your pardon.' She then said, with a flourish and a bow, 'Susana this is Nonnie, Nonnie this is Susana'. We gave each other small, tired smiles, said 'Hello' and began to get ready for bed.

'I did not mention your surnames, but of course, you know those don't you?' said the lady of the house. We were both tired out and wondered what on earth she was going on about. She then asked us if we could read which we both could. She then handed each of us a piece of paper. Mine had Nonnie Honan written on it and Nonnie's had Susana Honan.

Nonnie jumped off the bed and I stood, stunned for minutes. Neither of us knew that the other existed. We threw our arms around each other and started crying and then laughing and jumping. Mrs O'Sullivan, quietly opened the door, looked at us with a lovely smile on her face and left us to ourselves. We tried to work out our relationship, if any, but it was too late, we were too tired and any connection that we might have was too hard to find that night. We knew we had plenty of time to talk in the coming weeks and so it was off to a dreamless sleep for us both.

The next day we were given tickets to the Liverpool steamer and boarded it with Mr O'Sullivan's help. We arrived early and had

a cup of tea that was much nicer than coffee. I asked Mr O'Sullivan to write something in my special book and he did, a Celtic prayer, he had given to his daughters when they went to Australia.
In beautiful writing and addressed to me was the prayer.

*May the road rise up to meet you*

*May the wind be at your back*

*May the sun be warm upon your face*

*And the rain fall soft upon your fields*

*And until we meet again*

*May God hold you in his hand*

I was so grateful for the kindness they showed me that I sent them a Christmas message for the rest of their lives. This prayer was wonderful and comforted me as I had heard dreadful things about the Dublin to Liverpool crossing of the Irish Sea.

'The worst part of the entire voyage to Australia'.

'Irish emigrants were often left to sit on the deck with no shelter. Many had to go to hospital or had died."

'The trip was to take a day or two but once it was twelve days.'

The tides in the English Channel are amongst the highest in the world and with that amount of water moving in and out of the Irish sea with Wales, England Scotland in the east and Ireland in the west it was easy to imagine how cold, uncomfortable and dangerous it could be.

The good news was that attitudes, equipment and ships had altered from those days in the 1850s when ships heading to the USA were rightly known as 'coffin ships.' Mr O'Sullivan said 'Colonial government emigrants were now, by the standards of the day, well fed, adequately clothed and medically cared for.'

The crossing was calm. We were so excited about meeting each other and being on our way that the crossing passed quickly. We were half way across the Irish Sea when I remembered Caroline

Chisholm's pioneering work in the transport, safety and welfare of emigrants. I explained this to Nonnie and we both held my Saint Christopher medal and murmured a prayer of thanks. The Pope may not have sanctified her, but I had!

I had been impressed with Dublin's buildings and crowds, but Liverpool took my breath away. The ferry entered the River Mersey and was guided to a wharf by a tugboat and duly tied up. The wharf and harbour had been redeveloped about 20 years before with wharves of granite six miles long on both sides of the river befitting one of the most important ports on earth.

On the land side of the wharves were workshops, factories, chandlers, stores for wool, jute, cotton and grain, iron, steel, wood, stone, coal and uncountable amounts of equipment such as cranes, stationary and moving steam engines. Whistles, sirens, horns and people and trains coming and going created a cacophony of noise

This was the height of the Industrial Revolution that had started in Great Britain in the mid-1700s and Liverpool was the country's beating, roaring, thumping, smoking heart.

This was the time when sail was changing to steam. There were clippers and square riggers with multiple masts, steamers large and small and sailing ships with a propeller that could be used if needed. Some ships went to the ends of the earth, others plied their trade around the coast of Britain, some were fishing boats (big and small), some colliers, mostly working boats but some pleasure craft. There must have been several hundred ranging from tiny to massive and from all over the world.

It was an unforgettable sight and sound. Nonnie was open mouthed with wonder and confusion so I kept her close and held her hand most of the time. As I stood there, I had another epiphany and realised that Nonnie was five years younger than me, the same difference between my sister and me. God works in miraculous ways. Here I was bereft at losing Seamus and God had put Nonnie, who needed care and love, right where I had no alternative than to keep a vigilant and caring watch over her. I thought about writing a letter to Father McMahon asking him whether the number of epiphanies I had should be reported to Rome as maybe I was designed for the convent. I could see him chuckling if he read such a letter and that made me start laughing. Nonnie was still holding my hand and gave me a strange look but I tickled her, and she laughed as well.

We were met again by an agent of the Queensland Government. He took us for a ride in his horse drawn gig and we saw the three and four storey stone homes of the very wealthy business people of Liverpool. It was something 'way beyond our ken' as the Scots would say. The overnight accommodation was nice, and we kept our boxes there rather than leave them at the railway station. There were bad people called 'Liverpool Runners' who preyed on families and individuals by stealing their luggage and demanding a ransom for its return. A harrowing experience at best so we left our boxes and they were loaded onto the London train, like us, the next day.

Four other Irish girls, also bound for Brisbane, joined us on the London train. Nonnie was a thoughtful girl and when all was quiet nudged me and said, 'Didn't Mr O'Sullivan say that we were the only two Irish girls to be going from Dublin to London and Australia?' Grace O'Hea, the eldest of the others introduced herself and replied 'Yes that is right, but I came from London and the others were on the ship from Dublin the week before. When we got to Liverpool and had our boxes checked we all were missing something that was compulsory, so we were not allowed to travel further. Grace remembered the term 'Bloody Irish eejits' directed at them.

Once on the train we all became very excited and chatted about our homes, relations and fears. Mostly we just enjoyed the big fast train taking us through the industrial heart and the contrasting, beautiful fields of England to London.

It was a miserable cold, foggy day with a pall of smoke from the endless factories hurting our eyes and making it hard to see. It was dusk when we were transferred to another small train and taken to the docks area where we were bundled off the train into another dormitory building where we were fed and kindly, but firmly, sent to bed.

The six of us had kept together and were woken very early, told to wash and go downstairs for breakfast and then escorted a few hundred yards to the dock where our ship the *Gauntlet,* a clipper like we had seen in Liverpool, was moored. We were taken to a nearby iron walled building that was a United Kingdom Emigration Depot and were amazed to see about 300 people all waiting to board the ship.

We had to present papers and passed through some gates into a large area where we were mysteriously reunited with our boxes. We were also given a canvas bag each and told to pack essentials for the voyage as our boxes would be put in the ship's hold and when or how often we could get to them was unknown. I managed to keep the little bag Ma had made. We had to unpack our boxes and have the contents checked to ensure we had what was required. We packed our canvas bags, re-packed our boxes, joined the other girls and waited to be told what to do next.

After a longish wait we were ushered into another room and told to remove our outer garments by the three nurses stationed there. Although we had been examined before, conditions like measles, skin infections, scabies, lice or even smallpox could have occurred and lead to widespread illness or disease on board ship

33

and there was always the possibility of scurvy, syphilis or consumption, particular the variety called scrofula, in the neck. We were examined by the Surgeon Superintendent, Dr Henderson, who would accompany us on the voyage to Australia.

We were all modest and did not know what was worse, the freezing cold or the embarrassment of the physical reaction of certain parts of our bodies to the cold. Being hunched up and hugging ourselves dealt with both matters. It was not long before we were giggling at how silly we looked. Then we had our heads and bushes combed onto a piece of paper to check for lice. The latter indignation sent us into peals of laughter, embarrassed as we were.

Passengers were allocated to messes in groups of six and would eat and clean their quarters together. They did their best to put relatives and people who lived in the same areas together. The organising officer thought our group was near enough so we became Number Five mess. This sorting took all day but eventually we were shown on a big diagram where to go on the ship. The married people, with or without families, were in the middle part of the ship with single males in the bow and single girls at the stern. There was no communication between the compartments, and each had a separate hatch. Some ships had fencing on the deck to separate males and females but not the *Gauntlet.*

It was late by the time the formalities had been completed so we were fed on shore and shown to our quarters after being formed into messes, of six people as promised and I was made mess captain, given some basic rules to follow and went to bed.

It seemed no time at all that I was woken. As mess captain I had to rise at 0600 and give the water can to the constable to fill for washing. Good hygiene had been recognised as vital for an individual's health but also their fellow travellers. After they washed, I collected and served the breakfast, made my bunk and went on deck leaving the rostered girls of our mess to wash the dishes, scrub the floors with water, sand and hollostone to make them dry, clean and white. Cleanliness was like a creed Caroline Chisholm introduced. I thought 'CCCC—yes! Caroline Chisholm's Cleanliness Creed,' giggled and gave myself a little hug.

# 6

# The Real Journey Begins

When I was on deck I watched the sailors letting out or taking in the mooring lines and anchors so the deck stayed level in response to the rising or falling of the tide that could be as much as twenty seven feet. I was spellbound by the neat and tidy ship daylight had revealed. Anything that could be cleaned or polished had been. The decks almost shone. Ropes were coiled or hung where they belonged. Nothing was out of place and the sailors kept it that way. I had another new word, 'ship-shape', to go with port and starboard someone had explained the day before.

Soon the atmosphere changed. It was 14th October 1877, and the journey was now real. The die had been cast. Orders were shouted, there was bustle, creaking, bumping, banging, yelling and other noise. As my mates appeared on deck a small steam tug boat came alongside and a sailor threw a rope to a brawny seaman on the *Gauntlet.* He caught the rope, about an inch in diameter, joined to a thicker rope that he pulled aboard and looped it over a metal post on the starboard side of the stern and then repeated it for the bow with ropes from a second tug.

The tide was ebbing and some of the sails were catching a breeze, but the tugs were necessary to guide and pull the ship into and along the River Thames. The sailors were putting the finishing touches to the ship for the long journey to Brisbane. My messmates wanted to contribute, so we found some aprons and painted Mess 5 and CCCC on them. We now had a livery and were noticed.

Most of the big sails were tightly furled, the others were loose and as they filled with wind were attended by the crew. The sails working like this helped the tugs and also the steering and balance of the ship with a secondary benefit for passengers' comfort.

The day was foggy with the ghostly outlines of ship after ship passing behind us as we made way down the river into the dawn light with the unseen tugs puttering away and the rigging creaking impatiently.

The lifting fog revealed the paraphernalia of the huge city that was London; buildings, bridges, canals, cranes, railway lines, trucks, engines, ship building and repair yards for wooden and metal ships, paper milling, cement manufacture, timber yards, lead smelting, rope and sail making and massive coal dumps for steam to make power, and for heating and cooking and gas works. The engine room of an industrial power house was breath-taking; hard, cold, noisy, smelly and unfriendly.

We all knew how the telegraph had grown to affect everyone's lives. Off the port bow were six cable-laying ships at anchor. In time, Great Britain would own twenty four of the thirty ocean going cable-laying ships in the world. They were and wanted to stay a major world power. Despite the differences and disagreements between Great Britain and Ireland I could not help being proud that Ireland was part of this empire on which the sun never sets, and I suspected that my mess mates felt the same.

It was soon time to go below and organise the evening meal. It had been very cold but I had been comfortable in my cloak and hood. I was glad I wore the coat when we boarded because it would not have fitted in the bag.

The ship travelled 60 miles downriver and at dusk anchored

near to the southern bank of the Thames estuary sheltering close to the Isle of Sheprey in Herne Bay. There was a southerly wind, but we spent a comfortable night out of that wind and, again, I was glad for my cloak. It had been an exciting and tiring day so Mess 5 was ready and willing to go to bed early and slept well.

Before I went to bed, I made a list in my journal of the others in Mess 5 in my usual organised manner, well so I thought!

Nonnie Honan was 14 and travelling with people she called Uncle Patrick and Aunty Mary Hogan from Tipperary. They were distant cousins of her late father and cared for her as if she was their own. They all slept amidships with the other families. Patrick was a blacksmith with employment arranged in Warwick, 100 miles from Brisbane. Nonnie and I had not been able to work out any relationship between us as her mother had died during childbirth, and her father from typhoid fever soon after, but there was still plenty of time.

Grace O'Hea, a bonny slim colleen aged twenty two with, what someone said, was alabaster skin and shiny blue black hair under a scarf. Her parents from County Carlow had moved to London and she had studied there at the School of Nursing, the first in the world, established by Florence Nightingale at St. Thomas Hospital in 1860. She was keen to be a nurse in Australia.

Biddy Kelly 18, a laundress, and Betty Quinn 23, a cook and kitchen hand, were first cousins from Limerick. Both were big and strong with freckles, brown hair and always smiling or giggling at something that had happened to one of them but meant nothing to anyone else.

Sarah Murphy, 25 a widow from Wexford, was my height but thin and pale with a sad and resigned look. She answered questions politely when asked but offered little. She did not look as strong as Biddy, Betty, Grace and me and I knew I must keep a close eye on both Nonnie and Sarah. Next morning, I dressed, did my Mess Captain duties, had breakfast, and prepared to face the day that we would all leave Great Britain and Ireland forever.

That day indeed became memorable. The tugs had left so the crew set the sails and favoured by the southerly breeze we headed east past Margate and Ramsgate into the North Sea leaving the Thames River and entered the eastern end of the 350 miles of the English Channel, the protector of Britain for eight hundred years. The ship had to turn from heading east to south west and it became very rough with most suffering from sea sickness, some quite severely, vomiting everything until their poor stomachs were empty. The hatches were battened down. The smell of vomit and women, unable to wash, in the airless fug was hard to endure as the rough seas and the rolling and pitching of the ship continued for several days.

A consolation of sorts was that we made good time. Mess 5 found their 'sea legs' sooner than most and worked hard to do the chores of those who were still ill. The seasickness lessened when the hatches were opened and soon the sick passengers could keep water and then food down. Matron gave some of the sick girls arrowroot and that helped. I was thrilled that all the Mess 5 members, including Sarah, performed as well as other messes and better than most. Everyone pulled their weight under difficult conditions and it bode well for the future.

One day, in better weather, we changed course and headed north for Plymouth on the southern coast of England, almost at the western end of the English Channel. *Gauntlet* sailed into the large harbour and 'hove to', another new word for us, in a sheltered spot and dropped anchor. I noticed flags of different colours and shapes on a rope being run up a flag pole and soon their purpose became clear when a little steamboat came alongside. Five children and their mother were transferred to the little boat. A man with a sombre face stood silently on the deck watching and as they departed gave a little wave and went below. Many rumours swept the ship but no one ever found out the reason for their departure.

Next morning we left Plymouth and sailed southwest to the end of the English Channel and then the *Gauntlet* sailed west past Portugal, Spain and the western entrance to the Mediterranean, into the Atlantic Ocean and then headed southwest towards Rio de Janeiro in South America. We were, at last, in calmer waters and warmer weather. We passed through 'The Doldrums' a place of hot windless days and nights where sometimes the crew had to launch the long boat to tow the ship until they found some breeze. I could now relax physically and mentally, often on deck with a cup of tea, sometimes recording my thoughts that were slowly catching up with my body. The quarters were hot in 'The Doldrums' and my lasting memory was a sea of white bottoms gleaming in the scant moonlight filtering through the open portholes as the girls sought relief from the heat.

The *Gauntlet* was a beautiful thing, a fast sailing ship, a Clipper, designed to 'clip' time off a journey to make more money for the owner. It was one of the last and strongest ever built. Life was not boring on the ship. When the weather was good for sailing it was exciting and when the wind was scant, we played games of skill, fun and physical exertion. Grace was often asked to sing and did so. I loved music and remembered I had a tin whistle in my bag that I had with me on board. I had always liked that instrument, so common in Irish music, and had taken lessons. Another passenger had a spare tin whistle and let Nonnie use it. She was so excited and couldn't wait try it and did so with some success. She enjoyed singing with Grace and soon they made up acts that entertained others, particularly the children. There were lessons for children by teachers, a variety of reading matter and even a ship's newspapers of sorts. The newspaper's quality depended very much on the enthusiasm and willingness of passengers to contribute.

Conditions on these ships had changed greatly even before the end of transportation and, by the time of this journey, there were much stricter rules and requirement that the shipping companies and, by default, the crews had to follow. For example, rations in the past were only 75% of those for the Royal Navy and included salt meat and biscuits that were inappropriate for babies or the mothers so prostrated and dehydrated by sea sickness or diarrhoea that they had no milk for their babies, many of whom died. New rations were much improved and better than most emigrants had experienced at home. Canned meat and vegetables were an important part of our rations.

The crew including the Captain, a distant God like figure, had little to do with passengers. Dr Henderson was our leader in many respects and reviewed our health every two weeks, or more if required, particularly the babies, small children and mothers with child. He did rounds of the passengers' quarters every night and like Matron Bell was kind and approachable and very attentive to the needs of the passengers particularly our diet and ensuring we were drinking enough water. For example, lime and lemon juice were encouraged to prevent scurvy. Both Grace and I helped the Matron when things were getting out of hand with grizzly children or seasickness.

The bunks ran from fore to aft on both sides of the ship with a bench also running fore to aft and attached to the bunks. Then there was a passageway and more benches for eating the meals at a central table. The crew were not allowed below unless on duty.

These structures were almost the same on both sides of the ship. Straw filled mattresses and some bedding were supplied but predictably my cloak was a godsend. There was adequate eating, washing and drinking equipment supplied. A bunk was wide enough to be shared by two single girls or a married couple. Single men and boys had the same space as the girls but there were wooden dividers making two separate bunks. Seemingly it was quite proper for girls to be able to ease each other's fears and worries or share the warmth of their bodies, but not males.

One of the newspaper cuttings available on the ship quoted Governor Gipps in Australia stating, 'Homosexuality, going back to the convict days, was mainly an English pastime but not common amongst the Irish and incest was rare in Ireland according to the priests.' Grace and I were bewildered at that leap of logic assuming that homosexuals and those committing incest would unburden themselves to a priest.

There were four officers and 22 crewmen with shifts of four hours on four hours off, the standard practice. Time for roster changes was indicated by a bell being rung a certain number of times. I never did understand how it all worked and never settled properly to sleep because of the bells.

After 23 days, on November 13th, we had travelled nearly 3000 nautical miles and 'Crossed the Line', that is the equator, and, as usual for these ships there was a lot of hilarity and fun. There were cordials, tea and coffee to drink and a few other stronger beverages. Many the passengers were Irish or Scottish and liked a wee dram, as they used to say.

Special treats were brought out from the boxes that we were allowed to access for the first time. We were pleased to look at, eat or drink treasures from home and to take out clean clothes, needle and thread, wash our hair and so on.

At sunset, the clouds showed all the colours of the rainbow for an hour in the west and then those same colors were reflected in the east. It was not a rainbow but the eastern sky was red, changed to orange, then yellow, green, blue, indigo and violet. It took almost an hour for the display to finish. None of us, or the crew, had seen this weirdly reflected sunset before. I found it truly beautiful andI felt uneasy, but soon but brushed that feeling away. I went below to get some cards I had made for Mess 5 to celebrate. Instantly what we had just done hit me. We had passed the point of no return physically and mentally. We were now in the southern hemisphere. Ireland was the past and Australia the future. Somewhat settled I went back to the deck where Grace was about to sing folk songs in her beautiful Irish lilt accompanied by a flute.

I sat down and listened to the song. It was 'Red haired Mary' and the chorus was:

*'Take your eyes off red haired Mary*
*She and I are to be wed*
*We are seeing the priest this very morning*
*And, tonight we'll lie in the marriage bed'*

This was the song Seamus often sang to me when we walked home from church holding hands, replacing 'Mary' with 'Susana' of course. It was his gentle way of reminding me that we had a future together. Even though I was young I had wondered about his lack of physical expression. Holding hands when he sung this song and an occasional chaste kiss that was all the contact we had.

I remembered our Sunday walks when he told me that flowers smelt and looked nicer when I passed by. This was 'blarney' but was nice.

I also remembered that a month after Seamus died, I found Da sitting in his chair with silent tears rolling down his cheeks. That

43

upset me and I asked what was wrong. He looked at me in such a sad way and handed me Seamus's letter saying nothing. We both reread the loving letter with the awful news and sat there for a long time in silence.

Our young love was full of hope, love and dreams but they were dashed too soon and he had gone. Seamus was a true Irishman with his love of words, even from an English writer, Elizabeth Barrett (later Browning). She was mortally ill and wrote a sonnet to her husband and the lines that burned into my mind and heart forever were:

*'How do I love you let me count the ways!*
*I love you to the depth and breadth and height*
*My soul may reach-----------------' and ends with,*
*'I love thee with the breath*
*Smiles, tears of all my life, and if God choose,*
*I shall but love thee better after death'*

He said that to me many times and I was torn with the aching sadness and poignancy of Grace's song and Barrett's poem. I knew then that it was and always had been the love song that he knew would never come true. The poem had been his kind and gentle way of giving me something precious to remember through the years, an everlasting love.

I fled below and cried until I thought I would be ill. I had cried before for him, my parents and my country but never like this.

This was painful but I could feel the healing and thanked God for speaking to me through Grace. This became another secret memory I tucked into my memory box I called 'God's Grace.'

This gave me strength to cross the line between my old life and the new, emotionally and physically. I dried my eyes, went on deck and enjoyed the singing and dancing. We were allowed to stay up an hour later and it was quite dark when I went to bed. Just before going below I gazed, in reverie, at the incredible display of stars. One in the west was especially bright and a blue colour. I pointed it out and one of the crew said, 'That is Venus, the evening star'.

I was up early one morning doing my chores and happened to glance at the lightening eastern sky and lo and behold saw the same star. And indeed, it was Venus, the brightest heavenly body other than the sun and the moon but this time known as the morning star. I knew that was not true. It was Seamus keeping an eye out for me. His star said goodbye to me from the old world and welcomed me to the new. That became my second secret memory from that night. My grandma once said I was fey. I thought to myself, 'Yes the dear soul was probably right.' The morning star had brought the first day of the rest of my life. I was ready.

A few days later I was feeling dozy in my favourite spot on the deck on a sunny morning when a cold and wet thing hit me in a very soft and tender part of my chest, dropped on my lap wetting me and then fell on the deck and slipped over board.

'Beejaysus' I said 'Who did that, what was it?' Jumping up and challenging a pair of girls nearby who were laughing and holding what appeared to be an empty bucket. One said 'Susana, it was a flying fish.' I replied, 'Don't ye be taken me for an Irish eejit or I'll be havin' ye, English bints.' Just as I spoke several fish landed near me and I picked one up. It was pretty silver colour about fifteen inches long and six ounces of so. The amazing thing was that their fins acted as wings and they were as long as the fish and about seven inches wide. They could fly for a hundred yards.

Sarah heard me cursing and yelling and came out to see what was wrong. Like me she was fascinated by the spectacle and we watched in awe and silence. She soon noticed that they were being hunted from below by bigger fish and when they 'flew' Frigate Birds picked them off in mid-air. She looked at me with a little smile and proffered a comment as dry as a lime burner's boot. 'I think we can say that those fish are between the devil and the deep blue sea, don't you?' That moment changed her. We became quite friendly and she less sad, even happy at times.

# 7

# The Last Lap

The next day there was another beautiful dawn and a pleasant breeze. I had looked at maps of our planned voyage, but I was confused as the ship followed what was called the great circle route because the earth was a sphere. I finally got it sorted out.

We had left London on October 14th, 1877 when there was almost 11 hours of daylight and stopped at Plymouth. This took six days, much of which I was too sick to recall. We headed west from the English Channel and then south past the entrance to the Mediterranean towards South America and had crossed the equator at the longitude of 20 degrees west. This had taken us 21 days and we had covered 3300 miles.

The early emigration ships replenished supplies at Rio de Janeiro and Cape Town but, with the more developed ships, canned meat and vegetables and more sophisticated galleys for food preparation, these ships could now travel non-stop to Australia. Importantly, the curse of scurvy that killed an estimated two million seamen in the world in previous times had been recognised by Captain Cook and others as due to the lack of fresh fruit and vegetables that seamen were now given together with lime juice hence the American term 'limeys' for English people.

The good food, diet, fun with other passengers and the warm weather either side of the equator made it very pleasant although it fiercely hot sometimes. Inexorably we headed south into the

'Roaring Forties' and the weather became cooler, the wind stronger, the ship faster, more uncomfortable and more exciting. We did have the advantage of increasing length of daylight and in December there was only a pale sort of dark for a few hours so this made it much safer than in winter.

We saw dolphins, whales, often with big babies that had been born in the sheltered waters of Australia or South Africa heading south to their home waters. There were sea birds of all shapes and sizes and we were enthralled by a giant Albatross that sat in our rigging for a few hours. His wingspan was more than six feet.

Dolphins were a delight, often in pods of ten to fifteen riding the waves, jumping or just staying close to our ship. One day the weather was calm and I was leaning against the point of the bow looking into the water where a male dolphin was cutting through the water and crossing back and forth across the bow within a foot or less. He seemed to be communicating with us or maybe he was just having fun. I was lost in this magnificent sight and then it became even more beautiful.

A smaller female dolphin, likely his mate, swam alongside bumping him as if to tell him to leave that stupid boat alone and come with me. He actually had to keep his wits about him to keep close to the boat and then she did one of the most beautiful things I have seen in the animal world. She swam parallel and close to him and rolled onto her back and somehow swam lying on her back, facing him and tapped him on both sides of his face with her flippers then rolled over and swam away. Predictably he followed.

Sarah happened to be with me and saw this magic moment between lovers or playmates. It didn't matter - it was so beautiful. I had not seen the look on Sarah's face even when we shared the flying fish excitement. This was her epiphany and I thanked God she was leaving her pain behind in the old world and grasping the new. It must have shown as she took my hand and held it with a strength I was surprised she had. She looked at me, smiled, kissed me on the cheek and whispered, 'Thank you for understanding.'

As we sailed further south it became more exciting and I remember the speed the wind in the shrouds. We ignored any discomfort as it was of no account compared to the drama and beauty of the massive icebergs that shared the ocean with us for many days. We had become used to our ship being a big and safe haven but compared to an iceberg we were a little mouse compared to a horse.

It was scary in the dark sailing in those latititudes but it was brief in summertime. Our lookouts seemed to have cat's eyes and we kept well clear of icebergs. There was another compensation and that was the southern lights. These were magic, multi-coloured, ever changing writhing wraiths of mists. I knew the world was round but I had a sense, my Irishness again no doubt, that maybe the old paintings, the tales and legends about sailing off the edge of the earth that the old people told were true. Once we turned north, I was much more relaxed and happier.

Our journey was coming to an end. We passed the southern coast of Tasmania, sailed to the east of that island, and headed north to Brisbane arriving 20th February 1878. Our good ship *Gauntlet* had taken us to our destination in 129 days compared to the *Cutty Sark's* 100 days record.

Even though it was summer, as we travelled north along the east coast of Australia, we were well off shore and the breeze was cooled by the sea so we kept on our hats and other clothes. When we reached the channel into the Brisbane River, oh, how things changed. It was high summer and hot, but added to this, was the humidity of the wet season. To make it worse we had to anchor and wait for a tug so the illusion of a cooling breeze cruelly disappeared. Then the world hammered us with thunder, lightning and rain, that soon ceased and then the fiery sun reappeared. I had once seen someone steam some shellfish at home and now I knew how the shellfish felt. The summer of Ireland was friendly and soft, but this was fierce, unpleasant and something that could make or break newcomers. I made up my mind, there and then, that this was now my world. I would endure it and thrive come what may.

We were at the anchorage for two days to allow various officials to board and inspect us. I suspect that they were customs and health people. The ship carried, 62 married adults, 148 single men and women, 43 children and six infants. There were 266 souls on board, seven left at Plymouth and two babies died, leaving 257 to disembark in Brisbane. I could feel the presence of Caroline Chisholm in the care that the doctor and captain had extended to us.

With all these checks and paperwork completed, two little steam tugs spluttered out to attach lines to our bow and stern and take us through the mouth of the Brisbane River and into a very busy port. I had been very impressed with the solidity and grandeur of Liverpool and London. Brisbane was different. Hot, busy, smelly, green in parts but clearly showing that Brisbane was on its way to being a successful place even though it had only been proclaimed a separate colony from New South Wales in 1859. I felt weird when I realised Queensland was not as old as me.

There were abattoirs with cattle and sheep in the yards, associated tanneries and melting down works, timber and timber mills, wool and grain stores, uncountable bales of wool and bags of grain visible through the open doors, coal heaps, fish factories, railways and their associated paraphernalia, wharves with ships tied up taking on or ridding themselves of animal, vegetable, mineral or human cargoes. Other ships and trains were coming and going or waiting their turn in line and there were the inevitable horses and drays, tender boats, big and small fishing boats and ferries. It smelt to high heaven and the river was disgusting with all manner of human, animal, machine, ships and plant waste discharged into it.

Nonnie was gazing over the side of the boat and started pointing, jumping up and down and yelling, whether in fear or excitement I did not know. I ran to her and Sarah joined us. We looked over side and I thought my heart would stop. There was a giant fish in the water that was lazily swimming along at the same speed as the boat. It turned and looked at us and even though I only saw one eye it was unblinking and terrifying. While we were watching a dead dog floated in front of it and these huge jaws opened and gulped the dog effortlessly with not even a splash. It was as wide as a cow in the middle and longer than two cows with .a pointy nose and tail with fins. It was a dark colour with some stripe like marks.

Dr Henderson was on deck and came over to settle us down and told us it was a Tiger Shark looking for food among all the rubbish thrown into the river. He went onto to say that 'Australia had many dangerous sharks, known as 'man-eaters', so be careful where and when you go swimming.' It was certainly frightening and the way it ate the dog made us realise it could probably eat us in one or two mouthfuls.

It took all day for the boat to meander through this apparent chaos to a more pleasant area up river where we docked for the night near some palm trees and lawns. The day was almost done so the shadows lengthened and the sunset cast its rays onto the river. It was still warm, but a gentle, cooling, evening breeze blew. We sat on the deck drinking lovely cool lemonade, eating the remains of any treats and absorbed the air, the view, the short sunset and what one of the officers called 'ambience'. The contrast of the harshness of the day to the softness of the night was extraordinary and something I never forgot. I went to bed at peace and with a glad heart and told Seamus about the day. And faith! I believe I caught a glimpse of the evening star though an open porthole.

# 8

# The New World

After breakfast, tidying and cleaning our quarters, we were all in good spirits but also sad as we had become good friends and would be parting. We sat talking and as usual Biddy and Betty were giggling at something and Grace finally asked them what it was. Biddy went red and Betty giggled even more than usual and pointed at Biddy's left little finger that we had all noticed was stiff, deformed and pointed sideways. She went on to explain that it was only when Biddy fumbled something or drank with her left hand that they laughed. We begged and pleaded about why it was so funny and Betty interrupted. 'Well it's like this. Biddy had known a Martin McCarthy for years. God knows where he got it from but he always wore a kilt to anything special.' Biddy confessed that 'Sometimes I asked meself the old question ye' ask of a man in kilts and it made me feel all queer inside.' Betty then added, 'Biddy, Martin and me went to wake a few years ago and it was more about drinking and sex than mourning. Biddy and Martin were soon toastin; and dancin' close like.' Biddy joined in, 'I had always liked Martin and as the night passed, I started to think that maybe sumbthink' er um good might happen, ye know. I went outside to pee, and Martin came with me. We walked, well nearly ran, around the back of the building. He leant against the wall and looked away while I did what I had to and I think he did as well. I moved in front of him and we kissed and that stuff several times. It was sloping ground and it had rained and I had to be careful not to slip as we were like sort of movin' about a lot with his kilt in the air. Suddenly I did slip and Martin tried to stop me but only made it worse. Me legs went from under and I fell backwards, put out me hand to protect meself, heard a crack and then felt an awful pain 'cos I broked me little finger in three places.'

We were silent. It was funny but not funny somehow. Sarah was pale, sweating and looked faint, hesitated and then quietly asked 'What happened to Martin?' Biddy frowned and said 'The bastard finished hisself off all right and then he slipped sideways and hit his head on the wall and knocked hisself out. I thought he was dead, but he woke up later.' I laughed with the others, but Sarah looked like she had seen a ghost. She gave a convulsive cry and rushed on deck. I followed and found her leaning on the rail staring at the water and sobbing quietly.

I put my arm around her and sat her down in my favourite spot where she held me like she was drowning and sobbed to exhaustion. When she was at peace, I asked what was wrong because I was puzzled by her reaction. The story had tickled our fancy and was typical of our world. And may not have even been true. She sat quietly for some time and then with her hands twisting her wet handkerchief and looking like she had aged ten years said, 'Oh Susana. We were married for three years before I was with child and when I was about three months along the way we had some Guinness and whiskey one night and went to bed early to celebrate our good fortune. My husband was very excited as was I.....it was truly makin' love not shaggin. It all happened for him and then he clamped his hands on his head and moaned 'Jaysus Sarah, I feel like me head is going to explode –Oh shite I never had such a pain—please God make it go away' I didn't know what to do except get him a drink of water and hold him. He started thrashing around and in minutes was unconscious and a few hours later he died.'

I said nothing and could only hold her. She opened her eyes and reached into her pocket, opened her purse and showed me a piece of paper with 'apoplexy' written on it and said, 'That is what killed him and it was caused by the pressure in his head from what we were enjoying. Biddy's tale brought it all back to me, I killed him.'

We held each other tightly and both sobbed and Sarah seemed to settle down but unexpectedly Sarah pulled away and made a keening sound like I never want to hear again and moaned, 'Sadly, there was more. I was shattered, but there was some comfort in being with his child but I lost it a few weeks later.' I had seen and heard of countless tragedies in our accursed land, as my da described Ireland, but this was so painful I did not know what to do or say.

The day passed slowly as the crew readied the ship to move down river to a mooring but it was after dark before we were ready. As there was no wind, we once again used two tugs one at the bow and the stern. The night was warm and very calm and we settled down to sleep. I was exhausted and surprisingly, after the distress with Sarah, slept well. I woke at daybreak by a clamour on deck and saw that Sarah was not in her bed. With a sense of dread I threw on some clothes and rushed on deck. There was Sarah lying on the bloodied deck with a cut head, unconscious or dead.  Dr Henderson was by her side and had stopped the bleeding. He knew I was Sarah's friend and said I could stay but shooed everyone else back to their quarters.

The duty officer said that he had seen her walking in a strange way like she was asleep and did not know where she was. He said his mother had told him not to wake a sleep walker, so he watched and kept away but when she got near the railing of the ship she seemed to wake up and started to climb as though to jump overboard. Fortunately, he was a strong fit man and fast and in the act of Sarah throwing herself overboard he grabbed her around the waist and pushed his feet against the railing that was about three feet above the deck and dragged her back onto the deck. He saved them both, but Sarah cut her head badly on a piece of steel and was knocked unconscious.

Dr Henderson said she was alive and the bleeding had stopped. Crew members carried her to his working area and put her on a bench where he examined her more thoroughly, shining lights in her eyes and so on, sewed up her cut and dressed the wound. Matron helped as did Grace, to undress and wash her and put on night clothes I had fetched.

The Captain had contacted the police who asked questions of all and sundry. The police were satisfied after the doctor described her injuries and said she had been sleepwalking.

A priest appeared from somewhere and gave her the last rights in case she died.

Dr Henderson did ask me if Sarah was troubled. I thought very carefully as all of us were troubled in some way leaving our homes but Sarah's comments to me were private so I said, 'Not that I know.' There was little more I could do so I went to my bed and found a letter from Sarah, under my pillow. She wrote 'Please forgive me Susana but I cannot go on. I just know the fairies sent the sea monster for me because my lust killed my husband. Thank you for being so kind and my friend, goodbye and God be with you, Sarah.'

I lay on my bed, my mind in turmoil. Poor, poor Sarah; just when I thought she was beginning to recover from her awful loss. I did not know her at all it seemed. I have no idea what time it was, but I fell into a dream-filled restless sleep with fairies and sea monsters and Lord knows what else swirling around.

I awoke and was almost paralysed with fear when I recalled Dr Henderson's question. What was he thinking, did he know that she had tried to kill herself? This was a mortal sin. If she died, she would go to hell and would not be buried in consecrated ground. I had proof of what was in her mind. She was not sleep walking, she wanted to end her life.

I did not know whether it was day or night but I tossed and turned awake or asleep and then with a cold, sick feeling I remembered that when I fetched her night dress, I had seen an empty Laudanum bottle with her things. My faith was sorely tested. God was kind and forgiving but the Church was merciless. I kept hearing Da's voice about the Famine days and the church. I tore her letter into tiny pieces, ate them and threw the empty bottle overboard. I felt an intense calm and fell asleep. I was woken by Dr Henderson to tell me Sarah had woken and apart from a 'sore noggin,' had recovered but with no memory of what had happened.

Sarah was indeed awake when I saw her and she held both my hands in hers. She asked me what had happened. My answer was that fairies had made her walk towards the sea monster, but our dear God had sent a big strong handsome angel to save her. She looked into my eyes and held my hands again in her powerful grip and said, 'Thank you Susana, my true friend.'

I was so confused about what had happened and quite lost for a time but we were soon moored down river tied up at Queen's Wharf to disembark after we had made ready to leave the ship. We were thrilled it was over but, amid the joy, there was sadness. The six of had shared some good and bad things and we had managed. We learnt much about each other and importantly ourselves. Soon we would be cast into the wind like thistledown to land somewhere in this vast land.

Disembarking, like boarding, was an utter nightmare of noise, crowding, confusion, pushing and shoving but there was laughter and joking. We had reached Australia, again this was the first day of the rest of our lives. We all walked to the Immigration Depot B, except Sarah who was driven in a trap under doctor's orders and once again, somehow, we were in the same place as our boxes.

It was a splendid two storey building with a basement fronting William Street and a new three storey wing facing Queen's Wharf Road where we entered. There were three wards for females, males and married couples with kitchens and bathrooms and outside were earth closets attached to the building. These sanitary facilities were far more splendid than anything any of had seen or even heard of in Ireland and we were agog. Once again, I was not surprised that we had to leave most of our luggage at the wharf.

It took all day for the transfer of people to take place and the next day there was a medical parade. Dr Henderson had watched us closely and kept records. He sat between two Queensland doctors who checked us out, two at a time. It was simple and fast. The doctors had our paper work in alphabetical order and Dr Henderson had his in order as well. We sat down when our names were called and Dr Henderson confirmed that I had been seasick but nothing else, so that was it.

Next day we went through another process to be told or confirmed where we were to be sent and what we were to do. Patrick and Mary Hogan and Nonnie Honan were to go to Warwick about 100 miles south west of Brisbane where Patrick was to work as a blacksmith with a Mr Aimes and his wife Phoebe with a view to taking over his long-established business in due course. Nonnie would help her mother at home.

I was also to go to Warwick and work in the Oddfellows Home Hotel. Maybe someone thought we were related but that was fine.

Biddy and Betty were to go to Rockhampton 380 miles from Brisbane on the Fitzroy River 25 miles inland from the sea. They couldn't stop giggling when they knew that they would be at the same hotel.

Grace was to go the Royal Brisbane Hospital that was just 10 years old. And that only left Sarah who was still far from well from her injury. To make matters worse, the haberdashery shop where she was to work had closed down.

She had not told me that she was in that line of work and when we discussed it the next day, she said she was also a good seamstress, had been a waitress at times in what was probably the hotel where I had dinner with the O'Sullivans in Dublin, but I don't think I ever knew the name. She added that she had also been in charge of a section in a big shop that sold dresses to the ladies of Dublin. I knew now why she had such lovely skin, soft hands, a nice voice and lovely clothes.

The matron of the Immigration Depot was concerned about Sarah, as was I, as she was still very sleepy and tearful. I said nothing but Dr Henderson was a smart man and I am sure that he had an idea that there had been something else other than sleep walking going on. He talked to various officials about many things and knew that Sarah's planned employment was cancelled. He also knew the Queensland doctors at the Depot and asked whether any of them knew of a position that might suit Sarah.

A day or so later another doctor came to see Sarah who was now much better. A friend of his father said that 'Rosenthal,' a sheep and cattle station near Warwick, was looking for someone to manage the kitchen and cleaning staff and to organise functions for guests and would she be interested. Her misery vanished and she smiled at him and said 'Thank you, yes I would.' Time seemed to fly after that. The Hogans and Nonnie had already gone to Warwick. Next day Grace was to go to the hospital and Biddy and Betty to Rockhampton by steamship.

While we waited for news of Sarah's position, Dr Henderson appeared and asked if he could speak to me, so we had a cup of tea in an office he borrowed. After he shut the door he sat down and looked at me and softly said. 'Susana, this is not a fair thing I am asking of you, but I can't let Sarah and Nonnie disappear from my care and just shrug my shoulders and say goodbye. Sometimes things happen for a reason and you, Sarah and Nonnie, are going to Warwick. Susana, I know that you have been a friend and almost guardian to them. You have taken on more responsibility than a 20-year-old should ever have to. I am aware that there is much more to both of them and I know that you know or suspect the same. You have the courage and kindness to stick with them. They are lucky you are their friend. I know that they will need your help in the future.'

We had all broken the law probably. The Doctor said it was sleep walking, the Captain told the police who told the coroner and I had destroyed evidence of her intent. Sarah would not be labelled insane, immoral or whatever else. This was man's business not the Church's and I was content with that. The doctor trusted me, and I trusted me. I had sensed on the ship, as young as I was, that I had a duty to Nonnie and Sarah and I would not break that bond. That was my path in life for the foreseeable future.

At the moment I was about to say something noble to Dr Henderson my mind jumped to the song 'Foggy foggy dew' and the line 'So I pulled her into bed and covered up her head just to keep her from the foggy, foggy dew' and my heart lightened. I had the feeling Dr Henderson had read something in my face and smiled when I answered, 'Thank you for trusting me and thank you for what you have done for Sarah. I will not let you, her or Nonnie down.' He stood, shook my hand and said, 'I know you won't. Good luck' and amazingly added 'May the road rise up to meet you and the wind be at your back, God be with you.'

# BOOK TWO

# WARWICK

# 9

# An Introduction to Australia

We had to wait at the Immigration Depot to be told if Sarah had gained a position at Rosenthal. The telegrams the Immigration people had sent were soon answered and she was offered and accepted the job so we were both off to Warwick.

We were the last of our group to leave the depot and were driven to the station in a sturdy cart with our boxes, paper work and bits and pieces we had brought with us or acquired in Brisbane. God in heaven, it is going to be good to park our boxes and live like normal people.

Soon we were on our own in a steam train rattling and clanking its way out of Brisbane. We felt like queens, two of us in a section that could seat six. We tried all the seats, lay and lolled around and finally settled like adults in the seats we had been given. We steamed west towards Towoomba and then south west to Warwick on flat land to avoid the Great Dividing Range. We were now in the Darling Downs, a rich farming area.

I enjoyed the scenery, the colours, the tree lined creeks and other vegetation but my mind was drifting and I started thinking about the others from force of habit, especially Nonnie. She did her share of work and was friendly but quiet. She had spent most of her spare time on board ship and in Brisbane with her aunty and uncle, so I did not see as much of her as my other mess mates.

We did share a bunk and I kept a sisterly eye on her. She was a sad and pale child and did not have any monthly things as far as I knew. She did cry in her sleep but we had all done that. Sometimes she cuddled up to me as any desperate little girl might do, but at other times when cuddling, she acted older than her years.

She would have heard many conversations about female things include sexual stuff and maybe even seen it amongst our fellow passengers. I was puzzled during the voyage and still was. There was something at the edge of my thoughts that I could not bring out.

I soon forgot about bad things and enjoyed Sarah's company and chatter as she became more cheerful as we steamed and clattered towards our destiny. She talked about her husband and the future they had planned. He was a stone mason and with her skills as a seamstress, waitress and manager a positive future had beckoned and the pregnancy capped it off. Understandably she was struck down by grief and barely able to eat or drink for many weeks after the sad events. There was a refrain in her head from where she did not know, 'Our love was on the wing, we had dreams and songs to sing but now I am so lonely.' Every bit of her hurt and she could not think about something as complicated as going to Australia.

One lovely summer's day, a year after her husband died, she was walking alongside a stream near her home and sat down to enjoy the moment. As she gazed at the gently flowing stream a mother duck waddled down the bank and slipped into the water and a dozen ducklings unhesitatingly followed her, unafraid, into the strange new world of water. Ducks they may have been but this was life, held together with the glue of love and trust. Somehow deep inside she realised that she had not lost the gift of being able to love. The love she still felt for her husband and the dreams and songs they had shared came alive for her and as my da might have said, 'She girded her loins' and followed those dreams to Australia.

With her experience and mine it was like being in her skin and my feelings for her were far stronger than those I had for my sister. It was not sexual. We were two people alone in the world who understood and cared deeply for each other. It was nice to know that we were going to spend the near future in this new land together.

She was a different person, no longer the emotionally flat and sad woman I had known on the ship. She was peaceful, positive, smiling and enjoying the passing parade of a new country. She had left the dark place she had been in for so long and was in a place of light and laughter.

We both became silly and giggly and played 'I can see something new' and called out 'kangaroo', 'koala', 'emu', 'parrot', 'eagle' and so on.

We saw a dairy cow that looked just like 'Jessie the Jersey' I had milked for years and that brought a lump to my throat that soon passed. We talked on and on about how we would fit into this new world and went around in circles until we were both exhausted and nodded off to be woken by the train man telling us that Warwick was the next stop.

The train stopped at Milhill, a northern suburb of Warwick. We crossed the Condamine River by ferry and were greeted by our new employers at the wharf.

Sarah was soon on her way to Rosenthal and I met Mrs Frances Muller who had arrived in a buggy pulled by a lovely shiny black horse. She was the wife of Louis Muller who had built the Oddfellows Home Hotel. I was introduced to Tom Kennedy, the driver, who put my box under the back seat where Mrs Muller and I sat. He then swung lightly onto the front seat, untied the reins, flicked them and we were off.

We soon reached the hotel, an attractive and symmetrical building made of wood and sheeted with chamfered planks of wood, 'better than the usual weather board', so I was told. Mrs Muller was proud of the part that the hotel played in Warwick becoming a regional centre of 3,000 people and pointed to her Mr Muller's and her name on the front of the hotel under the red lights that were lit at night. She later explained that the lights and the names of the licencees were part of the new regulations for hotels in Queensland, to make them safer and more hospitable.

Mrs Muller and I went in the front door to a parlour, down a passage and a verandah to the outside kitchen where I was offered a cup of tea and fresh scones that I gladly accepted.

Tom, the buggy driver, joined us and when we had finished the tea and scones Mrs Muller took me to my room, with Tom following, 'To stow your gear'.

I was almost speechless. There was a single iron bed with a decorative bed head and foot, a bedside table with a kerosene lamp, a wardrobe with a mirror, a chest of drawers, a small table with a chair and a fireplace with an easy chair. There was a jug of water in a large china bowl and a soap dish on the chest of drawers. The bowl, jug and soap dish were matching white china with little roses painted on them. I had only seen such finery in the O'Sullivan's home in Dublin. There was a towel and cloth hanging on hooks in the wall and a matching mat on the floor.

Mrs Muller asked me to 'Open the alcove curtain please Susana.' I pulled the curtain open and there was a china chair looking thing that had a place to sit in rather than on and next to it was a cane seat with a lid a foot or more in diameter. She explained that the china thing was a hip bath that a person sat in and she lifted the seat on the chair and there was a china pot with a handle with the same little roses painted on it. This was a commode and she explained what was to be done with the contents.

The floor was polished wood partly covered by a large brown cowhide. I had my second lesson in Australian English after 'gear' describing my luggage. Tom told me later that the cowhide was 'red' and was from a Shorthorn bullock, a breed that was popular in Warwick and other parts of the Darling Downs. I was stunned by this room and said as much. Mrs Muller softly said 'It was our daughter's, but she is now married and lives in Brisbane. You are welcome to stay as long as you wish Susana.' I thought I was in heaven. I had a wash all over including my hair and put on clean clothes that I had washed at the Immigration Centre. I felt so wonderful that I lay down on the bed and before I knew it, I was fast asleep.

I was woken by Mrs Muller an hour later and invited to the kitchen where she busied herself getting our evening meal. There was a large fireplace with pans, saucepans, Dutch ovens and billies hanging over the fire, one with beans and the other carrots. I thought that would be a nice dinner to go with the bread and butter on the table.

She then put on gloves and pulled a Dutch oven onto the hearth and took off the lid. I was gobsmacked at the large piece of meat with a bone sticking out one end surrounded by potatoes and onions. I must have looked like a fish, staring, as she lifted the meat with a large fork, put it on a piece of wood and carved large slices that she put on our plates with the vegetables and gravy. She bowed and said, 'Welcome to our hotel I hope you enjoy the roast mutton.' I certainly did and ate all that was on my plate and the bread and butter pudding that miraculously followed.

I never forgot that meal and her kindness. I was keen to learn about my duties, but she would not hear of it that evening; it could wait until the morning. She made a pot of tea from a big pot of water that was boiling on the fire and we had cups of tea and chatted for an hour or more. She was interested to hear about home and the trip to Australia. It was all very nice. I helped with the dishes and said goodnight.

My beautiful bed was so different and I did not get to sleep for some time and then I dreamt of fairies, particularly the nastiest ones, and it was awful. I woke as the dream ended leaving me sweaty and shaking. Mrs Muller tapped on the door and as she did there was a loud, screaming, cackling noise outside my open window. I was terrified to my marrow, the fairies want to swap me with a changeling, must be a big one I thought. All this happened so quickly, I flew out of bed screaming to Mrs Muller, quite out of control, crying and panting and trying to explain that the fairies wanted me. I was hurt that she and her husband, who I had not met before, looked at each other and burst out laughing so keenly they were hitting their thighs and tears ran down their cheeks. After what seemed an age Mrs Muller put her arms around me, sat me down and told me that it was a bird called a Kookaburra also known as a 'Laughing Jackass' or the 'Bushman's Clock.' They were most raucous in the early morning, particularly if someone had fed them at that time. They were saying 'Wake up you lot, its breakfast time ya know.'

I will not even try to explain what truly being an Irish eejit feels like but believe me I know and have never, ever, forgotten.

With what dignity I could, I pulled my night clothes around me, retreated to my room, washed and dressed and reappeared at the table, had some breakfast, did the dishes and sat down with Mr and Mrs Muller to find out what I had to do.

I was not surprised. I had to rise at 5.30, milk the cow, light fires in the kitchen and elsewhere, help with meals, cleaning, making beds and when I got the hang of it, work in the bar. I also had to feed the chickens and help Tom in the garden.

That was my lot. I was so happy to be in Australia and especially at this hotel. These were definitely the first days of the rest of my life and few of those days passed before I knew I belonged- a lovely feeling.

# 10

# My New Life – 1878

We had arrived in Warwick in late February and soon autumn was with us; a lovely time of the year with the days warm and clear but getting chilly late in the afternoon. There were lovely autumn colours but not from Australian trees. Much to my surprise there is only one Australian tree, in Tasmania, that goes through the autumn process and loses its leaves.

I had kept my journal from the voyage and letters I had written while on the ship and posted them with up-to-date news of my arrival in Warwick. I sorely missed my family and friends, but on the other hand was very positive about what I had done. It would have broken my heart if they thought I regretted the decision I had made. It was a difficult balance because, at times I wished I was still at home. It was a price I had to pay and I would do that.

I decided to write at least one letter a month home on Sunday mornings. Before or after mass was an ideal time so I started writing immediately. I was tearful but felt close to my family and the times we walked home from mass together happy and laughing.

In winter the leafless fruit and ornamental trees in Warwick gardens reminded me I did not like the stark trees in Ireland in winter. The lovely gums and other trees were nicer to be around because they kept their blue- green leaves.

Mrs Muller encouraged me to knit as winter was coming. She

spun beautiful fluffy Warwick wool into yarn and helped me knit a little warm hat that look like a tea cosy. Later she taught me to spin wool and I made a jumper or sweater of my own. These were much lighter than my cloak but warm enough for most outings. Oh, I almost forgot - Mrs Muller had a friend who dyed the yarn Shamrock green for Ireland and to suit my shade of red hair. I also bought some twilled calico for under things. It was more comfortable than raw calico and very, very special for me.

It was cold milking early but otherwise it was nice and not as busy as it was in the summer. Mrs Muller was unwell for two or three weeks and confined to her bed. Once or twice when they were away, I had closed the hotel, managed the cash, cheques, bookings, records, receipts and so on. I asked her if she would like me to take on this task while she was ill because Mr Muller, to my surprise was not good at it. She thanked me and said that she would like that. I had my book keeping book from Ireland and put it to good use and with her help I managed to keep things shipshape. I thought I knew what had to be done in a hotel, but I still had a lot to learn.

Every Sunday I wrote letters, went to church, and sometimes stayed back with other people and Father James Horan, Warwick's first priest, now for about 10 years. I met young men there, at the pub, or the races who were nice enough and I happily chatted with them but there was no feeling in me for anything else. Seamus was still in my heart. It did not sadden me, it was rather nice. I could not, nor did I want to lose that part of me. I often thought of him during the peace and solace of the mass.

The first few months were physically hard and understanding the local way of speaking was tricky at times but, as soon as I relaxed, I started worrying about the task Dr Henderson had set me. It weighed heavily. Sarah was fine and enjoying the challenge at Rosenthal like she was born to it and, like me, she was content to keep her life simple. I saw little of Nonnie and that concerned me.

Tom and I shopped for Mrs Muller at the Pig and Calf sales. This was part of the very fabric of Warwick. Everyone and their dog would go, to buy, sell, look about, chat and yarn or just to be seen. For us Irish it was good craic.

Sarah did the same for Rosenthal and arranged to meet Tom and me there one morning. On the way Tom warned me not to wave my arms or make gestures with my hands or the auctioneer or his assistants might think I was bidding and 'knock it down' to me, meaning, 'You have bought whatever it is, give me the money and take it with you.'

I saw Sarah and she gave me a sort of salute. The bidding stopped and Tom said drily 'Let's go over and see what Sarah has bought.' I followed, puzzled. Sarah was talking to a man I had seen working with the auctioneer. He had a mother and father goose and six babies in a wire box at his feet and was demanding money. Sarah had no idea why this obnoxious man with his geese was yelling at her and getting angrier by the minute. I explained that the little two fingered salute she had given me looked like a bid.

We paid for the geese and a bag of grain and took everything back to the pub in the buggy and settled our new guests into the old shed to fatten for Christmas. Another job done! I gave an imaginary little two fingered salute to Dr Henderson, 'Begorrah, she needed watching', as my da would say in fun.

A mild winter passed and spring was beautiful. The gardens and countryside came alive with flowers, grass and crops growing and calves and lambs popping out everywhere. It was lovely. Our geese were getting fat, the big ones were eating a little grain, worms, slugs, snails and even a mouse one day, the little ones mostly grass and water. Tom told me our geese were a goose and gander and the babies were goslings so that set me right. The goose had a pink and the gander a blue collar. Tom told me geese mated for life and those collars meant that they had been married. I was so thrilled at this and said, 'That's lovely and for life?' He could no longer keep his straight face and shook his head and said 'Oh Susana, you are such a treasure, the collars are to take them for a walk.' 'Oh no I am not havin'any of that malarkey Tom, once bitten twice shy ya bloody spalpeen, try this for size, here eat this.' We were muckin' out a horse stall at the time and I threw a hand full of yucky stuff at him that he easily avoided. He then told me that you could walk them like dogs, and they would hiss at strangers, even bite them. I picked up two handfuls of muckins and rushed at him. He held both hands in surrender and said, 'True Susana I am not joshing you, it's as true as night follows day, honest.'

He was right. Many times, they chased someone off that looked like trouble. And the collars, yes, they were for a leash to take them walking and that is exactly what I did when I got enough nerve. They loved it, especially when I could find a puddle for them to splash around in and then open and shut their wings. They can fly, only a few yards, but I always held their leashes just in case.

As spring tuned into summer Tom took me aside to warn me about snakes. Saint Patrick got rid of the snakes from Ireland so I knew nothing about them.'Snakes are at their most dangerous in late spring-early summer, October especially. They sleep all winter and when they wake are horny and hungry and look for a mate and tucker. If people attack them, they are likely to bite with a full load of poison. Susana, me red haired beauty, you don't want that to happen as likely you would die.' Well, that was short and to the point.

He went on, 'There are two rules for snakes. One is, they are scared of you and try to keep away so leave them alone, don't attack them or they will retaliate. Secondly wear boots with heavy socks and bloody men's long trousers. They will protect you and help make a noise when you walk in the bush.'

The summer was wonderful, a similar temperature to Ireland except once or twice when it became unpleasantly hot. I became friendly with a group of young men and women from church and we had a lot of fun playing ball games, walking, and even acting out charades, a game that a visitor from France showed us. They invited me join them bathing in the creeks or river, something altogether new to me. Eventually I took the plunge, but only paddling!

To swim, I had to buy my first bathing costume, called 'togs' by the locals. Naturally I had to try it on. I went into a little room and undressed, put on the togs to show the shop girl and she approved. I then inspected myself in a full-length mirror. I was shocked about what could be seen or imagined about me. I paid for the 'togs' the girl had wrapped and fled with them in hand.

The next time I saw Sarah I told her about this and my embarrassment. We were at the hotel in the sitting room with no one else about. Sarah said, 'Go and put it on and come back here—NOW,' which I did. When I returned, she looked at me from all directions and said, 'Stop slouching, pull your tummy in, shoulders back and hold your head up. Now go into the hall open the door and walk back in like I said and look at me in the eye not at your bloody feet.'

I did all she said under her silent steady gaze then turned, did some other things and sat down when she said so. She was silent for ages. I thought I would burst from holding my breath and from the posture she ordered I was still holding.

'Susana you are beautiful, with lovely skin, hair and figure and you have an inner glow that few possess. You are confident in your ability to care for people and to get things done; be confident of your physical self as well.'

I said 'Wait here', threw a towel over my shoulders and went to the bar and asked Mrs Muller for two lemonades and returned to Sarah. I had read somewhere that 'A titter ran through the crowd' and I would bet that happened in the bar that night. We toasted our future and Sarah joined our bathing group.

When I wrote my letters home I avoided the bathing costume because Da and Ma would be embarrassed but I did write a few secret codes to my sister and her reply made it clear that Irish girls were not always modest. Once she and some girlfriends swam naked in a little hidden cove not far from our home. Much to their alarm the local priest had stopped on the cliff top and saw them in all their glory. They covered the expected places but Molly Conway whispered 'Cover yer faces. It's the only part of yer that he can identify.' And they did and were not recognised.

Nights were lovely, the twilight was much shorter than in Ireland and sometimes we ate outside, still a novelty for me. The year rolled on with Christmas coming and that meant roast goose for us and any patrons at the hotel. We sold two of the geese and used the money for decorations, chocolates and sweets. Mr and Mrs Muller, Tom and his wife Mary, young Tom and Gracie, their children and me were to have dinner together.

We served our four patrons first and then about two o'clock had our own spread I had proudly cooked. I was missing my family and Seamus terribly, more than I had done on board ship a year before. The kindness and acceptance by these good people soon cheered me and I shook off my miseries. Many times at home I had read letters or heard about how sad people were so far away and I certainly was but at the same time I appreciated the kindness of the people around me. But, maybe I was a little melancholy because I did forget many of the stories the Mullers told about the tin mining, pubs they had owned, life in Germany and Warwick itself.

I had not drunk alcohol in a hotel or wine anyway before but I had two or three small glasses of Reisling he imported from Germany with dinner and was very interested to taste it and hear him talk about how it matched the roast goose and vegetables. It was the first time I heard to drink white wine with white meat and red wine with red meat. I felt quite grown up and popped that wine lore into my memory box.

New Year's Eve was busy at the hotel and I was 'flat out like a lizard drinking', as Tom had predicted. It was a perfect night; people were outside and an Irish band was playing. A night for romance to be sure. But being hot, tired, sweaty, exhausted and having to work, that was far from my mind. I did sneak a pint of beer or two after closing, just what I needed. I washed and went to bed, wished Seamus Happy New Year and happily fell asleep and blissfully slept through the Bushman's Clock.

In the New Year work returned to normal. I felt very comfortable as the anniversary of my arrival dawned. I had enjoyed the summer and even started swimming and playing tennis with a nice strong young man helping me. I was over joyed with the warmth of the Mullers, Tom and Mary and their children who I often visited.

I joined the church choir, helped the children at Sunday school and did some embroidery under Sarah's instruction. Towards the end of summer, I helped Sarah at a ball held at Rosenthal. My, I certainly saw how the other half lived. I even danced with some very attractive young men when we had finished serving drinks. I stayed there that night and it was like I slept on air with the wonder of it. Next day was Sunday and Sarah and I had a nice long relaxing ride. My horse only walked but fast enough for me.

There were no beautiful white woolly sheep and lambs like we had in Ireland. They were a dirty, rusty red colour from the dust that surrounded them. Sarah told me they were Merino sheep and they grew some of the best wool in the world and we may have even seen bales of it at the Liverpool wharves. There were big strong Shorthorn beef cattle and calves. a few milking cows and uncountable kangaroos, emus and birds.

She then took me to a fairy glen where we saw koalas that walked on four legs and I was besotted by their babies riding on their mothers' backs or hanging upside down from their chests.

Sarah warned me to leave them alone. 'They have fierce claws and the tree they try to climb might be you if you frighten them.' We were sitting by a creek nearing dark and there was an ear splitting noise between a roar and a grunt, very loud and repeated. I didn't think of fairies, well not a lot, but it gave me hell of a fright. Sarah said, 'That was a horny koala.' Such a gentle, soft, cuddly creature making all that noise. It beggared belief.

We rode through a creek bed and I very nearly hit my head on an overhanging tree and remembered that lesson many times in future when I rode there at a faster clip. We returned to the homestead and I was taken the few miles home in a shiny, comfortable gig with a blanket around my knees.

# 11

# Nonnie – 1879

I hadn't seen Nonnie since before Christmas so I wrote to her and invited her for lunch at the hotel on Sunday, May 2$^{nd}$ her birthday It was nice to see her. We sat in the little sitting room and had a cup of tea and cslowhatted about what she had been doing. She told me she helped her aunt in the house and garden and her uncle in his blacksmith job as much as she could.

She was positive about Australia and said she had boy and girl friends. I proudly showed her my knitting and discussed other girly things when she became very serious and reminded me of her absent monthly bleeding on the ship. She said that all was fine after we landed for about three months but had stopped again. She had lost a lot of weight and was paler than before. She denied any chance of pregnancy. I was lost in this discussion but tried to reassure her.

The dinner was ready so I served beef broth, Irish stew with carrots, onion and potatoes and then rhubarb and custard for sweets and cups of tea or lemon drinks. She had a few spoonsful of soup and mopped up and ate some stew with bread and nibbled the dessert. She said she was hot and would like some cool air so went outside and I heard her vomit. No wonder she was thin. I made a comment to that effect and she said, 'Oh no, I need to lose some weight.' This was beyond me, so I gave her rhubarb and custard in a jar to take home and said goodbye.

This sorely worried me as no doubt it had Dr Henderson. I told Sarah, who visited later, as she often did on Sundays who said, 'These things happen; all women are not the same mentally and down there.' I was about to take some comfort from her comment when she added, 'I had a friend with that story and she died.' I just sat there, gulped and said something like, 'She bloody well died?' My head and everything else, was spinning. I was scared, felt guilty, afraid for Nonnie, afraid for me and Lord knows what else. I finally pulled myself together and asked her exactly how that happened. She explained that Beth, the girl she knew, had been chubby and everyone laughed at her and worse, shunned her. She stopped eating and lost weight but kept saying she was fat and her monthlies had stopped so that was a good thing. She was shunned even more and died alone in a deserted hut. They said it was suicide and buried her in an unmarked grave with no rites.

I found it hard not to vomit hearing this awful story that Sarah, the woman who shared my soul, told in such a matter of fact, callous and brutal way and I asked her, 'Why?'

She said, 'Susana, I am not a cruel or unkind person but there comes a time in people's lives when they survive or not. I had exactly the same trouble. Just like Beth I was chubby when I was fourteen and embarrassed by growing breasts, pimples, hair on my body and other awful things like the bleeding my mother had not warned me about.

My friends and even boys laughed at me and I stopped eating, lost weight and my bleeding stopped over two or three years and yes, I looked like Nonnie and Beth for that matter, but I still thought I was fat.

When I was seventeen, I started working in the Dublin shop that sold women's clothes and we had to learn about shapes and sizes of people. I became too thin to wear the clothes the ladies wanted to see, though I would have sworn on the Bible that I was too fat. The shop lady said I would lose my dream job if I could not wear the dresses to show off to customers. Deeper down there was a voice telling me that without the bleeding I could not have babies and that chilled me.

It was a strange world I was in but one day in our haberdashery shop my life changed. The man I was to marry walked in. We fell in love at first sight and after the usual courtship were married. I had to accept that I was wrong and force myself to eat proper meals. My weight increased and Lord! I started bleeding again became pregnant and you know the rest. Susana, the strength I found at that time carried me through my recent troubles. Let me know if I can help but I have things to do.' She gave me a peck on the cheek that was about as comforting as a splash of cold spit and off she went.

Hours later I went to bed with no dinner and barely slept. Next morning, I was drooping around doing my best, but Mrs Muller is no fool and took me aside and into her sitting room and asked what was wrong. Gulping and crying, I told her what was worrying me. She said she had seen such women's troubles before and they usually righted themselves but some didn't. I did not mention Sarah's trouble nor Dr Henderson's plea, but I felt better.

She was a practical person and said that if I wanted to help Nonnie I had to speak to Nonnie's Aunt and Uncle. Mary Hogan had sent me a jar of chutney so I bundled up some spinach and took it to her in return.

We chatted about her husband's job with Mr Amies and she said that he was very happy and his wife Phoebe had made her most welcome. She showed me their nice house made of slabs of wood with the chinks filled to stop the drafts and a wooden floor. There were two bedrooms, a parlour and a kitchen with a huge open fireplace that could roast an ox. They had simple but comfortable furniture and I could see the touches of a house-proud woman with money to spend she likely would not have had in Ireland.

It was a very difficult moment because I knew they had no children. Nonnie was their adopted orphan child. I had seen little of Mary on the ship or since. She was a big woman and friendly so we had the usual cuppa. And soon she asked what I really wanted.

I told her I was worried about Nonnie and wondered if she knew what was happening to her. She sagged in the chair and her face did the same. Almost in a whisper she said that she did and had feared that Nonnie was pregnant but she was not. It had been going on for so long and she was losing weight not gaining it. She looked even sadder when she offered, 'I never had much in the way of bleeding and could not have children'.

'Nonnie had only been with us a few years before we left Ireland and came to Australia. Her bleeding started when she was thirteen and a bright energetic, pretty, chubby, little girl. She had friends, enjoyed school and we loved her dearly, our gift from God. Then it changed. She became moody, her bleeding stopped and she lost weight but still said she was fat.

Then we found out why. My husband mashed his finger at work and went home early on the day I did washing at another house in the village. When he opened the front door, he heard Nonnie crying, 'No, no, no please don't. Not again, I am not chubby anymore.' He kicked her door open and there was his best friend doing things to Nonnie that sickens me to think about. My husband is a big man, as was his friend, but he picked him up and carried him outside, threw him in the horse trough and held his head underwater all the time screaming at him.

The village policeman, fortunately, came along and sorted it out after cracking my husband a few times with his stick and asking what the hell was going on. My husband was still so angry he could not speak. The other man said he had been talking to Nonnie and suddenly he was attacked and that was why his clothes were awry, whatever that meant. My husband grabbed the policeman's arm none too gently and dragged him into our house where Nonnie was cowering in shame. His friend was a printer and often used a special red ink that stained his hands and had marked her skin where it should never have been touched.

He was arrested, tried and found guilty. The judge gave him a choice as his family had been well respected people until this shame. Go to Australia and never return or you will go to prison for ten years. He chose Australia, alone, as his wife had disowned him. It was impossible for us to stay. We had trusted him. A good living church-going man who helped Nonnie with schoolwork. We searched, riddled with guilt, why we did not know what was happening. The only weird thing is that he often said 'I love chubby girls' and similar comments about her being chubby and often 'accidentally' tickling her in places that now we realise was dirty not nice.

So here we are in Australia and we thought Nonnie was over her bleeding troubles but that was not to be. Dear God, what can we do? I am afraid she will die'.

My heart ached for the three of them and for me. How could I help?

I offered to befriend her as I had done on the ship and would work something out. Mrs Hogan was pleased with that. On my walk back to the hotel, all I could think was 'Fools go where wise women fear to tread.' I talked more with Mrs Muller and a friend of hers who she called an 'earth mother' and Sarah, who had apologised for her shortness, as Nonnie's troubles brought back painful memories of her own youth. I even read a book somewhere about women's troubles that were rooted in our wombs. The Greek word, I think, for womb was 'hyster' or something that gave us the word 'hysteria for madness. All of this stuff made me more informed but no wiser.

My thoughts were scrambled, day and night. Did Nonnie see herself as fat? Was the absence of bleeding a reward for not eating? Did she tempt that awful man as he had claimed? I remembered her 'special cuddling' at times on the ship. I was worried, afraid, losing weight and showing it, but scones, jam and cream fixed that. Mr Hogan said he heard her say 'I am not chubby,' but when she had lunch with me, she said she was. That also went into my memory box, but I knew not what I would do with it.

I found her things to do at the hotel on three afternoons a week away from food because it repulsed her. She loved the geese and hens and enjoyed working in the garden especially in the company of the Bushman's Clock who she had eating worms from her hand. She mended some boxes and garden borders and polished things in the kitchen. After four weeks and with Mrs Muller's blessing I paid her ten shillings for her work. She was wide eyed with surprise. Struggling not to cry she told me that in all the times she had done things for others, no one had ever paid her anything.

We continued with this working arrangement and she certainly earned her money. It was not a gift.

She was very handy in the garden much to Tom's delight. For the first time I saw him smoke a cigarette at smoko as he was usually so busy. She often picked fruit and vegetables and one day, when I was cooking, I asked her to cut them up. I ate some raw carrots and cauliflower and noticed she had a few nibbles.

Once she ate a scone and an hour or two later I heard her moaning in the dunny and remembered her vomiting the soup I had made. When she came back, I asked her if she had vomited again. She said. 'No, it was runny at the other end and my tummy hurt.' Over the next few months she did not appear to lose any more weight and certainly was happier, more energetic and enjoyed the small pieces of fruit and vegetables we shared. One day she picked up a banana and asked about it as she had never seen one before. I told her how to peel it and fortunately didn't mention that I thought they were disgusting to eat and reminded me of boys' things. My face apparently revealed my thoughts because she looked at me, laughed, then ate the whole bloody thing.

# 12

# Ballarat to Warwick
## – Bill's Story

On a typical cold, wet, windy, August day in 1878, Bill to his mates, William to his mum, Tucker was camped with a mate, Jimmy Dittmar, in an old shepherd's slab hut near Ballarat in Victoria. Reluctantly he wriggled from his swag. Already partially dressed because of the cold, including shirt, socks and woolen hat, he only had to pull on his moleskin trousers, boots and wool lined sheepskin jacket.

A few drops of water on his face soon had him fully awake. They stoked the fire in the big stone fireplace, put a billy of water on to boil, a pan in the coals for their bacon and eggs and cut some damper to toast on a piece of wire Bill had twisted to the needed shape. When the water boiled, he tossed in some tea leaves, knowing how much from long experience and allowed a few minutes for the tea to draw then poured it into their tin mugs. They had no milk or sugar. They both sat on logs and ate from tin plates with the help of their sheath knives and used the toasted damper to mop up the eggs.

The day before they had followed a tributary of the Yarrowee River that ran through Ballarat. It was a difficult climb to the hut as rocks had been exposed from old gold diggings and many had rolled down the slope over the years and stopped against trees or other rocks. Up the hill from the hut the climb was just as bad.

They were both twenty and had been hiking, camping, birdwatching, fishing, yabbying and prospecting in these foothills of the Great Dividing Range since they were twelve. They discovered the hut when they were fifteen and it became their favourite spot. And there was another reason. Like so many of their mates and other people in Ballarat gold fever was like a rash that itched, and the hut was their itching post.

Over the years they did find gold in all sorts of places but only in very small amounts. After they found the hut their trips were much more comfortable as they could carry less and camp there in any weather.

They were both savvy about gold prospecting and knew that gold could be exposed or washed into crevices between rocks by heavy rain. This knowledge had led to three pounds in the bank.

When they had finished breakfast and cleaned up, they grabbed their breakfast plates to pan for gold in the gravel. They were lucky and found a small nugget, worth maybe a pound that delighted them both. Soon the rain started teeming down and it became unsafe so they went back to the hut as fast as they could.

After the essential cup of tea and a hunk of damper slathered with golden syrup, they started chatting and Jimmy mentioned that he had an uncle in Queensland who had a pub in Warwick that he had probably financed from tin mining at Stanthorpe.

'Where the hell are those places?' was Bill's reply.

'Warwick's 100 miles south west of Brisbane. Stanthorpe's 35 miles further south near the NSW border.' Jimmy told him.

'What do they use tin for, apart from tinned food?' Bill asked and after a long silence, Jimmy replied.

' Dunno, why?' Even a longer pause.

Bill put down his tea and leaned forward with his forearms on his knees and fingers laced together and softly told Jimmy, 'You know I am the oldest and would be first in line to get the farm but I have four brothers and I have always thought that it may be easier all round if I went somewhere else.

I am also worried about my chest. The last couple of years I have been short of breath in the winter when it is cold and I make wheezy noises when we cart hay and that stuff. Mum got me to see the quack and he muttered and mumbled, poked and prodded and listened to me chest and lungs. Then he told me that I have a weak chest that will get worse and I should move to a drier climate. Cobber, it hit me like a ton of bricks, as you would understand. Maybe this Stanthorpe joint might be just the shot.'

Jimmy froze. He was so shocked he felt like laughing. His fit, strong mate might have to alter his life because of a bloody weak chest. Bullshit! They sat quietly for a time, both looking down. Jimmy raised his head and said in a soft voice, 'Mate. Let's check if Stanthorpe is a dry place. My uncle will give us the good oil on that joint. I will come with you.' Bill looked up, smiled, nodded and said, 'Thanks cobber.' The rain didn't let up until late afternoon and they spent the afternoon talking about Stanthorpe and by the end of the day they had decided to go there for six months and give it a go. Next morning they walked to their respective homes and parted with a long, firm handshake, their eyes locked – two mates committing to something special.

Next day Jimmy wrote to his uncle in Warwick who had left the same village in Germany, soon after Jimmy's mother, 25 years before. He asked about the mining, jobs, climate, and accommodation in Stanthorpe. Bill took on the task of finding out how to get there.

Both boys spoke to their families as soon as possible and were encouraged to take the opportunity, subject to them doing their share of the work with the crops, shearing and lambing before they leave. A departure in May and return in November 1879 was agreed by all and would allow them to see winter and spring and maybe early summer.

It took a month for them to find what they needed to know. Bill was a methodical sort of a bloke and wrote everything down in a notebook with headings:

*1 Travel. Train to Melbourne via Geelong one to two days. Steam ship to Brisbane five days. To Warwick by train one day. Meeting with uncle etc, two to three days, Stanthorpe by Cobb and Co coach. Ten pounds should cover costs.*

*2 The easy pickings had gone and now the miners were digging trenches to look for tin but there was always a possibility of other finds, even gold, in small amounts Miners were employed in the larger set ups and there was always work in Warwick on farms.*

*3 Accommodation. Jimmy's uncle owned a pub in Warwick and one he leased in Stanthorpe so that was not a concern.*

*4 Climate was trickier. Stanthorpe was less cold and less hot than Ballarat and had slightly more rain. But on fewer days in the year. The winter was cold in the mountains but the days were usually clear in winter and invigorating. The main rains were between October and February in contrast to the winter rains in Ballarat. While it was not the dry climate recommended it sounded better than Ballarat.*

*5 Cost. Their savings plus five pounds from their dads would easily cover transport, clothes, food, tools etc.*

It seemed that the trip was going to happen so a departure date in May was set.

The remaining months seemed to take forever. The boys were busy prospecting, packing and re-packing and doing all they could to leave the farms in good shape.

Time passed and they eventually caught the train to Melbourne via Geelong, just as they had so many times before when they were returning to boarding school at Scotch College. They reminisced about those days. The first game of Australian Rules football was played between their school and Melbourne Grammar in 1859, the year they were born. Geelong football club was formed that year and was the team that they had followed all their young lives.

As the train followed the familiar track they talked more about football and that they lived at the time and place where the foundations of the great Australian game were laid.

They arrived in Melbourne, found accommodation and the shipping office; bought their steerage class tickets to Brisbane on a steamer and next day were on their way. The trip across Port Phillip Bay was uncomfortable, as was Bass Strait, but when they turned north and travelled up the east coast it was calm and relaxing. They berthed early in Brisbane on the fifth day after leaving Melbourne and caught a train that day towards Toowoomba. The line branched to East Warwick. They crossed the Condamine River by ferry and were met by Jimmy's Uncle, Mr Muller. After handshakes all round Tom the buggy driver helped them load their gear and then took them to the Oddfellows Home Hotel. On the short journey they were impressed by Warwick and Mr Muller's knowledge of the district and, in particular, Stanthorpe.

He suggested that they stay for a day or two and make sure that they kitted themselves out in Warwick as things were cheaper there and they might be able to organise to rent a hut or small house. ' But for now it was beer, whiskey, a nice dinner and a yarn.'

He was as good as his word and he delighted in finding bizarre excuses for them to drink alcohol while underage. The food was nice and reminded them of home and a great improvement on what they had eaten on 'the track.'

The whole evening was wonderful but there was one thing that made Bill feel something that he never had before. The Irish girl, Susana Honan, who worked at the hotel was gracious, polite, helpful and modest. She was pretty, with lovely skin and dressed nicely. Her voice and accent were like tinkling bells.

He was shaken by his thoughts and grateful he had said nothing and had not made a fool of himself. Earlier he had felt his face reddening and Susana, with a little smile said, 'Would you like some water, or perhaps the window open, Mr Tucker, as you look hot?' He mumbled something. Later on his way to bed he went to the kitchen for a drink of water. Susana was doing the dishes so he helped her and they enjoyed a cup of tea together with a small splash of whiskey. They talked for an hour and be damned if he could remember about what next morning. What he did remember was that she was a person he liked.

Next day the boys spent hours with Mr and Mrs Muller talking about the mining in Stanthorpe. There was so much to learn. Mr Muller offered the boys accommodation at the hotel he leased in Stanthorpe until they could sort something out for themselves and that was much appreciated.

The rest of the trip was a blur for Bill. He remembered going to the weird Pig and Calf sale the next morning and later Susana, while shopping for the hotel, took the boys to other places to kit themselves out.

They met another young woman at the sale, Sarah, who was very close to Susana. Like Jimmy and Bill, Susana and Sarah had background. But little did they know how much. Jimmy was quite silly with her, telling stupid jokes, showing off and the like but she didn't seem to mind. The four of them had a good time and Bill felt very proud driving the buggy and being responsible for these beautiful girls. Next day they were locked and loaded and boarded the coach to meet the mistress of their fate. Her name was Stanthorpe.

Bill remembered little of the first few months at Stanthorpe other than work, cold, sleep, eat and do it all again and again. He and Jimmy did some prospecting with little success and also worked in the trenches of other miners. Being farmers, part time prospectors and footballers in Ballarat meant they had never shirked long hours of hard work, but this was tough.

Digging mud in granite and sifting it on a slope for the hours of daylight with only ten minutes for smoko was very hard and it was fiercely cold. They were grateful for the heavy clothes they had with them and the oilskins and woollen hats Susana had suggested. They became stronger and their constant back aches slowly faded away. Spring was around the corner and they were earning wages, paid monthly, so things were looking brighter all around.

They often talked about how hard it was to work and look after the rest of living and how much their mothers had done for them in their lives. 'Not so easy on our Pat Malone is it mate?' Jimmy mused one morning as they struggled from their swags and scratched some breakfast together. They certainly appreciated their homes and mothers a lot more.

They had received a good education and that included English poetry and every boy's favourite was Tennyson with his 'Rollicking poems of derring do,' as someone once said. But he was also a Romantic poet and Bill remembered a quotation in his poetry book from school days. 'In spring a young man's fancy lightly turns to thoughts of love.' And in that cold, muddy, unsympathetic, uncaring slab of Queensland his thoughts turned to Susana and the spring to come.

He had had many girl friends over the years marked by holding hands, chaste kisses and occasionally his or her hands had 'accidentally' brushed forbidden places. His parents and church taught him respect for virginity for boys and girls before marriage. If that was not enough, what the devil had in store for transgressors and the shame of bastardry were potent forces in their lives. And if all that didn't work, what older blokes had told him about prostitutes, venereal disease and onanism was too frightful to even think about so he didn't.

Bill was a clear thinker for his age and cared about others. He was surprised to find out that Sarah and Susana were immigrants. He had thought he knew about the Irish in Ballarat and Melbourne and he was honest to admit to himself that he didn't really know the Irish at all. They were flotsam and jetsam that passed by him and his family in their well-ordered lives and they were Catholic; the fierce rivals of the Protestant people in Victoria.

His mother had a book of letters written by Rachel Henning, a woman of high birth, on how to run a household in Australia. She recommended that 'The Irish be kept in the kitchen and not let into the house, because they were dumb, dirty and ignorant.'

These two young women were the very opposite of Henning's view of the Irish. Sarah did not fit the picture he had of Irish people by a long shot and he liked everything about Susana. She was nice and he was happy to let that thought warm him on cold nights.

Bill, like Jimmy, was well mannered and had written to the Mullers thanking them for their kindness. Later he wrote to Susana and thanked her for being so helpful and told her about the diggings, their hut and some of the people he had met. She replied by letter that smelt so nice he kept it under his pillow.

Just when they thought it could not get any better Jimmy

received an invitation for him and Bill to spend the Christmas week at the Oddfellows Home Hotel. That was exciting in itself but the next mail carried a letter addressed to Bill that smelt enticingly familiar. It read 'Please come for Christmas,' in Susana's hand.

# 13

# Susana's New Admirer

Early in the year Mr Muller told me that he had invited his nephew Jimmy and his mate Bill to stay for a time as they wanted to see more of Australia before settling down on their family farms. He also mentioned something about 'Sowing wild oats,' that made no sense to me at all. Why come up here to do that and why use wild oats that have almost no grain in their heads. And they say us Irish have funny ways.

When the two boys arrived, I welcomed them and showed them to the room next to mine but one. After they had a wash and sorted things out, I took them in for dinner and once again Mrs Muller had made a wonderful meal with some vegetable soup, home-made German sausages, vegetables and gravy with cheese to finish. Mr Muller did make me laugh, as usual. He loved having people to dinner but it happened rarely because he worked in the bar most nights. He was excited about his nephew and his nice polite mate and gave them lots of food and drinks. 'Really genuine liquor' he proudly advertised. Beer confused him because it was made in Australia but, after several glasses each, he decided that it was a German recipe therefore that was alright and legal for nineteen year old boys. When he brought out the Tullamore Dew, he simple poured and there was no further discussion. I even had one and when people say, 'It is mother's milk,' that is so right.

The boys were good fun, laughed and enjoyed themselves and when they headed for bed I took the dishes to the kitchen and started washing them. I was thinking what a pleasant evening we had when Bill came into the kitchen and helped himself to a glass of water, excused himself and took the towel I had draped around my neck and started wiping the dishes. After the dishes we had a cup of tea with a tiny splash of Tullamore Dew and talked for an hour, about nothing really but it was pleasant. We said good night and went to our beds.

Next morning was the Pig and Calf sale. After hearing what it was and Sarah's mistake the boys would not hear of missing it, particularly as Sarah was to join us. Bill drove the buggy as Tom was miserable with a cold and had gone home to bed. The three of us drove to the sale and met Sarah by the gate. We did our shopping and helped the boys buy some supplies for their venture such as dried beans, peas and fruit, biscuits, jam, flour, salt, pepper, sugar, soap, medicine and so on. We had a gay time particularly when a pig escaped and about ten young lads eventually captured it getting filthy dirty in the process. We sat under a tree and had warm meat and fruit pies and cups of tea for lunch and exchanged stories about our lives. Bill was calm, quiet and smiled a lot and talked about his large family, their farm and his church where he played the organ or sang in the choir. I said my bit and Bill seemed interested.

Sarah was a polished and a more elegant lady every time I saw her and I was in awe of her. Her few years on me were showing and that was fine.

The night before, Jimmy had been funny, interesting, knowledgeable and sensible. Today he stammered and stuttered and said stupid things. It dawned on me that he was like a love sick calf and the object of his confusion was Sarah. He was simply besotted by this beautiful, pleasant, nice, older woman, the like of whom he had probably never been close to before. Sarah left for home and we went back to the pub and I helped the boys sort out their gear as best they could. We thought long and hard about what else they needed to buy next morning as there would be a limit to what they could carry on the Cobb and Co coach.

We had a quiet but filling dinner that night and played some parlour games but the boys were worn out and Jimmy far away in thoughts. An early night was welcome and next morning with Bill driving we visited the sights of Warwick and bought work clothes, boots, pots and pans, spades, shovels, picks, panning dishes, sieves and some greenhide trunks and hessian bags to stow gear, so they were all ready to go. While we were getting the gear Bill and Jimmy told us in some detail how they had prospected for gold in Ballarat in summer when it was hot and camped in swags and in winter when they camped in a secret hut they had found because it often snowed and or rained. They had found enough gold over the years to pay for their trip to Stanthorpe and the necessary kit to try for tin, so that was a good start.

Jimmy was still fidgety but Bill calmly went out about his business. He must have been excited about what lay ahead but I could not help notice, as he drove the buggy, that, despite his relaxed manner and smile, his eyes were everywhere and his strong hands gently held the reins in perfect touch with the horse. I felt safe with him. A strong, gentle and confident young man with black hair, brown eyes, slim and tall perhaps close to six feet as he towered over me. Mr and Mrs Muller spent the rest of the day with Jimmy and Bill telling them all they could about Stanthorpe, the weather, where hidden mine shafts were, how to go about looking for tin, some plants to eat if unwell or not to eat. It went on forever with maps and books scattered everywhere and the boys using inches of pencil leads writing in their notebooks.

It was all too confusing for me so I wandered off to bed. And yes, I did tell Seamus about the new boys I had met who will board the coach to Stanthorpe in the morning.

# 14

# More New Blood

The boys had written to Mr and Mrs Muller thanking them for their hospitality and later Bill wrote and thanked me for the help with his clothes and supplies. He added that tin mining was becoming more complicated with expensive stationary and wheeled steam traction engines driving saws, pulling trailers, shifting timber, digging drains and holes, drilling for water so much faster than the dear old draught horses and men. He also mentioned how he loaded tin, cut wood, cooked dinner, made tea and they were slowly making friends and some money. We knew this was the height of the Industrial Revolution and things would never be the same again.

I had settled down with a nice cuppa, as I now called a cup of tea, to read his letter that I was pleased to get but it was only about things. I tried to find something in it about him, his feelings, his thoughts and plans and I confess, about me. I blushed when I thought that, but I did like him. He was kind, quiet, gentle and nice and from what I had seen of men in Ireland and Australia they were rare qualities. I made myself another cuppa and read the letter yet again and realised that the thoughts I had about Bill were the words I had written on the card about Seamus at his funeral. Oh! Mother of God what has got into me? I looked into the dancing flames of the fire for a long time with my mind spinning and shed a few tears. For whom I did not know. Later, feeling alive and well,

I went to bed, chatted to Seamus and had a dreamless and restful sleep.

My kookaburra friend had gone away, maybe to have or make babies, but I was pleased he or she was back the next morning.

I had noticed that Mr and Mrs Muller were not as brisk and energetic as they had been when I first arrived eighteen months ago. They built the hotel more than three years before and had very little help since in managing the bar or taking in guests in the middle of the night as the hotel had to be open from10am to 4am. It was very tiring.

Tom and I were doing more and that was fine because they had been so kind to both of us. To save Mrs Muller I did the cooking when necessary and organised Lodge Meetings and 21st and 50th birthdays and welcomed guests. I loved my job and the standards of the hotel. I convinced many friends to use the hotel for parties, wedding receptions and sadly wakes at times.

This all needed recording, balancing books, managing cash, paying bills, ordering supplies, especially the high quality alcoholic drinks Mr Muller favoured and was so proud to serve to his customers.

I made time to write to Jane Moloney, my teacher back home, to thank her for what she had done to equip me to take these opportunities with book learning and confidence. As I wrote that letter, I pictured her in the far distance like looking through the wrong end of a telescope.

In about three months I received her reply. She was so excited and proud of me and stressed that it was me not her who was responsible. I could not agree and told her so in my reply but again I saw her in the distance. When I got my Christmas letters and cards from home, I learned that she had died soon after she wrote to me and had talked about me so much. When I thought about her, she was normal size. And they say there are no fairies in Australia; perhaps the bunyips do these things in Queensland!

I received another letter about the same time as Jane's, from Thomas Morgan the Junior Officer on the *Gauntlet* who had saved Sarah's life. I remembered him well. I had forgotten that he came to ask after Sarah at the depot, but they sent him off. He had tried to find Sarah's contact details in vain.

He subsequently decided to move to Australia where there were opportunities on land and sea. He signed on for the *Gauntlet's* last trip to Australia from London and was to be paid off in Brisbane in November. Dr Henderson was still the Doctor and he gave Thomas my address.

I clearly recalled the lie that had gelled between us when Sarah 'sleep walked.' We all knew what had happened and we all lied but I had never lost a wink of sleep. Dr Henderson cared and so did 'Taffy' Morgan.

I replied that I would contact Sarah and sent the letter to the shipping agent's Brisbane address. I had read his letter on a Saturday and gave it to Sarah the next day after church and we sat and talked about it for a long time. She was angry at Thomas 'spying on her' and showed her hard and private side that was so new to me. But her inherent decency shone through and she admitted that, 'I am so pleased with my world and if it wasn't for you two and Dr Henderson I would not be alive. Yes, I will contact him, perhaps he would like a job at Rosenthal.' Whether I am fey or not, that comment was supposed to show she was being outrageous and frivolous, but she meant every one of those last thirteen words.

It seemed like the last Christmas had only just gone but here we were only a few weeks from my second Christmas in Australia and what a to-do it was turning out to be. Would it be the first of many for Bill and me? How would Thomas and Jimmy get on? Perhaps they might fight a duel over Sarah? Oh, dear Mary, Mother of God I didn't mean it. Please don't let that happen. I was very pleased that Bill had been invited and sent him a little note asking him to accept the Mullers' invitation. His reply was much softer than his previous letter and he mentioned the flowers in the spring, lovely birds and how he looked forward to seeing me again. Seamus was happy about that, I am pleased to say.

Sarah wrote to Thomas and invited him to Rosenthal and said she would find something there to keep him occupied. Christmas day was on a Thursday so Bill and Jimmy would arrive the previous weekend. Sarah then told me she was nervous about meeting Thomas as she was mortified about attempting suicide and would have to face it all again. I appreciated what she said but here was a man who had saved her life and she owed him. I sat her down and said something like, 'Sarah you tried to kill yourself and I understand why. I have never had one angry thought about that but you should know that I ate your suicide note and threw the empty bottle of tablets, you had taken, into the sea. Thomas said you were sleep walking, the Doctor and the Captain confirmed that to the police'.

'Sarah, I do not know if attempted suicide is a crime but I am sure that telling lies to the police would be. The Doctor, the Captain and Thomas probably would have lost their jobs or even careers.'

'And me, I don't bloody know. Maybe gaol, maybe excommunicated. You told me to stand up and walk tall when I bought my bathing togs. You do the same now and be gracious and grateful to the man who saved your life. Remember you are that woman no more.' We were both surprised at my outburst and went our separate ways. A week later a huge bunch of roses was delivered to the hotel with a note saying 'Thank you Susana. I wrote to T. saying how much I am looking forward to seeing him and thanked him for what he did and the risks he took. Love S.'

That part of the year was always busy with parties and friends meeting for Christmas drinks. Tom and Susy, as we had named the geese, did the right thing and had a bigger brood than before so we were able to sell seven and still have enough for the pub, Tom's family, our expanding guest list and cash to buy bits and pieces.

# 15

# Christmas 1879

As it did the year before, Christmas week came with a rush. The *Gauntlet* was a week late due to a combination of rough seas and calm weather. The Merchant Navy had a long list of things Thomas had to do before he would be paid off. After banking his final pay, having farewell drinks with his ship mates, buying day-to-day clothes, a suit for Christmas and a broad brimmed hat, as Sarah had instructed, it was December 10th.

He caught the train, slept, woke up, boarded the ferry, crossed the Condamine River and disembarked at the ferry wharf. A lady was waiting in the shelter and even in the shade he could see she was beautiful with a natural grace and dressed in elegant riding clothes. He walked towards her and asked if she knew where Sarah Murphy might be.

She looked him, hesitated, smiled and said, 'Yes I do.' As she spoke she pulled some hair aside and exposed her scar. Poor Thomas was dumfounded and looked away but slowly turned back, looked again and remembered. They both smiled, hugged and held each other tightly.

I came from behind the shed and joined the hug. Sarah and I both cried and I believe Thomas was fibbing when he said he had something in his eye from the train smoke.

I had never felt like I did that day. We three were forever bound by what had happened.

Sarah had driven a buggy from Rosenthal and picked me up and now they dropped me back at the hotel. She doesn't miss a trick that one. I knew she had leather gloves in her bag but she asked Thomas if he would like to drive. He agreed as he had not had that pleasure for a few years. As they drove away, poetically into the sunset, they made a perfect honeymoon picture.

I had forgotten how handsome Thomas was with his fit hard body, above average height, curly black hair, blue eyes and fair skin, a real mixture of Celt and Viking. They were a bonnie pair and the emotion that radiated from that hug still warmed my heart. I said a little prayer and a rosary for them, it just seemed so right.

Thomas and Sarah would not be joining us on Christmas Day they would be at Rosenthal for the day as Sarah was the organiser of the festivities. We looked forward to getting together after Christmas.

In the short time we had Thomas told us that he had accepted a position with a Queensland shipping company that operated steamships in Australian coastal waters. He needed to move from the sailing ships to steam and a break from the long voyages would be a welcome change. He was to start in early January.

Bill and Jimmy duly appeared the Friday before Christmas as they needed to buy supplies and Christmas presents. They helped with the decorations and other preparations and met some friends for a swim in the river followed by drinks, pies and sandwiches, a nice way to relax after all their hard work. It was busy at the hotel so they had an early night. Jimmy asked after Sarah and I explained where she was, vague about whether we would see her or not. I asked him if he would help a friend of mine from Ireland, who came over on the same ship, get the place ready for Christmas next morning.

If he was Irish, I would have added, 'Now, don't you be sayin', bejesus me girl if ye turned side on and see you I can't.' But I did not, relying on his good manners. I also grabbed Bill and asked him and Jimmy to 'fix' the geese two days before Christmas so we could cook them on the day, starting very early.

Next morning, I introduced Nonnie and Jimmy and told them the scrubbing, sweeping, cleaning, pruning, picking, peeling and cutting fruit and vegetables I wanted done. I added, in my best Irish accent, that I had to work on these days. 'I cook on Christmas Day as a present for Mrs Muller and our cook, so if you lot be messing things up I'll be havin 'at you'. They laughed, especially Nonnie, Jimmy sort of smiled. I wanted to ask Nonnie and her family to Christmas dinner but thought that all the food might distress her so reluctantly did not.

The Christmas planning worked well, as did my helpers. The weather was wonderful and the food, fun and frolics left everyone full, with croaky voices. The wine was even better than the year before.

We exchanged simple presents. Later, in a quiet moment, Bill gave me an extra present. It was a copy of the calico bag my ma had made for me when I left home but with a buckled flap, a handle and a strap, made from fine, soft kangaroo leather, said to be the strongest for its thickness in the world. Words failed me. I had never owned, seen or held anything as beautiful as this and it was mine. I threw my arms around him with tears running down my cheeks and said thank you, thank you. When I let him go, he ever so gently, lifted my chin and kissed me gently on the lips and said, 'Happy Christmas Susana. Today is the first Christmas of the rest of our lives.' My life and his changed forever that day. In bed I went over and over how he smelled, his kiss, his arms about me, what he did and what he said. There was something I had missed. The bugger had teased me by repeating a favourite saying of mine. I had to get out of bed early and looked out my window and there it was. The morning star. The wonder of that night was now complete.

# 16

# A New Nonnie

Nonnie was more cheerful and enjoyed her work at the hotel but was still thin and ate little. Sarah asked if we could spare her to help get ready for the, always frantic, shearing at Rosenthal. All their workers would be busy bringing sheep in from outlying areas, washing them to clean their wool, making sure that the shearing shed, catching pens and yards were ready, unloading and storing new bales, preparing tar pots, making sure grinding stone wheels were working, checking the wool press, the big wool table, block and tackles and so on.

There were so many things that were left undone or done poorly at this time so she hoped that Nonnie would like to help with feeding the orphan lambs, geese, ducks and hens, collecting eggs, weeding vegetable gardens and looking after small children. It was nice of her to ask me first and I said that would be a great idea and Nonnie agreed. It would most likely be for six to eight weeks.

Tom was excited about it and Nonnie talked to him whenever she had a chance because she knew nothing about farms and farm animals, let alone a huge place like Rosenthal, with thousands of sheep and cattle. Tom had taken Nonnie 'under his wing' and prepared her as well as he would his daughter. She would be outside so needed boots, cotton shirts, hat, neckerchief, woollen socks, moleskin pants and a Le Roy raincoat because that time of the year it was likely to be wet. He insisted that she do this as soon as possible and to wear and wash the clothes and scuff the boots. This would make them more comfortable and look like she knew what station life was about. When Sarah collected her, she looked the part and happily waved goodbye to me and Tom.

Mr Muller suggested that it would do me good to have some time off and I would find the shearing interesting so I arranged to get a ride there with a carter taking supplies from the hotel.

The usually calm estate was a madhouse. During shearing there were 30 or so people involved and they had to be fed. There were people everywhere unloading potatoes, onions, pumpkins, flour, tea, sugar and other foodstuffs for the kitchen. Sheep were butchered every second or third day and carcasses hung in meat houses or salted. The main kitchen was going flat out and the shearers had their own cooks and kitchen in their quarters.

It was nice spending time with Nonnie. She thrived on looking after the chickens, geese, orphan lambs who had to be fed from a bottle, puppies and the children. She had not put on weight but looked more energetic, less pale and more talkative. I was beginning to feel positive for her. I had heard an expression in the pub, 'There is a light at the end of the tunnel.' I had put that in my memory box pulled it out and put it in the Nonnie box. She had to go through a dark tunnel but there was a way out at the end. I felt good about that and gave myself a hug and smiled.

Nonnie and I went for a long walk one day and sat down by a creek to boil a billy, make tea and eat our cold meat and tomato sandwiches. Nonnie whispered, 'Susana, I know you care for me and are worried about my weight and not bleeding properly but it is a long story, would you like me to tell you?' My answer was 'Yes.' But I am not sure I meant it. 'Susana, I was chubby when I started to mature and didn't like it but that man was kind to me and made me feel better about myself. He spoke and listened to me as an adult and was very helpful with some school work. He complimented me on my looks and said how many of the most beautiful paintings in the world were of chubby women. He was about 10 years older than me and over the weeks and months he had me believe he liked me as a young woman rather than a girl. He read me poems and sometimes sat close to me and touched me on the bottom or leg and would say, 'Oh sorry!'

I was flattered and liked the way he made me feel. I had lost my parents and although Aunty and Uncle cared for me there was little talk and affection. Once when I knew he was coming I dressed so that he saw part of me he hadn't seen before. He soon noticed and straight away whispered, 'How grown up you look' and cuddled me. It was nice and he gently kissed me and touched me in other places. I looked forward to these visits and thought that it was all a beautiful dream and he would take me away on a white horse one day. And then it wasn't nice any more. He made me do things that made me feel sick and ugly and others that were unnatural and hurt. I could not tell anyone, but it was not long before Uncle caught him, thank God.

After he was sent away, I was too guilty to eat and lost weight as you know. I probably cannot have babies. That is something I long for. To hold my own baby and look after it is what I pray for every night and now God has taken that hope away.'

Oh Jesus, Mary Mother of God, All the Saints and Angels save me. The bloody light at the end of the tunnel was the headlight of an on-coming train roaring on its way to destroy her and me. The air had become chilled as if an icy wind had blown. I put my arms around her and held her tight. She did the same and I again felt the desperate need and sadness in the 'strange' contacts on the ship.

She wanted and needed the touch and warmth of a fellow human not a filthy, sick, bastard swine. Mother Mary and the rest must have heard me because the chill wind disappeared and the air warmed. I felt an immense power in my chest and arms and I whispered to her 'God will mend you. You will have your babies and I promise you I will be there for you as long as you need me'. She rolled up in a ball and keened until exhausted, then sobbed and fell asleep. When she awoke, she had a shine in her eyes and a smile on her poor thin face I had never seen before. These bunyips must be exorcists as well.

On the way back to the homestead I asked about her health. She said she no longer made herself vomit but she had trouble at the other end going several times a day since being in Australia. She got scutters from bread, cakes, biscuits, batter and scones, as I had seen on one occasion. She did eat a small amount of meat, potatoes and other vegetables but as the family were better off there was more food made with flour eaten every day. That would make her lose weight but surely would not be enough to make nature turn off her ability to have children?

I told Sarah my suspicions about bread and scutters and she took Nonnie and me to see Annie, an old aboriginal lady a day or two later when Nonnie was feeling better. Sarah had an ear for languages and chattered away with this lady. I heard her say 'water' and she pointed at her bottom and then she drew stars and moon in the dirt and touched her lower tummy and made gestures of rain falling with her fingers and then shut her fist. So Nonnie's scutters were like water and her moon flow stopped. Sarah then showed her some bread and wheat grains and the lady shook her head almost violently saying 'No, no, no, no, no.'

She then stood up and walked over to a straggly plant with a small head that Sarah told me was Kangaroo Grass. She picked a handful of these and took them back to where she had been sitting, put the seed heads into a dish shaped stone and rubbed them with another stone until they were crushed. Then she blew away some of the grass leaving grains of flour. She pointed to the flour and then the bread and her mouth. She then rubbed her tummy and took her hand away with a big smile and reversed the closed fist and imitated the moon flow. This was exciting. If Nonnie only ate flour made from these seeds, would she would lose the scutters and get her monthly things back? Could it really be so easy?

Later that day we had a chat to the station cook who had been at Rosenthal for decades and was interested in Aboriginal food because, 'After all they were the world's first bakers'. She added that 'Native millet also makes good flour for people with this gut trouble as does, sorghum, ordinary millet, oats and maize and I have known people who have made flour from potatoes and also rice. The bread is not easy to make or as tasty but is a hell of a lot better than having the squirts and dying from eating bloody flour.' Sarah, Nonnie and I stood there in disbelief. Could this be fixed? Was her whole problem due to a physical cause rather than mind damage from her abuse? The cook, Peggy Jamieson, went one step further, 'You can work in here Nonnie and we will see what we can scratch up to make Nonnie Bread and Susana you can poke your nose in if you wish.'

That night Nonnie, worn out, went to bed early and Sarah and I had a long and relaxed chat about how far we had come in our adopted country and amongst other things, I asked her about Thomas. 'Susana he was lovely, I really enjoyed his company and part of me wants to see more of him but another part does not'. I must have had my 'What the hell are you talking about look' because she said.' I will explain. I do find him attractive and one night we had some lovely wine and whiskey and for the first time since my husband died, I felt warm and remembered how I enjoyed the physical and emotional pleasure of marriage. When I was displaying dresses, I used my 'come on' look I developed for a husband who hesitated to buy a dress his wife liked. He always changed his mind. I put that look on.' We were sitting on a sofa and one thing led to another and we held each tightly and gently kissed. Thomas lay back on the sofa and I lay with my head on his chest and my eyes closed. It was lovely and I did not want to stop when I heard his heart pounding, as was mine.

I just couldn't do it. I wanted to run, I remembered my husband's death and froze. Poor Thomas, he looked so crestfallen and I was almost crying. He was wonderful. He held both my hands in his strong callused ones and said, 'It is alright. It must be so hard for you.' He knew I was a widow but nothing else. We sat there for some time and then he stood up, still holding my hands, kissed my forehead and said 'Thank you for a wonderful time, I do hope we meet again.' All I could say was, so do I and thank you for being a real gentleman. Next morning, as planned, he left early to catch the train. So that was that.'

I arranged to go back to the pub the next afternoon with someone who was picking up shearers from the train and was waiting outside the kitchen to say goodbye to Peggy Jamieson and Nonnie who had not yet organised the bread. While I was thinking all this, I noticed a little iron figure of a beetle by the kitchen door. It was a foot long raised on two front legs with two feelers, the size of my middle finger, projecting from its head parallel to the ground. Two wings were folded on its back and sloped to the ground covering the back legs. Just then Peggy came out with a cuppa and I asked her if it was something to keep the fairies and maybe bunyips away. She looked around puzzled until I touched it with my foot. 'My Lord Susana you have an imagination. When anyone wants to come to the kitchen, they have to take off their big leather Hessian boots so they don't drag mud and goodness knows what else into my kitchen. They put one foot on the back of the beetle to keep it still and the heel of the other boot in between the feelers and pull their boot off, swap feet and do it again.'

She laughed and soon after I was settled into the coach seat swaying my way back home. As I started to doze, I realised I had thought 'home' not 'The hotel.' It was a lovely feeling.

# 17

# 1880 – Shearing

A few weeks later Sarah arranged a ride for me to Rosenthal as they were still shearing. On the way I noticed that many of the shearers from Warwick had found a relatively cheap and new way to travel. Instead of walking it was a common to see a shearer riding a bicycle, now with two equal sized wheels, wearing his cabbage tree hat for shelter. If he was from afar there would be a swag across his shoulders and a billy, frypan, water-bag and a cup hanging somewhere.

Nonnie looked a picture, colour in her cheeks, sun tanned stronger arms and her face had lost the gaunt look. She had been weighed on the wool scales and had gained a pound. The scutters had not stopped but lessened.

The Overseer was expecting Nonnie and me and walked us to the shed. The men were having smoko, most of them with a roll your own Bull Durham cigarette hanging from their lower lip and a tin pint pot of black tea in their hand. Soon they started shearing. There was an open area called the board with ten holes, about four by two feet in the wall each leading to individual pens where the tallies of sheep shorn could be worked out at the end of each two hour run.

There were ten shearers and each one walked across the board into pens of sheep through double swing gates and grabbed a sheep around the neck from behind and sat it on its bottom and dragged it across the board to their stand. They removed the belly wool and threw it away to be picked up and baled separately because this wool had been soaked with urine since the sheep was last shorn. They then turned the sheep in a succession of positions until after the last blow, meaning a cut of wool with their hand shears. When, somehow, the sheep was near the hole, it was pushed through, often bleating with joy. It was a wonderful stage with skilled performers.

The catching pens had been tightly filled before the shearers were at work by shed hands and had to be kept full so it was easier for shearers to catch their sheep. If they were near empty a shearer might yell 'Sheep O' or something less polite. Along the board worked the roustabouts picking up the bellies, then rolling up the fleeces in a certain way so they could carry them to the round wool table and cast it into the air holding a special part of it so that it fell on the table as gently as a mother putting a blanket on a baby. The roustabout then went back to the board to do it all over again, in the meantime sweeping loose wool away from the shearer. Sometimes there would be a call of 'Tar here Jack' meaning a shearer had cut a sheep and wanted 'tar', a mixture of lamp black, kerosene and tar, to cauterise the wound and the roustabout would get that as well.

The wool table was surrounded by three or four shed hands skirting the fleece by going around the edges and picking off dirty or prickly wool, throwing it under the table and then bundling the fleece up in a way so that the wool classer grabs the best part of the fleece to assess what grade it is. The fleece is then put into one of six vertical bins. Three marked AAA, AA, A, indicating quality of the fleeces and others for, bellies, locks, the curly wool on their head, and pieces of the skirtings they throw on the floor.

Near the bins is the home of the wool pressers fearsome

equipment. He puts an empty bale into the press, throws armfuls of wool into it jumps in and stamps the wool down at the corners and sides of the bale and repeats that until he cannot fit any more in wool in the bale. He then puts a wedge shaped metal grate on top, of the wool base down and attaches a long lever and cranks it down to force the wool down. When he can get it no tighter it is removed and wire staples put into the flaps of the bale and pulls them together. He then opens the press, pulls out the bale, rolls it onto the scales, records the weight (2-300 pounds) and then brands the bale. Then with a bale hook, strength and nous the each bale is and brands the are branded wih the name of the property and the class of wololsometimes two high, against a wall with a door leading to a loading ramp.

The shorn sheep in the yards are counted and recorded by the overseer or his offsider, often with the shearer doing the same with a piece of chalk inside the shed. The sheep may be sprayed or dipped depending on whether they have something wrong or it is the practice of the station and then put in a bigger yard or paddock until all the sheep in that mob have been shorn. They are then collected by the station hands and walked back many miles to their grazing areas where the shepherds take over. Some may be kept near the shed, for food as 'killers' or to be sold.

The bales of wool are put on drays pulled by horse or bullocks to Warwick, by train to Brisbane and ship to England. We may have even seen some on the Liverpool docks as someone once said.

We spent the two hour 'run' from smoko to dinner time in the shed and it was exciting, interesting and even romantic. The most successful shearer was called the 'Ringer' or the 'Gun' and he was at the end of the row so he could see how fast the others were shearing. The overseer told us the ringer in this shed was a new young fellow called Jackie Howe, born at nearby Killarney, whose dad was the town crier in Warwick.

I could not help watch him. He had black hair, was handsome and strong but what fascinated me most was his fitness and balance. He seemed to touch the sheep and wave the shears to make wool fall off and the sheep happily popped through the hole into the yard. He looked like he would not blow out a match. Some shearers were nearly as good but others, swore and hit the sheep, wore themselves to a frazzle wrestling them and it was only time before their tally was dropping off.

I never forgot the way Jackie worked, not only as a shearer, but as a model. Skill and strength are important but balance and gentleness or kindness really helps, not only in shearing, but in life.

There was a lot to like and admire about this whole process but the place stank and the shearers' quarters were even worse. Many shearers and other people hated washing and believed it was dangerous and unhealthy. That changed but it took a long time. The shearers and others who worked with them were seasonal workers. The station employed shepherds, farmhands, stockmen, horse breakers, blacksmiths, cooks, kitchen, maids and others full time.

There was another group I had not heard of, called Jackaroos. They were young men, usually but not always, from farms or stations who wanted to learn about the wool or cattle industry and worked at big places for several years to achieve that. They would take that knowledge back to their family farm, or to another property with the aim of becoming a manager.

They had single rooms in a separate block and ate with the family. This was to learn good manners, the management of money, buying and selling stock and even politics. This went some way to thank them for the long hours of work they put in often camping out in summer or winter and getting little pay. Wool, was so incredibly important that Australia was said to ride on the sheep's back. Many people who had squatted on these lands and were lucky with good rains, no bushfires and high prices made fortunes and became an Australian aristocracy. Their sons likely went to England to school. The training of Jackaroos to understand and fit in this world was all part of this new life.

Seeing the shearing and the size of the property was a real eye opener to me and I began to get a small grasp of just how big and progressive Australia was with a higher standard of living than the United States. In the time I had been in Australia the much feared and talked about droughts or floods had not happened anywhere near us.

Compared to Ireland meat and vegetables were good, plentiful and cheap. Families could eat meat every day and for a long time my tummy rebelled against this but I got used to it. Vegetables and fruit were easy to grow and many people enjoyed doing that for pleasure, sharing and eating. Something very special, compared to Ireland was the free access to rivers and the sea for fish or shellfish to add to the diet. We were lucky that we were given permission, where we lived, to do that but most people were not. Australia really is a special place.

I met interesting people at the hotel. Some were Danes who had fled religious persecution and and raised cows for cheese making near Warwick and I used to help at times. The Mullers liked their cheeses and the Danes liked Mr Muller's wines so I did the trading for them. The cheeses were the best I had tasted as were the wines!

I also met a larger than life man, Thomas McIlwraith, who was a politician, business man and owner of several sheep and cattle stations near Roma about 200 miles north-west of us.

In September 1880 he had been to Stanthorpe on business and stayed at the hotel on his way to Roma. He was Scottish and was born and raised in Ayr and he had followed his brother to Bendigo in the 1850s. In 1874 he had brought his business interests to Queensland. I was interested in his life at Bendigo because it had a similar history to Ballarat.

He was a massive man and touchy if things did not go well for him but I found him interesting. One night when it was quiet he told me he had tried long and hard to get a railway to Roma and on the 16th September this year it was to be opened and he did not want to miss that. I said, 'It is an exciting world Mr McIlwraith.' He bade me sit down and did so himself. He sipped his whisky, Scotch, not Irish whiskey, lit a cigar, blew a contended sigh of aromatic smoke and started talking:

'Susana, I moved my business interests and myself to Queensland and have no regrets. You are absolutely right about Australia and something I did earlier this year may interest you. My brother Andrew and I chartered a ship in the United Kingdom called the Strathleven, arranged for Bell and Coleman of Glasgow to install air compression and expansion refrigerator equipment in it and steamed it to Australia.

The ship loaded frozen sheep carcasses and butter in Sydney and then Melbourne and departed that port on 6th December 1879 and arrived in London 58 days later on the 2nd February 1880. The meat and butter were perfect. This will be a huge thing for Australia. Until now the only products we have exported from cattle have been tallow and hides. With the railways developing in other states the isolation of such a huge part of Australia will be no more and instead of walking, cattle will be transported by trains to ports and their meat shipped overseas. So, young lady this will be something that you will soon see on a large scale from the Darling Downs and much further away.

I have enjoyed our conversation but now I must go to bed as I have a busy day tomorrow.'

Australia was on the move. New industries, the narrow gauge rail way network expanding, the settlement of new land and growth in the cities and so on. I was told by our railway customers the narrow gauge was used to allow smaller paths to be cut for the rails to be laid so the program was quicker and cheaper.

# 18
# The Start of Something Big...
# Maybe

My work, Nonnie, Sarah and the experience of the shearing world had kept me busy. I did enjoy working in the hotel but some customers, or rather the world they lived in, did distress me. Some were soaked in blood from shooting kangaroos, cutting their throats, scalping them and then hooking the scalps on their belts until they had 2000. This was enough for the squatters committee to count and sign a voucher for presentation to the Marsupial Board who paid sixpence per scalp. In some places it was twelve pence or a shilling. In Warwick 100,000 kangaroos were killed in 1878 and 300,000 in 1879.

Another custom was battues when kangaroos and later rabbits were eating grass that was meant for sheep. Selectors collected dogs, horses and neighbours and drove the terror-stricken animals from the bush to open ground where they were killed with bullets or waddies.

Emus were killed by professional shooters, plucked and boiled down for their oil that is excellent as a lubricant, liniment and a pleasant smelling lamp oil. They were also killed for fun by would be 'gentlemen' chasing them on horseback, unhooking the stirrup strap and letting the iron run to the end of the leather and then swinging it to brain the terrified animal.

Kangaroo leather was lovely and a good skin was worth 10 shillings before tanning. Emu oil products were nice. I could understand the reasons and necessity for some of the killing by people who were trying to make a living or had spent huge sums on properties, but shooting harmless koalas for fun to see them fall out of their tree was a hideous thing to do.

I liked to think of nice things and one of those was going to Rosenthal where no one talked about battues. They were out of sight and out of mind. Sarah was enjoying horse riding as was Nonnie who had put on two or three pounds and scutters were less trouble with the bread that Peggy had made. No one said anything about Nonnie coming back to our hotel to work so she obviously liked working at Rosenthal and did her work well. I also enjoyed riding, as long as it was on Seamus. Yes, that was his name. A big white gentle gelding. He had belonged to an Irish man who had lost him in a gambling debt to the Overseer, who liked the horse but did not ride him often as he was too slow but was happy for me to do so. One day Sarah and I rode near the lambing ewes and unfortunately found two orphan lambs. We bundled them into my jacket. I remounted and Sarah passed them to me. She told me to go back home the way we had come and she would see if she could find any more and go home another way.

I did this and stopped at a locked gate. Seamus was very good and walked to the gate, close to the catch I had to lift to open the gate. It was stuck and when I leant over, I couldn't reach it because of the lambs in my jacket. I managed to slide off the horse with the lambs, open the gate walk through it with the horse and shut it. All I had to do was mount up. I could get my foot in the stirrup but could not get my other leg over because of the lambs. I had no hands to grab anything. Seamus was a good boy and stood still while I got a piece of wood and a rock and made a platform and put my left foot in the stirrup and pushed off the ground with my right. One push, two push and THREE push and up I went and straight over the saddle and landed on my back with my head between his front feet his sad eyes looking into mine. He gave a little neigh 'Eejit' in horse talk. Oh, I didn't tell Seamus about Seamus, I thought he, the horse, would be too embarrassed. Sarah had seen I was in trouble so back she came and we rode home and gave the lambs to Nonnie.

Sarah was happy and enjoyed her work. She was a great organiser and her touch was obvious in the kitchen and dining room. She had made a friend for life of Mr Muller when she ordered his wine for some of her very special dinners for people who bought sheep, cattle and wool from Rosenthal. He gave me a bonus of two pounds for my promotion of his wines, especially the Riesling. I was delighted to learn that she was teaching Nonnie needlework and I had a sneaking suspicion planning a dress for her as well.

Sarah and Thomas were writing to each other as friends rather than frustrated lovers but that was nice. He was enjoying the new challenge of steam ships and loved the climate and places he visited and often had time to explore. In Rockhampton, Thomas had spent a nice evening with Biddy and Betty. He found them hard to follow as their broad Irish accent had formed a weird mixture with western Queenslandisms. They were getting along well with the ringers they had met but they were vague about what that meant. Same name as the boss shearers but they were cattle stockmen.

Last, but not least was me. As mid-year came and went, I did not know the exact plans of Bill and Jimmy. Bill and I wrote to each other often and he said that they might stay longer as their fathers did not put in crops and instead had bought more sheep so they did not have to be there and if necessary, they could send money from their work at Stanthorpe. I missed him and remembered the Christmas present he gave me and the words he said and I thought that there may have been a little more in his letter but maybe that was unfair as he may have been worried about things at home. It was almost spring so I wrote back a cheery letter about my exploits at Rosenthal, but leaving out the Seamus episode. I was doing more management and cooking than ever. I did invite Jimmy and him for Christmas and said how much I would like to see him. He wrote back a nice letter thanking me and accepting my invitation. That gave me a pleasant tingle.

Tom and I went to the Pig and Calf sale often and sometimes bought a small pig or lamb that mysteriously disappeared with Tom and turned up ready to roast or have as chops or ham some weeks later. The man who looked after the yarding and sale of these animals was Gerry Muldoon and he was stone deaf. One day a regular seller of three or four lambs once a month, John Thomas, turned up with ten. 'G'day Gerry' said John, 'Mum died, and we have to sell all these to pay for the funeral.' Gerry as usual was gobbing away, talking meaningless drivel because he was so deaf and asked, 'By the way John, 'ow is your mum gettin 'on these days?' as he just kept unloading the dray. I wrote to Da about that and he wrote back that he was puzzled at why I thought it was so funny and I confess I found it hard to explain. I was used to Irish ways and I was clearly adopting some Australian ones.

Spring was soon in the air and it reminded me of a little ditty I heard as a child, 'spring is sprung, the grass in ris, I wonder where the flowers is.' Little things like that popping into my mind made me sad and miss home and Seamus but I accepted that it was part of my life but I did write to Catherine, my sister, to tell her about spring and ask if her children knew the ditty. Otherwise I was pleased with myself and relieved about Sarah and Nonnie. I had money in the bank as Mr and Mrs Muller did not charge board and lodging. I wore good clothes and did things I had never dreamt of in my life.

I loved my job and the people I met. One day a shearer from Rosenthal came to the pub and we recognised each other and over a drink he asked me what I thought of shearing. We had quite a chat and he mentioned just how good Jackie Howe is and predicted one day he would be the best shearer in Australia. He added, 'His dad, Jack senior, was a very good shearer before he became town crier and I will tell you a story about him. In the days of the early settlers people tried many ways to make a profit from the land and someone had some llamas for wool growing and of course they needed shearing and Jack senior was game. I was there when he fronted the animal and grabbed it but the llama released its foul, fermented, stomach contents in one fell swoop on his beautiful black shiny hair of which he was very proud. He threw his shears away and took half an hour of repeatedly washing his hair before it was clean. He then insisted that the llama must have a bag on its head. I was laughing so much the boss told me to nick off so I don't know whether Jack Howe shore the animal or not but he probably did as he did not give up easily."

I was planning Christmas and realised that a few weeks after that on the 20th February 1881 my bond time was up. I was scared as I would turn 23 in 1881. What would happen to me then? About this time Ned Kelly, bushranger, was hanged on November 11th aged 26, at the Melbourne gaol. I got a terrible start. He was only four years older than me. I had heard so much of him in Ireland and knew he had gone to gaol in 1871 for two years. His proud Irishness, even though he was born in Australia, made him a folk hero at home. I had always assumed he was one of the ex-convict bushrangers I heard of and much older. His last words as he climbed the scaffold, 'Such is life' carved the phrase, 'As game as Ned Kelly' on our Irish-Australian hearts forever. I made a promise to myself to learn more about this man and his fellows because it did cast a pall over Christmas for a time, but Bill's imminent arrival soon pushed that away.

I only saw Bill once or twice a year, so much different to Seamus and me. Letters were nice but physical company was better. The summer weeks went by, swimming, busy pub, pleasant walks and some nice letters from Bill. Nonnie was putting on ounces and blooming physically. Sarah had told me Nonnie and Jimmy were writing to each other and she and Thomas had settled into a friendship and were taking things as they came. She was pleased that he had been promoted so things were looking up all around. Sarah talked little about Christmas and I sensed she might have had ideas about spending it with Thomas as friends do sometimes!

Someone else was looking after the three couples and two local bachelors who wanted to try our famous roast goose and had booked in for lunch, so we sat down to eat at one o' clock Christmas Day.

There were the Mullers, Tom and family, Nonnie, her uncle and aunty, Jimmy, Bill and me. We ate our goose, the new ham and roast lamb and vegetables with the usual custard and pudding for dessert. We had white and red wine to match the meats and a Tokay that Mr Muller said came from Hungary with the sweets. We finished with tea and imported coffee that was nice for a change. The children had lemon drinks as white and raspberry as red wine in proper wine glasses. They giggled so much that someone would have thought it was real alcohol they were drinking.

This year we had a Christmas trees with presents all around, mostly funny little things, that made the kids and others laugh. There were Irish tin whistles Mr and Mrs Muller blew and laughed and slapped their knees just as they did when I thought the Banshee was after me. I knitted tea cosy hats, with the blue and white hoops of Geelong football jumpers, for Bill and Jimmy as they had often said how cold it was at night in Stanthorpe. I had made some sauces and preserves for the other adults and sweets for the children. I saw Jimmy wink at Nonnie and Bill wink at me and one of them announced. 'C'mon let's do the dishes. Mullers, you and Hogans and Kennedy parents stay here.' We were all happy and gay with the joy of life and the wine. There were many little smiles and touching between us. We took tea and coffee back with us to be greeted by the 'Derry Air' for God's sake. The Mullers could play the bloody whistles. Well that set us all singing and dancing. The quiet Hogans had beautiful voices and sung all sorts of folk songs. Before we knew dusk was upon us so that called for more food and drink.

We all went home or to bed late. Bill's path and mine crossed on the verandah outside our rooms and we looked at each other for minutes. He picked up my hand and gently kissed it, put it down and mouthed, 'This is the second Christmas of the rest of our life. Goodnight Susana. See you in the morning.' I was drunk for the first time in my life and stood there dumbfounded that Bill did not do something more affectionate. Damn it. I kicked my door open and threw myself on the bed and soon fell asleep. The bushman's clock woke me. After a drink of water, I lay back and remembered my one lovemaking with Seamus that ended so badly. Sleep came again and I woke up refreshed and at that moment I knew that Bill respected me and could see a future for us. I said the rosary for him several times. 'Being a Protestant, Scotch College you know, he needs a lot of help from you, Father in heaven.'

Later we met for breakfast and on the table was a hard, irregular parcel next to two candle sticks standing on a flat soft parcel. I unwrapped the first parcel and found a beautiful, leather bound book with a belt wrapped around it. The belt was two inches wide of the same leather and patterns as my bag. The book was 'For the Term of his Natural Life' by Marcus Clarke published in 1874. I just stared at it. I had read sections of it in 'The Australian Journal' on board the ship and once had told Bill. The man had a memory like an elephant and had written inside, 'Susana, you will have a better life in Australia than people in this book I promise. Love Bill Christmas 1880.' He laughed and added with a smile on his face and in his voice, 'The belt is to hold up those men's pants you be wearing when riding the horses so they won't fall off when you do.' I went red but laughed with the others. It was sweet and I gave him a big hug.

Mr Muller, with an open letter in his hand explained; 'Patrick and Mary brought their presents last night and asked me to give them to you this morning.' I opened the parcel and it was a table cloth with a giant rose embroidered in an oval section in the middle and at each corner a different animal, a king parrot, koala, kookaburra and kangaroo. It must have taken forever to make. It had been also wrapped around two polished metal candle sticks a foot tall with wide bases and each held two candles. Mr Muller coughed, cleared his throat and read 'Susana we are simple people and know simple kindness. The rose is for our Irish Rose, Nonnie, who will live to see these animals grow old due to you. The candlesticks are for you and the man you marry to always have light as you have given us.' He coughed again and blew his nose. My cup was overflowing as they say and so were my eyes for some time. Bill passed me a handkerchief I found out later Mrs Muller had made and given him for Christmas washed and ironed. He smiled and said, 'Well done. You are a very special person.'

And that was the light at the end of the tunnel for Bill and me I thought but, yes, there was another train on its way, bigger, faster and a good deal nicer than the first. Like any other day in an hotel there was work to be done and with the help of Bill, Jimmy and later Nonnie we did what had to be done and had a nice lunch left over from Christmas day. When we had finished Mr Muller asked if Jimmy, Bill and I would stay while Mrs Muller and Nonnie did the dishes and other chores.

# 19

# Here Comes the Train

Mr Muller offered tea or coffee that no one wanted and looked at some papers in front of him and paused. 'An Englishman called Shakespeare once wrote that, '*There is tide in the affairs of man that if taken leads on to fame and fortune, if missed he is a failure forever*' or words very much like that. There is something I want to discuss with you three that just might be one of those tides.'

I went pale and sweaty. Bill asked what was wrong. I could only stammer and splutter. 'Bill it's the bloody bunyips again; I read those words once before and the very next day decided to leave Ireland and go to Australia. It is scary.' After a drink of water and reassuring words from Bill, Mr Muller showed us a letter from Jimmy's father, Hermann Dittmar, who he grew up with in Prussia and had travelled with him on the same ship to Australia.

He passed the letter to us and it read:

*Good morning Louis and Frances.*

*I hope this finds you well and comfortable in that lovely hotel of yours. I know James is enjoying life in Stanthorpe and I appreciate what you have done for him.*

*I bring to your attention an opportunity that may interest you and /or perhaps James and William.*

*In recent years I have had more business dealings in Adelaide than Melbourne and have made valuable connections with the large*

*German population in that state.*

*South Australia is moving ahead very nicely and is leading Australia in mining income from copper and grain production, particularly since the British Corn Laws were repealed and grain can be exported to Great Britain.*

*In 1870-72 the South Australians did a wonderful job when they followed Stuart's Tracks and built the Overland Telegraph line, such an important thing for business and trading.*

*Since 1863 South Australia has been responsible for the Northern Territory and in 1876 announced they would build a railway all the way to Palmerston at Port Darwin.*

*A countryman of ours works near Quorn, north east of Port Augusta, at Woolshed Flat where the infrastructure and quarters of the railway are located.*

*He wrote to me that the railway finally started in Port Augusta in 1878*

*Of further interest is that a huge camel industry exists at Farina and Hergott Springs since Thomas Elder imported 123 camels and 12 handlers from India and located them at Beltana. By the time the narrow gauge railway reaches Hergott Springs there will be 2000 camels and 600 people there and in total 6000 pastoralists, farmers, explorers, miners, stockmen, prospectors, government workers, labourers and tradesmen living north of Port Augusta.*

*Since the early 1870s land has been taken up in northern South Australia and south western Queensland in the Channel Country, an area of 60,000 square miles where the Georgina, Diamantina and Warburton River, Cooper Creek and their countless tributaries on their way to Lake Eyre create a paradise of grass for cattle when they flood.*

*The recent news of sheep meat being frozen and sent to the United Kingdom has been of great interest to cattlemen in that area.*

*When linked with the railway under construction. It could be a 'goldmine.'*

*I have met a Douglas Field in Adelaide who recently wrote to the Member for the Gregory electorate in Queensland advising that he and a number of friends planned to start a store in the north of South Australia to supply goods to that part of Queensland. It would however, be preferable for it to be at Diamantina Crossing where a settlement, Birdsville, had sprung up only a few miles from the South Australian border so he applied for a grant of land there from the Queensland Government and was successful.*

*I also know a Robert Frew who coined the name Birdsville and has a store there. He told me that in three months he imported goods to the value of 5000 pounds.*

*I am sorry my friend to take so long to get to the point but Frew highly recommends the building of an hotel.*

*All the goods and services in that part of Queensland come from South Australia and there are thousands of cattle being driven 700 miles to Adelaide at present. This year the rail reached Hawker 215 miles from Adelaide, next year it will reach Beltana, Farina in 1882 and Hergott Springs, 300 miles south of Birdsville, in 1884. Loading there, a busy town of 600 people, will save the cattle a walk of 400 miles.*

*I asked Frew the obvious question as to why he didn't build an hotel himself and he said he already owned Pandie Pandie Station nearby. He also understood that licensees of hotels in Queensland had to live on the premises and that was impossible for him.*

*Are you interested in pursuing the idea further? I believe I know someone who would and could build a hotel.*

*Yours sincerely Herman*

We were mute, still and stunned. I had no idea why I was even there. The silence dragged on until Mr Muller coughed and said.

'We are too old for that challenge but what about you?'

Jimmy said that he was content to return home and be a farmer one day probably sooner rather than later and was not interested at all.

Bill looked into the distance and eventually offered that he had some interest. After the meeting, with the help of a stick drawing pictures in the dirt, he explained to me how the stock routes of the Northern Territory and the eastern half of Queensland and the Northern Territory did or could go through Birdsville and on to Hergott Springs.

I still didn't know why I was there.

Next morning after breakfast Jimmy and Bill went off somewhere to talk more about the Birdsville idea I suppose. I was tidying up and Mrs Muller invited me to bring us cups of tea to her office.

She greeted me with her usual smile and asked me what I thought of the letter from Mr Dittmar. I told her I wondered why I was there, but it was interesting. Her reply left me utterly amazed and I knew not what to say or do. She said, 'Susana you have been a pleasure to have in our home and your work is excellent. I believe you have the personality, skills and the indefinable knack needed to run any hotel. We are well aware that your bond ends in February next year and you are free to go wherever you wish. My husband and I would be happy to allow you to manage this hotel and teach you what we can if you are interested in the Birdsville proposition.'

I thanked her but confessed I would be far too afraid to go to Birdsville. She reached out and took both my hands in her old wrinkled ones, looked in my eyes and almost whispered, 'Susana, it is obvious to me that Bill adores the very ground you walk on and the air you breathe. I am sure he would go with you.' After what they call a pregnant pause I whispered, 'Yes I think so, and I would like that.' 'Last but not least Susana, we have lost our daughter and you being with us has been a joy we thought we would never feel again and we would like to help you as we would her.'

All I could do was cry and say thank you and I am sorry about your daughter over and over and then when I was empty of tears we sat in silence for a long time until she said, 'Thank you for listening. Think it over and we will talk again tomorrow' and kissed me gently on the forehead.

I went to my room and lay down but sleep would not come and my mind was churning but amongst all this confusion some thought were becoming clear and they were simple. I love Bill and this is an opportunity for me to meet my destiny with him side by side. I dozed off to be woken by two draught horses called Bill and Jimmy in the passage outside my room. I went into the passage and Bill was waiting by my door, Jimmy had disappeared. I said, 'Bill I must talk to you.' Just as he said, 'Susana I must talk to you.' We both laughed and walked outside holding hands to our private little spot in the garden with its lovely Jasmine smell and sat on a bench we knew so well. We argued about who would go first, Bill pulled a coin from his pocket and said winner goes first, you call. I called heads and it was tails so Bill went first.

'Susana, I think this idea has merit. The cattle industry in the Northern Territory has really gone ahead since the telegraph in 1872, and in 1878 Nat Buchanan over-landed cattle there from Queensland and many others followed him. The Channel Country is doing well, and cattle are being fattened there from the Northern Territory, Queensland and also South Australia. With the train soon going to Hergott and the export of frozen meat developing the future would appear to be bright and a pub in the middle of all that would likely be a good business.'

'Another thing is that I have seen the doctor at Stanthorpe. My chest is not improving as much as I had hoped as there are so many cold and wet days here and Birdsville will certainly have less of those. I know nothing about running a pub but Mr Muller told me an hour ago he has a friend in Stanthorpe who is looking for a steady chap to learn the ropes in his pub so he can take some time off.' My reply was that Mrs Muller would train me as the manager of their pub so I would be useful in Birdsville. He said, 'That is wonderful' and gave me a big squeeze just as the dinner bell rang, so off we went. He was unusually quiet during dinner and appeared puzzled. I put on my quiet face and ate my dinner just saying 'yes' and 'no' when I had to. His puzzled look nearly made me burst with laughter.

When we had finished our meal and had done the dishes Bill went outside and came back with some jasmine in his hand and eventually mumbled, 'Do you want to come to Birdsville with me?' I nodded. 'But do you know what that means?' Another nod. 'But we are not married.' A shake, this time with downcast eyes. Then his beautiful blue eyes lit up and his smile was a mile wide. 'Do you mean you want us to be married?' Another nod. But I could not keep it up 'Yes, Yes, Yes please!' Bill put on his hat, swept it off again and went down on one knee, gave me the Jasmine flowers, held my other hand and asked me to marry him. I accepted and we had a proper kiss and sure enough there was the evening star in the west and that made my day complete.

# 20

# What Now? – 1881

We were beside ourselves with joy and could not resist telling Mr and Mrs Muller, who were delighted, as were Jimmy and Nonnie but they were the only people we told for the time being.

Hard headed planning was difficult in a dream, but we tried. We had to tell our parents and for the first time I considered sending a telegram but that was impersonal so we both wrote a letter to my parents with Bill asking for my hand and he wrote to his parents telling them that we were now betrothed but not publicly. The next thing was to tell Mr Dittmar that we were interested in his proposal. Easy to write but to move to the middle of nowhere and find a pub ready to go was a crazy idea and we started to panic. Mr Muller asked, 'How would you eat an elephant?' We looked at him blankly. He answered, 'One bite at a time'. That made us laugh and settle down.

We really did not know where to start so Mr and Mrs Muller prepared letters for Mr Dittmar and his friend. Plans for Bill to work in a pub at Stanthorpe were hatched and a letter written and I was to start as manager of 'our' pub in the New Year after we had time to enjoy our special moment. We formed a rough plan of us working for a year or two and then Bill going to Birdsville, maybe in 1882 to organise the building of a pub. Somewhere, somehow, before then we would get married. In the mean time we would work hard, save money and do what we had to do to become publicans.

The next few days and New Year's Eve passed in a beautiful haze. We talked and talked about why we loved one another and our future. I will never forget Bill saying to me, 'Susana, I think you are the prettiest girl I know, you are clever and have a heart as big as the outdoors, but most of all you are nice. I like as well as love you and want to spend the rest of my life with you.' I remembered Sarah telling me that she and husband had a love that grew wings. They had dreams and songs to sing and that is just how I felt and when I told Bill he smiled like a cat that ate the cream. Like all good things the week came to an end and Bill had to return to work and he carried the letter Mr Muller had written to his publican friend.

Mrs Muller told the staff about my new role as it was time for her to take things more slowly and asked them be as kind to me as they had been to her. I was pleased that no-one seemed jealous or angry and they gave me a little clap and shook hands or gave me a peck on the cheek.

It was so different being the one who had to plan and answer questions and I fumbled along. When I thought hard, I knew most of the things to be done such as meals, cleaning, making beds, staffing the kitchen and bar and I liked the contact with my fellow workers and customers.

I was used to ordering, paying bills, getting and giving receipts and recording what I had done day by day. Mrs Muller opened my eyes to how important it was to keep financial records in what she called journals and ledgers to know if the business was successful or not. She touched on budgets but said that could wait but what couldn't wait was knowing what hours staff worked and how much to pay. 'A business would rise or fall on how fairly staff were treated' she said often and I never forgot.

The work had always been physically hard but now it was mentally hard as well. I was proud to have the responsibility but doing my work, bookwork, sorting out squabbles and checking supplies. Planning ahead was like I heard someone say once, 'Having a lot of balls in the air at once'. I went to bed with my head spinning, bone tired every night but with a pad and pencil under my pillow. I became very good at writing in the dark. Every night I talked to Seamus and slowly introduced Bill to the conversation. Did I like my life? Yes indeed! After my little routine at night I slept like a baby.

The weeks rolled by, and my sister Catherine sent a photograph of her, her husband and children and Ma and Pa in a well wrapped frame. They had caught the little steam ship to Limerick where a photographer they knew had set up shop. I was overwhelmed with emotion. Her children had grown so much, she looked older as did my parents. I had that photograph close to my bed that night and for the rest of my life. The next day I wrote a tear stained letter and dear Bill added some lovely words thanking them for the gift (it was for both of us) and some other nice words that would have melted the Blarney Stone about how lovely I was blah blah. Perhaps those words came from 'Blarney Stone? Bill and I wrote to each other weekly and I had to chuckle to myself at times. Here we were, young and in love writing loves and kisses and then about our Birdsville venture, something that would terrify most people older and wiser than us.

When February rolled around and my three years bond had finished, I received a long letter from the Immigration people wishing me well for my future in Australia along with some formal documentation. I answered it and thanked them for what they had done.

When I had a spare moment, I wrote to Grace and found out

she had completed her studies and was second in charge of a new ward at the hospital and was stepping out with a handsome young doctor so that all sounded very nice.

I wrote to Biddy Kelly and Betty Quinn as all I had heard about them was from Thomas and that they were still at the Criterion Hotel, owned by a Mr and Mrs Curtis, where they first worked and had some romantic interests with a couple of ringers.

It was my usual gabby letter to these wonderful friends and after a few weeks I had a reply from Betty.

*Hello Susana*

*It was nice to hear you are doing well with a boyfriend and all and have a good job. Biddy and I are well and happy in our world although it's a bit different to what we thought it might be.*

*We both like men and stuff as you know but it all got too hard. All these ringers seem to want from girls like us is a bit of this and that; 'Thanks' if we are lucky and then goodbye. I can understand that as I am a bit like it me self. But we want more. I am 26 now and Biddy 21 god bless her.*

*I don't want you to get the wrong idea but we have slept in the same bed together more times than we can count on the ship and in our homes full of babies and little ones. Yes, there have been many, many nice 'comfort cuddles' as we call them.*

*We have a little house with only a big double bed and decided that would be our way. It is much simpler and we are very happy and relaxed about it all without the risks of the other stuff. And the strangest thing of all is that we must look happy and well because we started getting noticed by some very nice men. One was a Tom Jackson, an actor and shearer, who is in plays and recites poems. Six months he ago moved in with us and we share everything together. We think he is true to us. I don't think he would have the strength to elsewise be.*

*He has some funny friends and the three of us were married in the water of a creek and later got bits of paper saying he had two wives. We still laugh a lot particularly when he told me he is part Scottish and I can picture him in a bloody long kilt, that to do its job would near reach the ground me thinks.*

*We are blessed and full of joy, food, drink and Tom—it is called makin' hay while the sun shines and he did help me write this letter-he is nice.*

*Oh yes, Biddy is with child. Both of us have done our share of shaggin 'and never been with child so we look forward to that.*

*Fair winds for you lovely girl we will never forget you.   B B Baby and T*

I did not know whether to laugh, cry, be angry or what. They were kind, cheerful and had few pleasures in their lives except each other. I wrote a happy letter to them because I was happy for them.

This had added a little spice to my life, the weather was good as was work. I often had a moment of joy thinking about our life to come. Bill had missed writing a letter or two but he was working hard so when I had my first letter from Bill for a while I sat down with a cuppa and opened the envelope. I unfolded the letter and started to read it with a smile on my face and a warm feeling but that changed to a cold sweat a tight chest and paralysis.

The letter read:

*Dearest Susana*

*It is hard to write this letter but I must. My parents and I have written to each other several times and they will not agree to me marrying a Catholic in our church. I have tried so hard and told them you go to mass every week where I haven't been to our church for months.*

*I am happy to marry in a Catholic church as I believe God knows who is a good and godly person not men in churches who make the rules.*

*What's more they refuse to attend your church to see us married. I have spent these last few weeks sorely troubled as I love my family and church and feared I might not be able to commit to our marriage.*

*I talked for hours to our minister in Stanthorpe and told him my troubles. Amongst other things he explained, 'Rules and customs help us to live from day to day in our families and communities but they don't suit everyone all the time. My own belief is that those who have love in their hearts, care for another and live Christ's teachings and the 10 commandments can marry anywhere in the sight of God'.*

*Susana, forgive my momentary lapse. I have found the strength I was lacking in his words. I want you to walk by my side and be my friend forever, no matter where, because we will always be in God's sight.*

*Susana I was so sad when my parents said what they did but my spirit is singing since I wrote this letter. I was going to tell you something when I next see you but I feel so close to you I can't wait. I am sure you were sad at the start of this letter but I hope pleased by now and maybe ready for a little story.*

*After my talk with the minister we had a cup of tea and started talking about the Geelong Football team as he came from there and our mood lightened and even more so after a glass of whisky.*

*When I was leaving, he shook hands with me and said, 'Oh there is something you can do for me Bill.' I thought he meant some money in the poor box so I reached into my pocket. 'No, I do not want money but if this conversation gets out, I will be sent to Birdsville and you will surely see me wandering in the desert with a crook in my hand looking for lost sheep. If you do, please say g'day and give me a drink of water, Good night lad and God will be with you.'*

I slept like a baby.

After a long wait I had a letter from my parents with their consent but reminded me that we must be married in a Catholic church and my husband had to convert and our children had to be brought up as Catholics. I saw the hand of man in this and wrote as much to Bill.

He replied and repeated what he had told his parents about being happy to be married in a Catholic church and for the children to be brought up that way. He was not too keen on the conversion but he would go along with it if that is what it took. We decided to live by the view of his minister and see what happened with the Birdsville plans. This had been a difficult and unpleasant subject and we were both glad we had resolved it in the way we had. We went about our business knowing that we would be married but we did not know when or where but we were both happy we had made the commitment to each other in our hearts, minds, bodies and souls.

There was so much to learn about running any hotel and I enjoyed the people part of the business and was getting a feeling for the paper work. I was hopeless with mechanical things but Tom was good at that, as was Bill. I started getting plans, on paper at least, and wrote endless letters to Jimmy's father, Mr Frew in Birdsville and Mr Field in Adelaide and many others. We were in a hurry but time was necessary to learn enough and to earn money to get a start.

Then one day Mr Muller received a letter from Mr Dittmar that surprised and thrilled me. He said that, if we bought some land they knew about, he and Mr Field would build the hotel and we could lease it from them or work for wages until the way forward was clear. This needed a personal discussion with Bill. Mrs Muller wanted to visit Stanthorpe to help their friend, where Bill worked, with his paperwork and invited me to come along. She said she would be our chaperone. I had never heard the word and when she told me it was a two legged chastity belt I blushed to the roots of my hair.

I enjoyed the trip, the conversation with her and the bookwork and spent a wonderful time with Bill. She wasn't the best as a chaperone, but our mutual respect for each other took care of any wayward conduct. The plan in the letter was that the building would be finished in late 1882 or early1883 as there was a meeting of the Licensing Court on April fifth 1883, so Bill would need to be in Birdsville by late 1882. I was delighted at this turn of events but disappointed it was going to take so long. Before this meeting Bill and I had a long and private conversation and swore to each other that we would put every fibre of our being into earning money and otherwise equipping ourselves for this venture in all respects and would marry when we had a home and hotel.

# 21
## 1881–1882

The year was flying by. Sarah was still finding her way with Thomas and did spend Christmas with him in Brisbane and was comfortable being friends. I resisted asking further.

Nonnie was thriving. I saw her every month or two when she was in Warwick seemingly having been captured heart and soul by life at Rosenthal. The passing parade of edible, sorry, eligible Jackaroos no doubt helped that happy state. One day she whispered, 'The girl stuff is all happening proper like you know and my tummy is fine.' That was self-evident from the way she looked with more weight and a happy heart. Christmas was, as always, pleasant and it was wonderful to see Bill and to be wrapped in each other's arms and dreams. The venture was unfolding, we were saving and learning about being publicans and about Birdsville. Back at work in 1882 I was able to fill my time with work, dreams, writing letters to Bill, my family and messmates and spending time with friends.

I knew I was extremely lucky. I was comfortable in Warwick and at Rosenthal and thought I had a reasonable idea of Australian life but the death of Ned Kelly had a strange effect on me. His death and that of Ben Hall and others meant the end of the bushrangers or 'Wild Colonial Boys' as they were often known. Since the colony started there were about 2000 bushrangers and most led short, brutal lives. In the early days they had help from friends who hid them, held their cash, lent them horses and were sympathetic jurors. But times had changed, they were no longer romantic, and many were ruthless killers who robbed any and every one.

The police had repeating rifles and pistols, the telegraph and trains made it easier for the police to travel and catch them and large-scale land clearance and settlement took away many of their secret hideaways and tracks. The use of blacktrackers hastened the end of many, particularly Ben Hall. When the laws were changed to allow police to shoot at someone they thought, rather than knew, was a bushranger, the end was inevitable.

Bushrangers were said to be the result of convictism, but this was not all on one side. Public sympathy for the bushrangers was not so much a sympathy with crime as a protest against tyrannical rule. I pondered much on this and asked questions of many. Opinion varied so much I had to accept that their history, although recent, was no more. My thoughts should be about the world to come for Bill and me. That I could influence.

I enjoyed mixing with our customers at work and talked with them about all sorts of things and learned much about the real Australia. One quiet day Gerry Muldoon, the almost deaf chap who ran the Pig and Calf sale, was having a drink with a couple of mates. As usual, he was yelling and I heard him say, 'Yair I know that there were some white people killed by murdering black fellas but we never give 'em a fair go. I was at the races in Toowoomba about 25 year ago and that murdering bastard Billy Fraser shot a young blackfella strapper, for no reason, right in front of me while I was watching the horses in the mounting yard. They reckon he had shot an Aboriginal woman in the main street of Rockhampton not long before that. He never went to trial for those or any other killings.'

I interrupted with three beers and asked about Billy Fraser. Between Gerry and his mates and other people later, I got the story. Fraser's father had owned Hornet Banks station in the upper Dawson River area about 250 miles north of Warwick but died young and Billy, the eldest child, took over. He drove bullock teams to make ends meet and once when he was away as many as a hundred local Yeeman warriors attacked the homestead. His four sisters and mother were raped and killed, three brothers and two hands were killed. His brother Willie was left for dead but later raised the alarm. The reason the men from the local tribe had attacked was because Fraser, his brothers and the native police had repeatedly raped their women. They enacted a biblical revenge. Billy earned a certain heroic notoriety at their funeral by holding up a tomahawk and promising to bury it in the skulls of the murderers. He went on a rampage and was said to have killed 100 blacks himself and with the hatred unleashed, the squatters, white and native police, killed a further 200 people. In 20 years, there was no one of that tribe left alive. A year or two later near Maryborough close to the coast a similar thing happened and local blacks killed eleven whites in revenge and suffered similar losses and yes, Billy Fraser was said to have been there 'helping.' In both these massacres any blacks the white vigilantes, or their black troopers found were killed.

I quietly asked questions about Warwick. I was told about a butcher who was attacked by five Chinese, armed with broken shears they had made into weapons. He surely would have been killed but Jimmy, an aboriginal flew into the fight with his waddy and knocked them all unconscious. Sadly, he was killed somewhere else by others of his race simply because he was from a different tribe. There was one tragedy where some local black people set a trap for a white man who had raped many of their women but he escaped and told other white men about the trap and they shot several blacks.

Warwick people were publicly angry and ashamed about this tragedy. I was to learn that many things happened out of sight and out of mind but Warwick seemed more peaceful than other places I had heard about. Someone told me that the population of Aboriginals in Queensland at the time of white settlement was 100,000. By 1880, there were maybe 10,000 remaining.

These thoughts made me sad but as happened so often in my time with the Mullers they shone a light in the dark places where I hid. This time the light they shone was dramatic, surprising, infinitely kind and generous. I was having a cuppa and chat with Mrs Muller when she heard Mr Muller in the next room and called for him to come in and poured him a cup of tea as he sat down. She smiled and said, 'Perhaps you would share what you told me last night about Susana, my dear husband.' He looked embarrassed but she held his hand and said, 'Go on she won't bite you.' He looked at me and whispered in a trembling voice, 'You know you have become the daughter we have lost and have been a joy to us both. You have probably saved the life of my dear wife who was in such a decline when you first came. I feared for her life but since then every morning she wakes and welcomes the day. We both would like to help you as if you were our own daughter. Please accept this this as a small thanks for the joy and love you have brought us.'

He handed me a piece of heavy paper rolled up with a green ribbon tied in a bow that I removed and unrolled the paper. And then it dawned on me that it the title to a large block of land on the corner of Frew and Adelaide Streets in Birdsville with my name on it. I struggled to get a word out. 'What is this?' Mrs Muller smiled gently and softly said, 'The future for you and Bill dear girl.

It is the land where your hotel and house will be built and you will own it.'

I could not talk and sat there with tears rolling down my cheeks in torrents. Mrs Muller was crying and Mr Muller was dabbing his eyes. I ran to them and put my arms around them and held them tightly. My nerves were ragged and could not talk sense. I nearly fainted and then with Mr Muller helping me, I stumbled off to my room. As soon as I lay down, miraculously, I fell asleep, but not before I thanked God and told Seamus and Bill the news.

The timing was perfect as next day Bill was to arrive en route to Birdsville. This planned departure was bittersweet as we really did enjoy each other emotionally and physically. Our future was looking very positive indeed but we did not know when we would be together. Hard as it was, we kept our promises to each other to wait until we were married to taste the joys of marriage. A few tidbits in the meantime were most enjoyable. Bill was with us for a few days and all too soon he was gone. He left on the 19th August 1882.

# BOOK 3

# LONG JOURNEY
# TO THE
# PROMISED LAND

# 22

# Bill's Journey

My final few days with Susana were a dream. We became physically much closer but did not break our promises to each other before our wedding. More importantly we cemented our friendship and revelled in what we were facing. We had land in Birdsville and money to start building an hotel there. Susana had saved most of her pay for several years. It was truly a God given gift that the Mullers did not charge for room or board and I had a few pounds from prospecting and savings from my wages. I was sad to leave but it had to be, I confess that the train trip to Brisbane and about half the steamship journey to Melbourne was a blur. But I enjoyed the last few days of the trip. I played cards with other passengers and had a good look through the ship guided by an officer I had known at school. My home in Ballarat was on the itinerary. I was surprised and pleased to be treated as an equal by my parents. Like many young people, I had the illusion that my parents were much wiser now I had grown out of my teenage years. I had discussed everything I knew about Susana and my future by letter but face to face contact was invaluable. They were both wise in financial matters and in employing people. I learned much in a short time and could barely talk when Dad enclosed 20 pounds in his vice-like handshake when we said our goodbyes.

Another train trip returning to Melbourne and then to Adelaide by ship where I had meetings with Mr Field and Mr Dittmar, usually at the South Australia Hotel opposite Parliament House or the Adelaide Club on the other side of King William Street. Both holdings were on North Terrace. I could not help notice how many distinguished people they knew. We confirmed the arrangements that had been worked out by mail between Susana and me, the Mullers and these two gentlemen. The hotel building had already started and it would be ready to open in early 1883. They had Mr Muller's 75 pounds and 50 pounds from Susana, me and my father. Mr Field was owed a few favours and believed we had enough money to build the hotel and fit it with basic furniture. Susana and I were expected to provide linen, glassware, crockery, cutlery and other things.

All they wanted was that we purchase our alcohol and other goods and supplies from their business in Adelaide. It all seemed too good to be true and I tossed and turned trying to work it out. It really went back to the life-long friendship of Mr Muller and Mr Dittmar and how, in the absence of the Muller's daughter, Susana had filled that space. I was jolted by the memory of a Scottish folksong, Bonnie Mary of Argyle. The last two lines were. 'Your goodness was the while. You have made my world an Eden, Bonnie Mary of Argyle.' Susan had certainly done that for them. Susana's goodness and decency were unconditional and this reward unexpected, but appreciated. I was dumbfounded by the realisation that, with luck, we would be able to establish ourselves financially in a short time. I could not help but notice the value of personal contacts. Another was Adolph Zucker, a fellow countryman of Mr Dittmar who worked at Quorn, the heart of the new railway. He knew when it would reach Farina or Government Gums only a short distance from Hergott Springs that was the stepping off point to Birdsville. They both also knew a man with a string of camels who worked out of Farina carting supplies to the ever growing railway line and had organised him to help me get to Birdsville from the railhead at Farina.

But that was all in the future. I went to bed early and tossed and turned all night often in a cold sweat. The recent events had caught up with me. Eventually I struggled out of bed, washed and readied to shave. I did not recognise the pale, gaunt, fearful, face and then the horrid truth that it was me. I was deeply and mortally afraid of the open razor in my hand, put it down and collapsed on my bed. I lay there in my state of utter exhaustion and awoke dreaming of my proposal to Susana and her answer of 'Yes, Yes, Yes please,' each word louder and more definite than the one before. I had thought little about that but now I realised the intensity meant more. She was alone, maybe still a little afraid, loved me, but most important trusted me to look after her forever. She trusts me, I repeated several times. Then I had a wonderful sleep and when I looked in the mirror the next morning, I saw a strong, happy, determined young man. That young man, shaved, dressed in moleskins, blue cotton shirt, boots and wide brimmed hat, slung his swag, picked up his bag and strode down the stairs, crossed the road, boarded the Great Northern train and faced the first day of the rest of his life.

There was a mixture of people on the train, farmers befitting South Australia's reputation for grain and wool, business men in suits, school children with and without parents. Women in their finery returning home after shopping in Adelaide, two policemen with their families going to where and for how long I did not know and a few young fellows about my age looking like stock agents and stockmen. The train went north to Terowie, where we changed trains from wide to narrow gauge and then to

Peterborough and Quorn, a total distance of about 240 miles from Adelaide. The country did look in good heart with crops and pasture doing very well. The main area we went through was the mid north of South Australia that had become world famous for its strong merino wool and grain. As we travelled north the country became less attractive. One of the young men I yarned with told me that from 1863-1866 The South Australian Government Surveyor, George Goyder, had drawn a line that marked the border between agricultural land for farming, and pastoral land that was better for the grazing of sheep and cattle rather than crops. This Goyder's line turned out to be very accurate and sadly prophetic for many who settled there believing that 'rain followed the plough'.

One chap excitedly pointed out where we crossed that line south of Quorn and the country was certainly different north of there. We had reached the Flinders Ranges. They were magnificent and being in an arid area were different from any other ranges I had seen, running 260 miles due north from near Port Pirie. We approached them from the east as we neared Quorn, the main town in the Flinders Ranges. While we made good time from Adelaide to Terowie on the new standard gauge rail we slowed from there to Quorn on the narrow gauge. It took about 13 hours all together and we stopped at Quorn for the night. Quorn was a hive of industry and some of the night and the next morning were spent loading the train with the myriad items of gear and equipment, rails no longer made of iron but the stronger steel, wooden sleepers from Western Australia, water, food, hammers, shovels, picks, crow-bars and many other things. There were workers from all over the British Isles and Europe, particularly Germany.

Most of our passengers from Adelaide left the train in Quorn and were replaced by workmen, often countrymen who were fit, wiry and strong and wore the same tough clothes and boots. Many had red neckerchiefs to signify their loyalty to their particular workmates. My mate from the train told me that they were called 'navvies' and built railway lines with little else than picks, shovels, a few horse-drawn scoops and dynamite. They, or their mates, had built the Navigation Channels or Canals in England, hence the name. They were said to have had rations of a gallon of beer and a pound of beef a day. About 50 of these men sat in groups with an easy familiarity from working long and hard together and being on their way to do it all again. We left after lunch and in a few hours we reached Hawker, sixty six miles away and due north of Quorn and stayed for the night. We had passed through magnificent ranges and settled down for a meal and cups of tea after someone lit a fire and boiled a giant billy.

I will never forget sitting on my unrolled swag watching the most spectacular sunset in my life. Not only was the western sky a maze of colour, it lit up the cliffs to our east and showed their beauty. They were rough, harsh and forbidding in the fierce sunlight but at sunset and dawn they were a soft and beautiful sight. As the sun set into the infinite flat saltbush plains, I felt close to God and his works and felt Susana's presence so powerfully that I turned to look for her but had to be satisfied with the evening star peeping over the ranges as I lay in my swag. I felt peaceful and determined and had a wonderful and refreshing sleep.

We started at daylight and steamed 80 miles towards Beltana where we stopped to take on board some more navvies who were joining their mates from Quorn and moving to the work camp at Farina for the Hergott Springs section of rail. I was sitting next to a stockman who worked at Beltana sheep station owned by Sir Thomas Elder who, amongst other exploits, was the first person to bring camels to South Australia in 1867 to cart freight. These animals had made the settlement and development of hundreds of thousands of square miles of Australia possible. I had heard the train called 'The Ghan' many times and asked my stockman mate why. He told me that the cameleers were mainly from Baluchistan and Afghanistan hence the name. Unfortunately, he also told me about the problems in Beltana they were having with navvies, particularly as that one section of railway had finished and another was started. There could be new contractors who would not necessarily employ the existing workforce. People would need to move and if they had families it was more unsettling. Grog, gambling, fighting and even murder were features of these camps. I must say the men who boarded the train were quiet and looked thoughtful.

It was only 50 miles to Farina. It took us a bit over two hours. The South Australian Government had founded Government Gums in 1874 but the farmers called it Farina, a name I recalled from my schoolboy Latin, meaning 'flour', so it was indeed a place of hope. For many years it prospered but in 1882 there was a drought and little or no grain grew in northern South Australia. The adage of rain following the plough was wrong and Surveyor Goyder was right. My new acquaintances had left at Beltana and I dozed off and was lost in my dreams, lulled by the click and clack of the train wheels, of how to explain to Susana the unfolding vast world of mountains, endless plains with their blue stumpy bushes and beautiful gum trees lining mostly dry creeks and all bathed in an infinite cloudless blue sky.

I was woken by the train slowing and stopping in Farina. There was a wood and corrugated iron goods shed with an arched roof, a single line running shed, loading platform, a water column with a 50,000 gallon tank filled from a five million gallon tank three miles away. The station master had a house and there were a few others, but the main accommodation was tents for the fettlers, gangers, engineers and navvies. There were iron huts away from the main camp for the Afghan cameleers.

I soon found a spot under one of the famous gums to set up my simple camp. I had my swag and bag and had bought some cooking kit at Quorn. The station manager said I could eat with the railway folks. He said that the man Mr Dittmar had asked to take me to Birdsville was up the line carting rails and sleepers on his camels and would be back in a day or two but I was welcome to give a hand with a mob of cattle that was due soon.

The next two days were hot and still but I was comfortable under my gumtree and enjoyed the rest. When it was cooler, I had a walk around and as far as I could see there was stony hard red dirt covered by millions of pebbles called gibbers, a hard place to live and lay down a railway. It had been very quiet but I saw dust in the north and then heard cattle mooing, men yelling and stockwhips cracking and a mob of about 100 Shorthorn cattle, red by nature and by dust, appeared. The drovers soon settled and watered them in a large yard and left them overnight. Next day a train was expected with trucks to take them to Adelaide. I had a yarn with the drovers and they told me that the cattle had come from Clifton Hills south of Birdsville. It was settled in 1876 by the Broad family and was the biggest station on the Birdsville Track, almost 300 miles away. It was one of the very places we had heard about in the Channel Country and I had followed that dream to Farina at least. One of the drovers asked me if I wanted to give them a hand in the morning and I agreed.

Next morning we put a few of the cattle into crushes and removed their horns as they may have hurt man or beast. We then divided them into groups by size because the railway track was rough and the cattle trucks small, only holding about ten cattle. They were not well built, so small animals could be damaged or killed by big ones slipping and sliding around. There was no drafting yard so the drovers moved the cattle in a circle past a gate. The drover worked a particular animal though the mob as they circled the yard and when he neared the gate the gateman opened the gate in front of it as the drover shouldered it through the open gate that was quickly closed. It was not long before the 100 cattle were drafted into five lots of 20 of similar size. The cattle were then loaded onto the train when it arrived. I was pleased with my day's work and almost enjoyed my sore and stiff muscles that were the price and reward for a hard day's work. I had a wash and changed my clothes and joined the others for the evening meal but returned to my camp soon after.

I had made a cup of tea and settled on a gum tree stump to write to Susana when the station master walked over with another man about my age. He introduced him as Mohammad Baluch, the man I had seen last evening with his six fellow cameleers camping nearby, but away from and downwind from the cattle. There were about 50 camels. He explained that he had been working at Farina transporting goods to and from the camp that was responsible for the next section of rail to Hergott Springs but now that goods and equipment from Mr Field, Mr Dittmar and for me had arrived in Farina for transport to Birdsville that would be his next job. I was welcome to join him and his countrymen. He asked me to be ready at the goods shed at dawn, then wished me good night.

# 23

# A Very Different World

I hurriedly wrote to Susana and rabbited on too much but I was excited. I felt welcome and comfortable in this new world we had dared to dream about. It was a wonder I slept but the day's toil took care of that. The noise of the camels being loaded woke me early. I had a cup of tea and a hunk of damper, a wash, put on myhat, rolled my swag, slung it over my shoulder, grabbed my bag and walked over to the goods shed. There were 50 camels being loaded. Each cameleer was responsible for seven or eight animals. To be loaded, the camels, wearing their harness, knelt when their cameleer said 'Hooshta.' They were all obedient but made the loudest groans, moans and the most pitiful wailing I have ever heard. The noise mixed up with the smell, farting and piddling from these massive creatures, in the half light, was quite an experience. When they were loaded the cameleers gave a short sharp whistle and they stood up and after more pitiful wailing, quietened down.

Everything the camels carried was tied across their harness and not tied to it, so balance was critical. After loading my gear, as shown, onto a smallish female camel, Mohammad told me to walk alongside her so she would know me if and when I rode her. He explained that each camel had a nose peg inserted so that if it baulked, or threw its head back, the peg would come out without the injury that would occur if the peg was put though tissue. A string from the nose peg was tied to the crupper of the camel in front. They usually travelled eight hours a day and did not stop in the middle of the day so as to reach their destinations as soon as possible. Camels could walk all day for as many days as it took, with as much as half a ton on a big bull, but they could not tolerate standing with a load. Stopping at midday wasted time to unload and reload. I complimented Mohammad on how quickly the camels were loaded. He explained that his camels and men were experienced but the most important thing was that he had already been informed what was coming on the train by telegram and had told the others so they knew how to load each camel.

Soon we were on our way to Hergott 30 miles away with the string of 50 camels quietly walking north into a beautiful morning, with the sun rising above the ramparts of the Flinders Ranges warming the cool air. They walk at two and a half to three miles per hour so travel sixteen to twenty four miles a day. We reached Hergott Springs early afternoon the next day. I was leg weary but again enjoyed the feeling of stiffness knowing I was getting stronger and fitter. I did not enjoy the dust as it made me cough, but less so than the cold wet weather.

In the years we had been planning this venture I had learnt much about Australia in practice and theory. I had met business men and avidly listened to their conversations and certainly the importance of camels in the development of Australia's outback was familiar to me. I knew that Thomas Elder had introduced camels and cameleers to Australia in 1867 and by the 1880s Hergott Springs was the centre of what became the 'Inland camels communication network' and known as 'Little Asia.' My new friend Mohammad was not a talkative man but walking alongside him for two days and in the camp at night I heard his story. He had been in Australia from Baluchistan for about ten years and worked camels with his uncle at Beltana who left him some money and camels when he died. He bought more camels and slowly increased his string and worked between Quorn, Hawker, Beltana and Farina from 1879 to 1882, taking goods forward with the building of the railway and, in the reverse direction, wool from sheep stations to the trains as they reached further north. The railway was on schedule to reach Hergott Springs in early 1884.

The next big section was to Oodnadatta but Mohammad knew that Hergott Springs to Oodnadatta was about the same distance as from Port Augusta to Hergott Springs so he had a mind to settle at Hergott Springs. There he had access to the Channel country via the Birdsville Track, where cattle stations such as Clifton Hills, Pandie Pandie, Roseberth, Mount Leonard, Monkira and other stations had been established in the 1870s in South Australia and Queensland's Channel Country and were reaping the rewards of a train line that was creeping closer and closer to Hergott. The track from Birdsville to Hergott and the railheads had become a very busy place. Farina had also progressed by developing links to Blanchewater, Murnpeowie, Innamincka and stations north and east such as Cordillo Downs and Nappa Merri where the camels took goods and stores and returned with wool. They were able to do this because in 1870 Harry Readford stole 1000 cattle from Bowen Downs in central Queensland and found his way, on what became the Strzelecki Track, to Blanchewater Station in South Australia 110 -120 miles north east of Farina. This provided another stock route between South Australia and Queensland that rivalled the Birdsville Track.

About ten years after Elder introduced camels in 1867, cameleers had made Hergott the centre of the camel industry in Australia. There were about a 100 cameleers and even at 30 camels per string, 3000 camels went to and from Hergott. These men and their animals went to Birdsville and into Queensland, to the Northern Territory and to Broken Hill and elsewhere in New South Wales and to Western Australia.

They played a huge and essential part in the building of the Overland Telegraph that was completed in 1872. I liked geography at school and had a map of Australia in my head and knew that Western Australia was about a million square miles. With pencil, paper and fingers I realised that the area the cameleers covered with their freight deliveries and loadings was about the size of the biggest state in Australia. I kept that calculation between Susana and me, because I was afraid people would laugh at me for saying such a thing.

We stopped and camped a short way outside of Hergott Springs and stayed two nights. Mohammad was unloading and loading stores and putting some of his other camels into the string. He was happy for us to spend a day resting before the 300 mile trip to Birdsville so I had time to explore. Hergott had been recently surveyed and blocks of land had been allocated. It was busier than I had imagined. A feature was the 'Great Northern Hotel' a large stone building that would not have been out of place in any country town. It was two stories 83 x 46 feet with a bar room 22 x 46 feet larger than the dining room of 17x16 feet. There were fourteen bedrooms and a bathroom upstairs and an annex with eight bedrooms each having air brick openings to draw off heated air. There were stables and 20,000 gallons of water in an underground tank.

I really had my eyes opened. The planned railway would divide the town with most shops and businesses on the south side facing the railway yards. I counted four stores, a butcher, wheelwright, the Town and Country Bank, two saddlers, a Chinaman's store in a building that the Local Court used, as did the Church of England. The population was about 600 with half being 'Afghans' and most of them were single. I was really stopped in my tracks when a man pointed out an open mud brick building with walls about three feet high with a gabled roof thatched on long sticks held up by six or eight posts, with water connected for washing, in the main street. It was the first mosque in Australia.

The size and scope of the trading and freighting was almost beyond me. If 50 camels each carried five hundred-weight, that is twelve and a half tons and there may be at any one time, from Hergott alone, 100 camel trains or strings working. They would be carrying about 1200 tons in total to their destinations and perhaps the same amount on their return. If they made two trips a year that could be 5000 tons that the camels carried through some of the toughest country in the world.

These numbers and the fantastic hotel I was in love with made me almost light headed. I had a meal and a couple of beers in the hotel and grabbed a quiet spot and wrote to Susana, while a mob of about 500 cattle passed through heading for Farina and the train.

# 24

# The Home Straight

In horse racing terms, with 300 miles to go, I had turned into the straight and the finish line of Birdsville was in sight. There were a number of versions about how Birdsville got its name. The first man to journey from Birdsville to Hergott was Percy 'Baldy' Burt who had built a store at Diamantina Crossing. 'Burtsville' was a worthy recognition but Burt was a modest man and refused this recognition. Another school of thought was that Robert Frew was the first to use 'Birdsville' as he did not want his opposition storekeeper to have the town named after him and of course there were flocks of birds in the area on the banks of the Diamantina River. So, who really knows?

We broke camp early as usual. The camels slept in between their packs that made loading more efficient and we were soon on our way, due north to Birdsville. Camels were hobbled and often had little brass 'Zungwalla' bells so the cameleers knew where they were. Mohammad also used Australian made Condamine bells and found them very effective. He used the large and therefore louder ones on bulls as he had found they were more determined to find feed than the cows who learned to just follow the bull's bells.

Next, we would leave the main Track fifty to sixty miles north of Etadunna and travel north west to Cowarie station and then make a bee-line north across country to Clifton Hills, then Pandie Pandie and Birdsville. I asked him how long it would take and he smiled and said something like, 'As Allah wills.' As we left Hergott I was excited with the sight, sounds and smells of the air, plants, camels, sandhills, stony plains, dry creeks with their lovely gum trees getting a drink from heaven knows how deep in the earth and the everlasting blue sky. I must have been jumping around too much because I did become tired well before midday and Mohammad noticed. He suggested that it was a good time to ride my camel friend as only carried a riding saddle and a few bags of cameleer's belongings. He took her out of the line and after a 'Hooshta' or two she kneeled and made a noise I could only think of as 'camel keening' as her fellow camels kept walking. Mohammad gave me enough instructions to help me to mount, behind the hump and hang onto the reins. He whistled and up and off we went. As we had been left behind, she and Mohammad's camel trotted to catch their friends. I initially found that unpleasant but soon settled into the camel's walking, rolling, soft ride.

I was happy, thrilled and excited sitting on a bloody camel on the way to Nirvana. The physical and mental effort of the last months and years caught up and I fell asleep. I had never experienced a feeling like I did that day. The day was warm and still. I drifted off into a world of peace and love for Susana and these wonderful people who had my future and life in their hands. A phrase from the Bible, 'A peace that passeth all understanding' was so apt. I woke when the camel kneeled. I had slept all day and we were now setting up camp. Mohammad put out his hand and helped me dismount and said, 'Welcome to our world my friend.' I had dinner and slept a restful sleep and when I woke, I felt I could move mountains.

After another two days we reached the Clayton River and then four days later Etadunna, established by the Lutheran Mission, Killlalpinina, ten miles or so to the west. We had a very pleasant night as the station people thought highly of Mohammad's team and when they saw our dust a rider came out to check it was us and fired three shots in the air. This was the signal to light a fire and roast a sheep that we all enjoyed, and I had a rum, or two, with the station hands so slept well again. I had seen dry creek or river beds from Port Augusta to Hergott as was understandable in such a dry country but when we headed north I was hoping for better. I had heard of Cooper, Warburton and Strzelecki creeks, the Diamantina and Georgina rivers and Goyder Lagoon. And I never forgot these names and their role in creating the Channel country and our dreams.

The first highlight was to be Cooper Creek that crossed The Track twenty seven miles from Hergott just north of Etadunna on its way to Lake Eyre. Eventually I asked Mohammad where it was. He said we were in the middle of it with sandhills and some reedy looking things occasionally and added that it rarely reached Lake Eyre but had good permanent water near Innamincka. He added that it started in the Great Dividing Range way up in Queensland as the Barcoo, was joined by the Thompson River and was over 800 miles long second only to the Murray Darling system. The Diamantina River started north of Birdsville and ended 560 miles later in Goyder Lagoon that we would pass and emerged as Warburton Creek that drained into Lake Eyre only a few miles from Cooper Creek.

The next section was to Cowarie, a four day stage of 90 miles. About two thirds of the way we headed north-west off the main track and were treated to a similar feast at the station. It was owned and run by August and Isobel Helling, who were having a hard time of it, but despite that, treated us royally with yet another wonderful meal. I was stunned to see a post office box there and said so. August looked at me and gently said, 'Bill you have realised the potential of this area as have we and many others. Many leases have been taken up and there is a line of shearers, shed hands, pastoralists, workers, well diggers, fencers, hawkers, other travellers and them buggers who are wanted or not wanted down south. Our post office opened in 1877. In the first year it dealt with 342 letters, some addressed to 'Jack' with a brand sketched on the envelope. It took time but letters were usually collected by someone.'

Isobel looked after the post office, fed drovers and others and cared for her four children including a little boy on her hip only six weeks old. While I was helping her tidy she told me that apart from her family she also provided the Aboriginals on the station with blankets, rations and medicines. I realised how little I knew about the life of a station woman and how hard it must be to have the right stores in the right amounts, something I would have to learn very soon.

As I walked along I thought about how positive the news was. The post office was five years old and there must be many hundreds or even thousands of people use the Track each year. It fair put a spring in my step.

Clifton Hills was easy to find, we just followed the Warburton River for three days. On the second night we camped by a pool of water and had a wash and drink and the camels likewise, well the drink anyway. This was the highlight of a tiring journey and revitalised men and beasts.

It was the time of day when the moon aligns with something or other on earth and animals hunt, drink, eat, and seek mates. There were parrots by the hundreds, all shapes, sizes and colours, kangaroos, emus, rat-like creatures and even a dingo, slinking through the firelight. The high pitched noise of insects and the calling of birds was a joy to hear. Mohammad and I sat next to each on a log taking it all in. Somehow the subject of prayer came up. I knew his people prayed five times a day but I had not noticed a midday prayer and asked him why. He replied, 'Our prayers are when we give ourselves to God and think of nothing else. In a mosque with our brothers it is a ceremony but the essence is between us and God. He understands our world and does not expect us to halt the camels but you will notice that around midday we are quiet and although aware of the camels our conversation is with God.' I thanked him and went to bed where I had a word to my bloke about the mysteries of life.

The cattle we had seen from Port Augusta to Clifton Hills were mainly red, roan or white Shorthorns, red Herefords with their white heads and chests and a few Black Angus but there was something strange about one mob we saw on Clifton Hills. They were young with weird light coloured marks of various shapes and sizes scattered around their mid-sections. When we reached the station homestead I asked about them. The manager laughed and said, 'Yair they're a rum lot. A few years ago I drove some cattle down to the mid north not far from Adelaide to sell and there were some Belted Galloways for sale. They are Scottish cattle similar to Angus with a white belt anything from six to eighteen inches wide around their trunks. They told me they were hard doers. They were going cheaply and as we had feed I bought a few including some bulls. When I got them home I ran them with our normal Shorthorns and bugger me Bill, they stood out like lighthouses against the red sand and the red cattle when we muster so I get a few more every now and then. What you have seen is the belt trait persisting in the offspring.'

They also kept black and white fox terriers around for snakes and rats so on my travels my mind wandered to black and white spotted dingoes, but I never saw any. Clifton Hills was a huge place and we continued on our way following the route of the Warburton Creek to Goyder Lagoon and Alton Downs station for 50 miles. This was on a tributary of the Diamantina River that we would follow to Pandie Pandie and then Birdsville after crossing the border into Queensland.

Mohammad told me we had been following the stock route rather than the Track since Clifton Hills as it was shorter. It suddenly dawned on me that this was our promised land The Channel Country. I threw my hat in the air and screamed 'Susana. We have made it!!' Mohammad smiled. He understood.

The weather was good, the going easy, the camels happy and Mohammad said they knew they would have a rest soon in Birdsville. After four days we pulled into Pandie Pandie that Robert Frew established in 1876. Here he was, larger than life, the very man who instigated this venture to put a pub in Birdsville. After the unloading and the evening meal he and I settled in the kitchen for a yarn. My chin was mostly on the table when he told me his story. He not only had this station, but he had taken up Annadale, Alton Downs, Planet Downs and Haddon Downs at various times. And he had a store in Birdsville of course. He did take me under his wing and we yarned until midnight. With liberal doses of whisky, the evening blurred as he told me as much as he could about the history and people of Birdsville. He asked me to supervise the unloading and storing of his goods at his store and said there was a reasonably comfortable shed where I could camp, 'Because, young Bill, there's no bloody pub there mate until you make one.' He roared with laughter slapping his large thighs.

Spirits did not sit well with me in large amounts so next morning I was not feeling well at all but summoned the will power to swallow a huge piece of steak, damper and tea. That helped.

I got my gear and walked unsteadily into the painful sunlight to see my camel in front of the string kneeling with all the others standing behind her ready to go. Mohammad was standing next to her holding the reins. He removed his hat, bowed and said, 'My friend, thank you for being part of our world and appreciating it so much. It is our honour to ask you to lead our humble camel string into Birdsville and then almost picked me up and lifted me into the saddle. A much stronger man than me. I was proud but embarrassed at my condition amongst my teetotal comrades but somehow survived the first hour or two and then enjoyed myself immensely. My camel liked being the leader as well. It was fifteen miles to go and about halfway there we crossed the border into Queensland. We finally arrive outside Mr Frew's store mid-afternoon with camels strung out down the street behind us.

It was not long before a crowd had gathered and I was teased as the 'great white leader', 'lazy bastard' and so on. Fortunately, I dismounted without making a fool of myself.

Mohammad, as always, had thought ahead and Mr Frew's goods were on the leading camels so it was not long before they were unloaded and the camels camped on, what I found out later, was the racecourse. I was thrilled to see that some of the goods were addressed to me at The Royal Hotel, the name Susana and I had settled on. About half the camels had been 'emptied' but there were still goods on the rest for stations like Monkira, Mount Leonard, Innamincka and other stations east of Birdsville where the camel string was headed to unload and then pick up wool, sheep and cow hides on the circuit back to Hergott via the

Strzelecki track. From Hergott to Birdsville had taken seventeen days. Later, over a cuppa, Mohammad told me he had once done it in three days on a big bull lightly loaded to get an urgent message to someone. I could only shake my head in wonder.

As always the camel string left early and headed into the dawn. As it did I had a lump in my throat and tears in my eyes, as these wonderful people, who had taught me so much about life, disappeared. I had an epiphany, a word and concept Susana had taught me, that these people added the final touch to my journey from a boy to manhood. The welcome and farewell and the unloading tired me physically and mentally. As the camels disappeared I remembered a school master say carpe diem every morning as he burst enthusiastically into the classroom. It meant seize the day and that is what I did. I squared my shoulders and attacked the tons of stores, mine and Frew's that had to be sorted, checked, recorded and stored. That night I spread my swag and collapsed. For the first time I did not talk to Susana. Next morning, I woke tired and sore but proud of what I had done and rarin' to go.

# 25

# Birdsville – The Die Is Cast

The next few days passed in a blur. I wrote to Susana, my parents, Mr Field and Mr Dittmar and busied myself with sorting out and storing what goods were mine and what were the store's. Then I wandered around the town. One hundred people lived there and there were two stores (Groth and Frew), two shops, a police station, two blacksmiths (Bill Clarke and Allan Harris), two butchers (Fred Bowman and Bill Ridger) a baker (Bob Bates), cordial maker, a boot maker (James Hern), saddler (Chas. Morton), auctioneer and commission agent (Samuel Smith) and a customs officer (E Ward) camped in a tent and postmistress Mrs Ward. I had not thought of customs but Australia was made up of independent Colonies and there were various taxes levied on goods going from one colony to another. I remembered Mohammad going to talk to this man. The dealings were in cash, a tidy sum with all the cattle and freight moving north and south. I suspected it would not be long before the customs man had a building with somewhere to keep his money. It did strike me that people must be very honest in these parts or alternatively there was nowhere to go to get away from the police.

The main building, the hotel, was being built by Wally Maxwell and it was coming along with the walls about half built so I had plenty to do aside from helping at Mr Frew's store for a very handy wage. The weeks flew by and soon Mohammad turned up with roofing iron and posts strapped to his camels, so we were really on the way when that arrived. The building was planned to be similar to the Oddfellows Home Hotel in Warwick. That was not surprising with the requirements of the recent Hotels Act. There was a bar with an entrance from the street and a second entrance led to the dining area, lounge, two bed rooms, a wash house, cellar and separate kitchen and dunny.

Typical of outback buildings in these parts, we used local sandstone blocks held together with a dehydrated gypsum, sand and water mixture. There was a steep iron roof supported by wooden bearers and a roofed verandah on two sides held by wooden posts. There was a horse trough and hitching rail at the front. Christmas and New Year came and went but it meant little with Susana so far away so I worked even harder at the building and got through it somehow.

I made the necessary application on 26th February 1883 to the police district of Windorah for a licence to sell fermented and spirituous liquors and it was granted on 24th April 1883. Somehow I managed to sort out the money, stock the hotel with food, alcohol, linen, cutlery, crockery and glasses and employed a cook and cleaner. I was so missing Susana. I had way under estimated the time things would take and the costs. Susana's income was critical to the whole venture and as the house had not been started there was nowhere for her to live. We expected the hotel's bed rooms to be well used so, while our dream was happening, the joy we had imagined was not.

I soon got to know the locals and some of their wives and felt welcome and settled but as always Susana was missing and that hurt. August Helling often visited and one night over a beer he confessed that he was worried about what may be turning into a

LONG JOURNEY TO THE PROMISED LAND

drought, something he had seen before and he had already lightened off his cattle numbers. He hoped he could get a mail or freight run to supplement his income. He had already carted wool to Hergott and alcohol back to us. Eventually we opened the hotel on the 1st May 1883 by good luck and with some logic, as the traditional May Day in Europe was long preceded by Roman and Greek celebrations and those folks knew a thing or two about having a drink. Mr Frew helped as did Wally Maxwell, our builder, who wanted to show off his building. Wally surprised and delighted me when he made a speech and unbeknown to me had put a plaque on the wall that he covered with some building material that he unveiled. It read 'Proprietor: William Albert Tucker.' He had left a space for Susana's name and his dear wife Joyce gave me a sketch of the plaque she had made that I sent to Susana. Two barmen volunteered and the police sergeant Arthur MacDonald and his constable looked in every so often, a boon later in the evening. And so it started and kept going the same way for weeks and months, making a lot of money, but it was very hard work and drunks could be aggressive and dangerous.

I mentioned August and Isobel and soon after we opened a Murray O'Brien and his wife Pat came to Birdsville and stayed at the hotel. He was an interesting person and had been the manager of the biggest sheep station in New South Wales and a big one in the north-west of South Australia until it was sold. He was representing a group of people interested in the triple potential of the Channel Country. The potential to fatten cattle, the railway reaching Hergott next year to tie in with the establishment of a frozen meat trade with Great Britain. He was in the process of setting up premises to do this but in the meantime he asked if he could use the hotel and that was fine. He had the nick name 'Banger' and voice to match and was good company and a great story teller. He was canny and had made it known that he was available to manage stations. This was a master stroke as the demand for leases and their stocking had outstripped available managers. He had taken two years to work his way up the track to Birdsville. The knowledge he d gained was valuable, beyond price, to investors.

He introduced me to two Aboriginal people who lived in Birdsville, Eadie and Eddie, from one of the stations he had managed. I was delighted that they agreed to work at the hotel. Eadie did the cooking and other kitchen tasks and Eddie the yard work, lighting fires, looking after our stables and so on. They were a great help and made it a lot easier for me to run the place.

The first Birdsville races had been held in September 1882. They were regarded as unofficial for some reason but were a great success and 150 people, including me, were looking forward to the event in 1883. The races were held on a straight course of a mile marked by 15 fence posts with a platform for the judges. Pat, Eadie and Eddy helped me set up a food and drink tent and Robert Frew and Johann Groth and their wives helped during the day. After the races it seemed that everyone was in the pub or milling around outside. There was an ocean of cash with bookmakers and punters settling their bets. The tradition of settling bets at Tucker's pub started that day.

Murray was on the receiving end of more cash than most. He was a real racing man and knew a lot about horses. It helped that he had ridden many of the horses who raced that day on the stations where they lived. The crowd was noisy but orderly, no doubt helped by Murray shouting the bar several times despite Pat's protests. I will never forget the clean up the next day. We were all tired but we prepared for the second day of the meeting. That was also very successful and a highlight involved a very well-known man. Susana loved Australian history and had told me about a book written by Rolf Boldrewood called 'Robbery under Arms' published in serial form by the Sydney Mail for a year or so and she had followed this avidly. I happened to notice Pat reading the same story one day as she was also great reader. The author had written about Harry Readford's extraordinary feat of droving 1000 stolen cattle into South Australia from the middle of Queensland on what became the Strzelecki Track to the railheads in South Australia and the Adelaide markets. He had been given the name Captain Starlight similar to the grandiose names of many bush rangers.

Harry Readford was staying at the hotel and I pointed him out to Pat. Later in the afternoon Pat, a very ladylike woman, with a little beer on board, walked over to Readford and passed him a little notebook and asked, 'Would you sign this please Captain Moonlight?' He was a big man, stood up, took off his hat to reveal a white bald head that set off his black beard, bowed and said. 'My pleasure madam, but I am Captain Starlight.' He signed that name, returned her pencil, kissed her hand bowed again and put his hat back on. As he was about to sit down, he stood up and pulled a chair out for her to sit and that she did. He then introduced her to the two men with him, Sylvester Browne the owner of Sandringham Station on the Mulligan River and his brother Thomas from Victoria. With impeccable timing he told Pat that she probably knew of Thomas. She looked puzzled and then was struck speechless, a rare thing for her, when Readford added. 'He also goes by the name Rolf Boldrewood, he's the bastard that gave me that stupid name, Captain Starlight and told a lot of lies about me. He has come up here to look for characters in another book. Perhaps you might get a spot.' I will not embarrass Pat further but speechless and looking 'like a stunned mullet' for the afternoon would cover it.

Murray told me later that Readford had organised a drive of 2000 cattle from Queensland to Brunette Downs in the Northern Territory, where he was manager, but a mob of cattle he was to pick up further north had been quarantined with red water fever. As he knew the way to the Channel Country he had arranged for Murray to buy a mob of 500 cattle that he and two other drovers, with an Aboriginal man to look after the horses, would pick up from where Murray had yarded them and re-join the drive to the Northern Territory. I couldn't wait to tell Susana about Boldrewood and this enormous droving venture that, while quite normal in the world of these fellas, were far beyond my experience.

When the dust had settled after the races and things actually returned to normal, I wrote a long letter to Susana and told her everything I could and, apart from her absence, how well things were turning out.

# 26
# Drought – 1884-1885

Christmas and New Year 1983-84 in Birdsville came and went in a sea of money, food and grog. I enjoyed the experience and had become part of the local mob and was given a lot of help behind the bar and in the kitchen. The pub was doing well but I could not build a house for Susana as quickly as I had wanted. The Birdsville Hotel was being built and the Tattersalls Hotel was planned soon after, so opposition was coming. The other factor was that my chest trouble was getting worse and the near constant breathing of tobacco smoke and dust did not help.

I was able to put aside a reasonable amount of money and when a new builder came to town, I was able to start building a house and a licence to include a billiard room was approved.

In mid 1884 Johann Groth approached me about selling the hotel and licence and offered a good price. Susana was most unhappy at this turn of events as she had her heart set on us running a pub together. I understood all this, so I told Johann politely we would leave things as they were and perhaps look at it again in twelve months.

We continued on with the pub and building the house and billiard room and near the end of 1884 they were finished and the hotel was still doing well. The hotel was built of stone with an iron roof but the house and billiard room had foundations of stone but was mainly timber and corrugated iron with a verandah much like the hotel. It was difficult and took a long time to get things built in Birdsville but when underway, adding a few more rooms to the house for accommodation or storage would be an option. As soon as my billiard tables arrived on bullock wagons and were reassembled in place we were open for business.

There had been good seasons and many more travellers but I was worried that, with Tattersalls Hotel under way to join the Birdsville and Royal Hotels, that three hotels would struggle in a drought or any other slow-down in business. Also as much as I tried to deny it was finding it physically much harder to do my work. After seemingly endless letters Susana and I decided to sell the licence but not the land and building. There would be rent for the hotel for four years where I would work part time and still keep the books at Mr Frew's store so I should be alright for money and be much healthier and Susana was also keen to work at the hotel.

I looked forward to driving a light dray to Hergott to catch the train to Adelaide where we would marry, have a honeymoon and return to Birdsville the same way.

Susana was happy about this and asked Mr Field all sorts of questions about churches, receptions and so on and from her letters was as pleased as punch. As the year moved on I certainly found the work harder, my cough was getting worse and my anxiety about a drought was increasing.

August Helling told me that he had sold all his cattle bar a few breeders and had bought a Cobb and Co coach that had become available from somewhere a railway had taken over. He hoped that it would arrive early in the New Year at Hergott. Jim O'Brien, no relation to Murray, the previous mail man at Farina, who August knew well, had been moved to Hergott earlier this year.

Over the years August and Jim had discussed mail and

transport and the rough old carts really were not good enough with the flurry of settlement that was happening. Jim decided to put things in motion to introduce a mail service by coach and August made the necessary application.

One day in December Robert Frew, Murray and August were in the pub and I took them into the lounge where we had a meal and a few beers. They had been through many droughts between them, so I asked them about this one that seemed very serious.

August almost whispered. 'Bill somehow ya bloody know. Ya get a feelin' ya bloody water. Whether it is the birds, the ants, the black fellas going walkabout, the wind, the sky, I am buggered how but somehow ya know. Some you can buy your way out of, some you had to walk away from.' I expected 'Bullshit,' 'Lot of bloody nonsense' and the like but Murray and Robert Frew looked at the table, August and me and nodded their heads. It was the essence of their experience. It fair spooked me that did. More beers followed.

I explained about Susana. August said he might be able to find some feed for his horses and use his coach on the mail run instead of the current packhorses. He reckoned that he could do it but not later than April because of the feed situation.

I had never made a decision anywhere near as difficult as this and doubted my dad or his family had done so. One night as I tossed and turned, I recalled fishing with my uncle in a little boat in the estuary of the Hopkins River at Warrnambool on the Victorian coast, south of Ballarat. I was six and it was cold, wet, windy and rough and I was scared. My uncle looked at me and said in a kindly way, 'Bill this is when you make up your mind whether to fish or cut bait.' Funny, I never knew before what that meant. The choice was stark. A small chance of a very risky trip succeeding or choose between Susana and the pub. I wrote to

Susana in great pain saying that everything was off as it was not safe for her to come to Birdsville at that time. I chose to cut bait!

Another Christmas passed. It was like the world had stopped. Endless heat, burning sand, copper sky and nothing moving. On and on and on. But in March 1886 there was thundering rain and floods between Hergott and Birdsville and August was successful in his bid to introduce the mail coach. It was time to fish. I arranged for a telegram to Susana to tell her to be in Hergott by mid-April 1886 and we will be married in Birdsville in early to mid-May at the Police Station.

# 27

# Susana's Final Time in Warwick

I was surprised that the dream of having our own hotel and working together was to be for such a short time but Bill's logic was hard to argue against. It was often said only one thing was certain in the outback-drought. I could tell something else was worrying him, perhaps his health. Once I had thought long and hard about this I was happy. We would both be working together and the hotel would only be rented for four years so by the time we married, set up home, ran the billiard room and maybe served meals the time would fly.

I likely would not come back this way so this Christmas would be even more special for all of us. The place and date of our marriage would have to fit in sometime, somewhere as well. Mullers, Hogans, Tom Kennedy and his family, Sarah and Thomas and Betty, Biddy and Tom with their children, all the way from Rockhampton, were here. It was a wonderful few days and as good as any of the Christmases we had experienced despite the absence of Nonnie, Jimmy and Bill.

In the morning of the 27th of December I was woken early by Mrs Muller knocking on my door. She said that Mr Muller had had a turn of some sort. I sent one of the maids to get the doctor who lived nearby and went back to the room to sit with Mr and Mrs Muller. He was finding it difficult to talk and pointed at his drooling mouth. The doctor soon arrived and examined him carefully. His mouth was drooping at the left corner, as was his lower left eyelid with tears running down his cheek. His upper left eyelid would not close. The doctor pointed out that the many wrinkles on the left side of his face and forehead had disappeared. Mrs Muller was quick to say, 'His rough, old, lived in face, is as smooth as a baby's backside.'

The doctor described Mr Muller's condition as Bell's caused by damage to the facial nerve that made muscles of the face work and I could see what he meant. The cause was unknown but most people recovered in five to six weeks. He would need to be hand fed and to have his eye padded but the pad was not to touch the eye as he could not shut his eyelids or blink.

He suggested that we make a tea of willow bark and give it to him four times a day. It was known to contain a substance called salicylate that had only just been found in the willow bark liquid that had been used for centuries for pain and inflammation.

This condition did improve slowly and he was better for the six weeks' rest and more like his old energetic self although Mrs Muller clearly felt the strain. Bill and I had talked about our wedding plans in Adelaide but the Catholic-Protestant divide between our families could not be breached. We really had enough of this and agreed to get married in the police station at Birdsville.

Fortunately, Mr Muller recovered. I don't think I could have left if he had not. Both he and Mrs Muller knew what was happening and understood. Their encouragement made it much easier for me and Bill.

Even though I had been planning this for two years or more collecting and making clothes, linen and the like, it was a nightmare. Mr Hogan made me a beautiful Australian cedar trunk, bigger but matching the one my da had made with a section to store my candle holders. His skill was not restricted to metal work.

I had waited so long for this and the tension and rushing was unbearable but somehow I managed and got through the parties, farewells and the sadness of leaving the place and people who had made my life so wonderful over what was now exactly six years.

I was so sad to leave the Mullers but it had to be. Then I received a letter from Bill.

It read:

*My Dearest Susana.*

*I have some bad news for you. I have been somewhat dishonest with you in the hope that things would change. August has not yet got the go ahead to take the mail from Hergott to Birdsville. There is no water in the 100 miles from Etadunna to Cowarie and hundreds of cattle have died, teamsters have abandoned their loads to save their animals and people have died at the station. The Hellings have moved to Birdsville. It is far too dangerous for you to attempt this journey or for me to come and get you.*

*I do not know what to do other than to keep going hoping things will work out. You are safe in your job and with friends. You would not be safe coming to Birdsville and I could not bear it if anything happened to you.*

*Please let me know what you want me to do.*

*I am so sorry but please hold on to the hope that things will work out.*

*All my love Bill*

I had taken the letter to my room and sat down amongst the mess that was to be my nicely packed luggage and opened and read it and read it again and then threw it on the ground, jumped on it screwed it up and threw it against the wall.

Rage burned through me at his deceit, lying to me, sweet talking about the wedding and honeymoon in Adelaide and then I dissolved into tears. I knew what a broken heart must feel like.

When I stopped, I took the letter to Mrs Muller who sat me down with a cuppa that had a good draught of rum in it. She just sat there quietly while I cursed and raved and cried. Mr Muller had come in and I continued my tirade that seemed to go on forever. I then asked the question, 'What in God's name do I do.'

They were silent. Mrs Muller moved as if to speak but Mr Muller gently touched her on the hand and she stopped. He knew it was tough time for me, unbearable in fact. 'Do you think Bill has willfully deceived you rather than suggesting an optimistic, but incorrect and dangerous, thing to do and secondly do you want to spend the rest of your life with him? We will talk in the morning. We do love and care for you both.' He touched my cheek and left the room. More crying, more rum, maudlin was the word. I went to bed exhausted and slept deeply.

Next morning I felt disgusted in mind and body but managed to eat some boiled eggs, toast with plum jam and tea, cooked by Mrs Muller and served by Mr Muller dressed in his best suit looking ever so serious. I had to laugh even though it hurt my head. He looked quizzically at me with his head turned like a crow, his eyes bright and his hand palm down on the table. I answered, 'Yes and yes.' I covered his hand with mine. Mrs Muller followed until there was a sandwich of six hands on the table. We looked at each other and someone, I really cannot remember who, said. 'We will make it happen.'

We soon sorted out that I would carry on as best I could at the hotel. I was sad and lonely but these were the cards I was dealt. I spent more time at Church and that was a help. Soon my natural optimism took over, but Christmas was certainly quiet and peaceful, something I needed. With help, Bill and I got though what could have been the end of us but love found a way. We both wrote a letter a week. I used some black Irish logic to comfort myself that the longer it was without rain the sooner it would come. And it did. In March 1886 it rained a torrent on the Birdsville Track and surrounds. The Hennings had move back to Cowarie and rain would bring feed. I received a welcome telegram Bill had arranged from Hergott. '*August has the contract. Be in Hergott mid-April 86. We will marry in May. Bill*'

Mrs Muller and Tom took me to catch the train to Brisbane in Warwick itself as the line had now crossed the river. It was a sad parting with the usual hugs and tears. I had mixed feelings but it was time to take the next step in my life. Sarah met me in Brisbane and took me to the ship I had to catch to Melbourne and Adelaide. She gave me a parcel to open later. The ship docked for 24 hours in Melbourne, the second city to London in the British Empire. I gawped at the gardens, buildings, theatres, shops, restaurants and hotels.

A fellow passenger on the ship told me there was a painting I should see in the upstairs bar of Young and Jackson's hotel on the corner of Swanston and Flinders Streets. I found my way to the bar and stared, stared and stared some more. It was a front on, life size, picture of a totally naked girl perhaps 16-17 years old. Her hair was very dark and piled on the top of her head that she turned fully to her left. I had never seen anyone posing in such a proud and confident way. From what I had seen of naked, dark haired, women her body hair was scant. On the way out I saw a notice about 'Chloe,' as the painting was called. It had been painted in 1875 but the original was still in France. What I saw was a copy. I was flushed, embarrassed and felt guilty as there were men in the bar, but I also felt a strange stirring in my body I did not like.

A copy of the painting was a penny and I put it in my bag knowing I would find a use for it one day. I had a cup of tea at a nearby hotel. Among other scrambled thoughts I wondered what affect the real painting would have on me, let alone the real girl. I looked in a mirror and I was red in the face and very flustered so I drained my tea, had some water, left the hotel and walked back to the ship.

We left Melbourne next morning, steamed through Port Phillip heads and turned west into Bass Strait. Fortunately, the weather was calm because those waters could be extremely rough. Two ladies invited me to join them for a cup of tea in a lovely sunny spot on the passengers' deck. I thanked them and sat down and ordered a cup of tea from the steward. We chatted about the usual things and one asked me if I lived in Adelaide. I said 'No, it will be a short stay. I am on the way to my new home in Birdsville.' I had enjoyed the theatre in Warwick and these women reminded me of a melodrama about two ladylike, unmarried, sisters who owned a boarding house and were sharing a cup of tea and cucumber sandwiches with one of their young lady boarders. There was a rare lull in the conversation and the girl gave a little sob, dabbed her eyes in the way young ladies do and confided that she was in a very delicate state of health and would be leaving soon to take some country air and would return in about six months when the Spring Racing Carnival was on.

Just like the ladies in the play, those two in the ship, spluttered, coughed, looked away, took their little fans from their handbags, unfolded them and fanned themselves, burbled nonsense about heat, blacks, flies, murder and other things and flapped off to their cabins claiming headaches. Whenever our paths crossed on the ship, they gave me sorrowful looks and went for their handkerchiefs and fans and scuttled out of my way.

Something was gnawing at the back of my mind and it popped out. When I returned to the ship after seeing Chloe, I had trimmed her picture because it was too big to hide unless in a pocket of my bag. The anxious ladies always patrolled at the same time, the same place and probably took the same number of steps and had the same conversation. I waited behind a big pipe thing that let air into the galley. When they came near I spoke to them and they stopped. I thanked them for the information they gave me about Birdsville and I asked them if they would write down their names for me. Bemused they nodded. I ratted around in my bag and said 'Goodness gracious I have left by notebook in my cabin. Oh! It doesn't matter, just write it on the back of my picture that is a wedding present for my fianceè and handed it towards one of them face up. I had chosen my spot well. They both sat down on the nearby bench with the strangest looks on their faces and sort of gurgled. I made my saddest face, struggling to hold back tears and said, 'I am sorry you don't think I am pretty enough for him,' took Chloe back, and walked off, a picture of abject misery.

Later in the voyage I had the pleasure of meeting some gentleman at the hour when the sun was over the yardarm. That was apparently a clarion call to have a drink of alcohol, preferably gin.

That was fine by me and in conversation with then and during dinner they filled in a lot of gaps in my knowledge about South Australia. The State grew more grain than any other colony, had a large and wealthy copper mining industry and grape growing for wine production had started. One of them knew more about business than the others and mentioned the railway that was being built towards Alice Springs. It had just reached Hergott Springs, only 300 miles or so due south of Birdsville and would be a great boon to the cattle industry in those distant parts. When I told him that I would soon be on that train. He dragged on his cigar longer than before and wished me luck as did the others. I thought 'only' 300 miles. Mother Mary, that is the bloody length of Ireland, maybe I heard wrongly! Just before we finished our coffees and port the men discussed the failure of the Commercial Bank of South Australia in February, only a month or so before, so maybe things were not as good as they appeared. The calm weather of late summer and early autumn persisted all the way to Adelaide. We followed the Victorian and South Australian coasts until we entered Gulf Saint Vincent, steamed past Adelaide and entered the Port River and duly docked in Port Adelaide. The trip from Warwick had taken a little over a week. It was a long journey in miles but a far longer journey in my mind was in front of me.

After we had moored, we said our goodbyes and left the ship. My gentlemen friends helped with my gear and we boarded the noisy, rattly little train for its eight-mile journey to the city square mile with north, south, east and west terraces the boundaries. Our little train ran from Port Adelaide to the north west point of Adelaide and passed the magnificent stone Newmarket Hotel that had been established in 1847 and rebuilt for a lady owner only two or three years before.

Opposite and over the railway tracks were thirteen acres of stock yards and an abattoir. We rattled alongside North Terrace for about half its length to the unfinished station that was going to be another magnificent stone building. I was directed to the Terminus Hotel on North Terrace directly opposite the station where I booked a bed for the night.

The hotel proudly advertised Adelaide's water flushed sewerage system, the first city in Australia to have such a thing. After a perfect demonstration of its capabilities and a wash, I brushed my hair, went downstairs and joined several others from the ship waiting to travel the next day. I was asked by a bar maid if I would like a drink. I replied, 'A small beer would be nice.' She returned with a glass of beer and said, 'Here's a butcher luv, cheers.' This was more folk lore. It was a glass holding seven fluid ounces and was the size that butchers drank lunch times at the Newmarket Hotel. They would eat lunch in groups and just as in Ireland everyone in a group or school would buy a drink in turn. In Australia it was called 'shouting.'

I had beautiful grilled lamb chops, potatoes, carrots and beans with apple pie and cream to follow. It was fit for a queen. After a second beer and cup of tea I was full up and went to bed about 10 o'clock and fell into a dreamless sleep. Next morning a porter took my luggage across the road to the station and I boarded the train to Hergott Springs.

The train was comfortable and the trip pleasant. I had pored over Bill's letters and maps and knew, more or less, what to expect as we headed towards the Flinders Ranges. He was certainly correct when he described the raw beauty of them. The country in all directions away from the ranges was flat and the ranges were probably not all that high, but majestic, coming so vertically out of the plain. The train stopped at Quorn overnight and I stayed at one of the three hotels and again had a nice meal of chops and vegetables washed down by beer. I noticed next morning that the train had several more freight cars attached full of rails, sleepers and all sorts of other gear bound for Hergott Springs that was now the rail head for the next section of the line to Oodnadatta.

Hergott was 340 miles from Quorn so we left soon after dawn, stopped at Farina to pick up equipment and people then travelled overnight. Sleeping in the seats was uncomfortable but I managed to snooze and woke when the train stopped with a great deal of noise in Hergott Springs. Some wag had quipped that the Ghan went from the back of beyond to the middle of nowhere. When I woke in the morning and saw the flat land stretching forever, I believed it but when I saw the beautiful hotel I changed my mind, to a certain extent at least.

Bill had booked me into the hotel so this is where I headed with a railway man pushing a trolley he had loaded with my luggage. I had a wash and change of clothes. When I opened my travelling case, I found the parcel from Sarah that I had completely forgotten. It contained a night gown and other under things that I am sure she had made. They were beautiful, very bold and made me blush when I thought of Chloe at the hotel. Typically, she had enclosed a lovely hand painted card and written, 'The way to a man's heart is supposed to be through his stomach and your cooking will sort that out. I have always believed that another part of his anatomy is the way to his heart, and these should make sure of that.' I wrote to her straight away and said how happy I was that she and Thomas were now lovers. Somehow, I knew.

I wandered around Hergott ticking off the things Bill had written about and had a nice snooze in the afternoon and dinner at the hotel. Enjoying my roast mutton I was at peace with world. A feeling that I had not had for a long time.

As I finished my meal and was enjoying a cuppa, a bear-like, bearded man with a loud voice introduced himself. He was August Helling, the coach man. I invited him to join me in a cuppa and he did. He told me that everything was set for the morning and he would like to leave no later than six o'clock.

He asked about my luggage and said he would load it tonight but to keep a bag with things for the trip. He was pleased when I told him I had done that. He anticipated the trip would take six or seven days because the Track was in good shape. He had a light load as I was the only passenger and the mail was not heavy. We would be stopping at various stations overnight but sometimes we had to camp out so Bill had sent a swag for me with nice new blankets and sheets.

# 28

# Susana – The Track

Breakfast was ready at 5.30 am so I was ready for the coach at 6 o'clock. I put my bag in the coach and accepted Mr Helling's invitation to sit next to him on the driver's seat. It was April the first, not an auspicious day for a fey Irish girl but I thought if I got through that alright the journey would be fine and so it was. It was a gorgeous morning, cool and still with the last rays of dawn fading. I had dressed, as Tom Kennedy told me years ago, in my well-worn, hat, cotton shirt, long moleskin pants and boots. I felt his silent approval. Here I was with a man I had never met, driving off on a week or longer camping trip. Strangely I felt reassured rather than frightened. I remember Bill's calm hands driving horses and this man handling four rather frisky horses gave me he same confidence. Bill would never put me in danger so I was calm, relaxed and allowed myself to dream. The country was rough. There were rocks and sand but grass was growing everywhere from the rain. I became absorbed in the moment and heartened by the stories August, as he insisted I call him, told me about the good times following the bad.

He had spoken to his friend Edgar Chapman who owned the Mundowdna Run a few miles south of Hergott. They had a bit of an outstation about 50 miles up the Track called Dulkaninna and we could stay there that night. I gawped at that, 'You mean they have a farm 50 miles long? He just looked at me and said, 'Yep and that is not uncommon and by the way we call farms up here stations.' 'We can do sixty to seventy miles a day but fifty is a good number and doesn't knock the horses or us about too much.' At midday we stopped for a rest, tea and damper with salt beef. The country was getting less rocky and sandier and August said that would continue. About four o'clock we reached Dulkaninna. I helped August unharness the horses, rub them down, put their nose bags of chaff on and hobble them. This took more than an hour. I then took my swag into a little hut, had a bit of a wash, brushed my hair and joined in making dinner of steak grilled over the fire and spuds cooked in the coals. We cooked enough for breakfast and lunch the next day. Then salt beef, damper and spuds.. I enjoyed watching August make the damper and bury it in the dying campfire and made up my mind to learn how to make them on this trip. It looked easy but I knew how fickle bread baking could be and baking on an open fire must be harder than on a stove.

The next day we stopped at Etadunna for lunch. I remembered Bill's letter where he mentioned Killalpaninna Lutheran Mission where local Aboriginals were ministered to and cared for and how tough it was.

Soon after Etadunna was the dry Cooper Creek and then the infamous Natterannie Sandhills. Bill had told me how the camels walked over them with little trouble. August told me I might have to walk and even push the coach. The sandhills were so difficult the difference of my weight being in the coach or pushing might just make the difference between us getting over them easily or having to partly unload the coach and ferry the goods over the hills.

We were travelling light and the horses were fresh and strong so we made it easily but stopped soon after and camped on the edge of Sturt's Stony desert as we had done our fifty miles that day.

We did our chores and set up our swags an appropriate distance apart on either side of the coach each with our own shovel and ate and slept well. I tried to make a damper but failed — it was too wet. Next day we were headed for Cowarie about 50 miles away on the stock route. It was north-west and off the actual Track but a shorter distance to Birdsville than if we had stayed on the Track. August was sure we could manage and it was a nicer trip. The track to Cowarie meandered through the Cowarie Sandhills and about half way we came across a family or small clan of Aboriginals camped on a pool of water in Derwent Creek. They looked in a bad way, thin and exhausted, with a sick old lady and a mother with a baby. The men carried their boomerangs and spears, the women only a digging stick. August could converse with them after a fashion and knew that they had come a long way north from the Tirari Desert and were heading for Yellow Hole, near where the Derwent Creek joined the Warburton Creek, still ten to fifteen miles to travel. They were waiting for the old lady and young mother to be rested. If they had not found water they would have had to take their chances on reaching Yellow Hole because the others would have left. August said that the grass and water would soon bring animals and plants for them to eat.

We drove to Cowarie Station and as soon as the coach pulled up several children and a woman with a two year old came out and welcomed him with great enthusiasm. August helped me down from the coach and introduced me to his wife Isabella and their children and welcomed me to their home. When I saw the post office Bill's story came back to me. How could I have forgotten his name? It is all too hard sometimes. We had a nice meal with a bottle of wine. We discussed how great the rain was and Yellow Hole would be full. They had just returned to the station as he had to sell his cattle because of the drought and had bought the stage coach. He could make ends meet with the mail contract, but passengers were the icing on the cake. My trip was the first for the coach so time would tell.

Before we went to bed Isabella brought up our wedding. Bill had discussed the date with August and he had arranged with the O'Briens for Susana to stay with them. Isabella offered to come on the coach, with the children, to help and be my bridesmaid if I wished. She simply added, 'August has told me what a truly nice person you are and we have enormous regard for Bill. It would be our great pleasure to help and brides need someone with them.' Once again, I gave my impression of a stunned mullet at this kindness from people who were battling for their very survival. I had given up having a bridesmaid, sadly, but now I simply said, 'Yes, that would be lovely' and hardly cried at all! August went to bed and Isobel and I talked and talked and talked.

I was given their guest bedroom and slept well even though I went to bed very late.

In the morning she bundled the children up, collected clothes, food and water and we all piled in the coach and off we went. Goodness knows what time August got out of bed as he had already changed the horses. We followed the Warburton River. There was water in Yellow Hole and a few other spots he knew. The next place was Clifton Hills where Bill had seen the weirdly marked cattle. No one was fussed at the coach load of people and kids that had landed on them. Alton Downs was the next station where we planned to stop and was 80 miles further. We decided to camp at Goyder Lagoon still on Clifton Hills and stay there two nights as a treat for the children and the big people. It was something we all needed and deserved and a fantastic and relaxing experience. This time the damper was too dry.

Alton Downs was owned by a man named Whittington, a Director of the Bank of Adelaide, so we were on hallowed ground. He, of course, was not there but we were welcomed by the manager, Lindsay Noel, another man hewn from stone. August had left some young horses and he wanted to swap them for the ones we had. They would benefit from finishing off our journey, now less than 50 miles. We changed the horses and had some damper with Golden Syrup they called Ringer's joy. I thought it was Cocky's joy. Must depend on whether you work on a farm or a station. My damper was not successful again as this time the fire was too hot.

The last wee bit of less than 50 miles seemed to take forever. I will never forget the sight of that little town of tin, stone and dirt; not a flower, a tree or any grass. August had stopped to let it sink in that I was here. Now this surely was the first day of the rest of my life. There would be no more. The children, Isabella and I were in the coach. August tied the reins and got down from the driver's seat, opened the coach door and asked me to sit in the driver's seat. He helped me up and then sat next to me and pointed to a particularly bright roof reflecting the late afternoon sun. He gave me the most beautiful smile shook, my hand and said. 'That shiny roof is your life to come. You and Bill are some of the nicest and most decent people my wife and I have ever met. If you have trouble, and you will, we will be here for you. Now get a'hold of them ribbons and take us to YOUR PUB.' He smiled to himself when I picked up and flicked the reins and called quietly 'Git up now' and the four of them did. We pulled up in front of The Royal

Hotel and August wisely took charge of the horses while I walked into the bar. Bill was in a little nook behind the bar, with his back to me, so I breasted the bar and said in my best Irish accent, that I find hard to do now, 'Do I have to take off me bloody shirt or somethin' to be gettin 'a bloody drink in this poor bloody excuse for a bloody pub?'

# 29

# The Wedding – Bill's Story

The 11th of April was a Friday and coincidentally the birthday of a friend who had recently died but it would do as a wedding date. Although no one could be sure, the information I had was that Susana probably would arrive in time. I could not contact Susana once she left Hergott so I just carried on running the pub and organising the wedding and the follow up-party on the Saturday and Sunday. Pat and Murray O'Brien were towers of strength and Pat quietly suggested that Susana stay at their place and get ready for the wedding there. That suited me fine because we had always wanted to do the right thing and be married before living together.

On the 9th of April I was in my nook, the room behind the bar, and our barman was looking after four customers. There was the usual murmuring that time of the day but it grew quiet. Then I heard a hand or something bang on the bar and rough female voice with a very Australian accent yell, 'Do I have to take off me bloody shirt to get a bloody drink in this poor bloody excuse for a pub?' I had been 'miles away' but soon woke up and ran into the bar to see the four blokes, sort of silent and a sunburned woman with the top three buttons of her blue shirt open and bulging breasts flopped on the bar, covered in dust, with a big hat pulled down over her eyes. I was gobsmacked. Time stood still, as did I. Then she took off her hat winked and shook her hair down. I jumped over the bar and we hugged and hugged and jumped in circles.

Naturally I shouted the bar that suddenly became much busier with August and his family and passers-by who had followed the female driving a coach, tying up at the pub and going in. And of course, the good Police Sergeant MacDonald wondered what was happening on a quiet afternoon.

I only remember two things about the rest of the night. One was telling Isabella about this woman with a horrible Australian accent demanding a beer and threatening to disrobe, I suppose it was dis-shirt. Susana became cross and said it was her best Irish accent. We started to argue and then just laughed and fell into each other's arms. The other was Isabella taking Susana to O'Brien's place and telling me to be there at seven in the morning for a wedding planning meeting - and of course I was.

# 30

# The Wedding – Susana's Story

I had a real treat from Isabella and Pat O'Brien, who I had just met. After I had a bath, they washed and rinsed my hair and tidied up my finger nails and toenails and applied powders and creams to some other bits of me. Some eau de cologne dabbed in the right spots made me smell nice and completed the new me. Sarah had taken care of my under-things, I had bought some new 'going out' shoes in Melbourne and Mrs Muller had given me a parcel and said, 'It is a dress, you will know when to open it.' This surely was the time and it was. The dress was white cotton with lace trimmings and high neck. There was a veil as well with a coronet of hand-made flowers to attach it to my hair and bless her the flowers were shamrocks and Sturt's desert peas. Ireland meets the outback! I had always tried to look nice but this time I felt beautiful, inside and out.

We were married in the Birdsville Police Station by Sergeant MacDonald reading from a dog eared, fly specked, cigarette burned, Police publication. It was not what I had wanted but as other options were shut it was fine by me. I was driven by August in the coach and he gave me away. Isabella was my bridesmaid and her dear little daughter Mary a flower girl be-decked with a posy of wild flowers we had picked on the way. It was a tight squeeze in the coach but we managed. Murray was the best man and although Bill and he wore old borrowed suits they looked splendid. The service was brief and then came the ring bit. Murray, smooth as you please, presented it, with a bow, to Bill who slipped it on my finger as slick as you like. Then we kissed, signed some papers, left and walked to the hotel.

There were quite a few people watching and chucking confetti of straw, saltbush, newspaper or whatever. I looked at my ring and Bill whispered, 'It was Mum's mother's ring, but she wanted you to have it and hopes it will help to bring our families together. It joined the ring Seamus had given me on my right hand- I knew I would never need any more rings. We did our best to formalise things with an official table and speeches by Bill and the best man but Robert Frew got into the act as did Wally Maxwell, the pub builder and Johann Groth. We had a few funny and ribald make-believe telegrams and real ones from Mr Field and Mr Dittmar. Each had put ten pounds into my bank account. The meal Bill had organised was excellent and included a magnificent three level cake that would have melted in the summer. There was singing, music and dancing and then we sneaked off as it was bed time. It had been a long, long wait. I had heard and read ghastly stories about wedding nights but ours was the best experience of my life and Bill said the same. We celebrated both the evening and morning stars and in between as well. The stars were so bright I just knew Seamus was happy for me. The morning star faded faster than I had seen before. I knew Seamus had gone as he no longer had to watch over me as I was in safe and loving hands.

# 31

# The Real World... and a Baby

The next two days were a blur. Many of the guests had travelled a long way and one day was not enough to catch up with their mates by a long shot. I had a wealth of experience in pubs and a very good eye for trouble or otherwise and I could tell that our guests liked and respected Bill and that made me even happier. One of the many conversations I recall was with Isabella who mentioned that, although they had gone back to the station, August was going to persist with his coach until it was clear which way the wind blew. There were people coming and going from the north, south and east so he hoped to get some of that business and if that didn't work droving was another option opening up after the rain. If ever people deserved to succeed those lovely people did. Even though they had been married for years and had the children to show for it when Bill and I watched them drive away with the sun just appearing they looked like they were going on their honeymoon they were so happy.

So that was it, to work and work we did. Johann Groth had taken over the hotel licence in 1885 as planned. From then and for the next two years it was very confusing as one of his relatives, then someone else and then Johann again held the licence. The effect of this was that Bill, then both of us, ran the pub. That was good for the bank balance, but we also had the billiard business and boarding house to look after. Bill ailed more with the work and I was tired as well. Johann Groth offered to buy the land and hotel so we happily sold it for 260 pounds almost double what it had cost.

The rain in March, although brief, had damaged Birdsville, so many of the people who had fallen on bad times found work repairing buildings, roofs, fences and so on. The cattle industry came good once again and we saw how the Channel Country deserved its reputation of recovering from drought after rain. In weeks the country was green. In months there were cattle coming and going every which way.

Sadly, there was also bad news. I had written to Mrs Muller about the wedding but it was a long time before she replied. Her husband had died soon after I left. His Bell's palsy was getting better but something went wrong with his heart and he died. She did not want to upset me at such a time. Life goes on but I really ached for this kind, lonely and lovely woman who had made my life for me. I never did find out what happened to their daughter. Maybe I was the only one they ever had. I was deeply sad, so much so, that I felt sick to my stomach and vomited most mornings.

My sadness eased but the vomiting increased. Worried I told Pat O'Brien who asked about ladies' things and confidently laughed, 'The illness is being with child.' I was going to have a baby. God I was embarrassed. How could I not have known? Bill and I were both ecstatic. Not only did cows respond to the country coming to verdant life and have calves, I would be doing the same thing in May 1887. Dr Milne kept a very close eye on my weight, diet and fitness and everything went along quite well. I used to visit one or another of the three Chinese vegetable growers on the river bank, Ah Chee, Ah Nee or Ah Ping with their clever system of pulleys to bring water up from the river. I am sure that more greens, potatoes, watermelons, pumpkins, tomatoes, cucumbers and other vegetables and less salt meat was good for me

On May 1st, 1887 a baby girl we called May was born. The birth was no fun but when Doctor Milne put her in my arms I forgot all about the bad stuff. The saying, 'God's in his heaven and all's right with the world!' popped into my head when I looked at this little mite. A baby, a husband, money, a job and a home. What a wonderful country. Bill wrote a telegram and sent it to Hergott as soon as he could for despatching to both sets of grandparents. I was still writing once a month to home but I wrote a longer letter than usual to my parents. I felt different with a baby and now knew how they felt about me. As best I could I thanked them for what they had taught me about life, love, respect and kindness and I now understood why. I had reaped a rich dividend. If only I could see them, but that was not to be and made me very sad for a few days but May soon turned that into joy.

A week in bed, a few days reading and rest and I was ready to get on with our lives. We were still busy but found time to meet friends for cups of tea and go for walks. We sat at home under our verandah in the evening after dinner and read or just talked while I fed May. It was a peaceful time for us but we were busy enough to earn a good living. We had some interesting people to stay with us. One was Thomas Browne better known as Rolf Boldrewood. Bill had met him at the races when Thomas was on the way to see his brother Sylvester Browne, who had taken up Sandringham station in1877. I delighted in meeting him. He was very knowledgeable about Australia and I had read pieces of his book 'Roberry under Arms' in the newspaper. I was thrilled when he told me that the book itself would be published in three volumes the next year and he told me where I could get it.

For the first time since I had been in Australia I had a quiet peaceful Christmas and New Year and shared it with my wonderful little family. I had never been so happy in my life. It was very hot but were used to that and like all weathers it changed and autumn was with us. It was just less hot but it marked another special time in my life, again with child I was. I was not worried with the sickness this time and managed my chores and May was now sitting up, crawling and getting teeth when she should. When I was about three months into my time Bill told me that Tom Merrifield had asked him if we would look after his Tattersals Hotel from early July in 1889 to the end of 1890 and Bill was keen to do that. We discussed that for a time and I agreed. Bill then suggested that we go to Ballarat for the birth, expected in March 1889 and stay at his parent's place. I would get to know them, and we would at last, have a break from work.

We had been helped financially by his parents and Mrs Tucker had sent beautiful hand-made dresses and little jackets embroidered with wild flowers that grew near Ballarat for May. She had a sense of humour and included a Sturt Pea very much from our desert world. She also wrote lovely letters and I could tell she wanted to do what she could to make us part of her family, despite the religious differences and I agreed wholeheartedly with that. She was delighted when Bill asked if we could go to her home for the birth.

Murray always like billiards so he was glad to look after the place and Eddie and Eadie knew what to do so we started our planning. Like all parents we were surprised by the amount of stuff we needed to take for May but it was a labour of love. August Helling's coach to Hergott, train to Adelaide and train to Ballarat. Easy when writing it down but it took about ten days.

It was lovely to meet and get to know Bill's family, particularly his mother. She was like a real mother to me. I had not forgotten to contact my own parents and wrote once a month as always. We received probably their first telegram at our wedding. Amazingly, it arrived on the day. I missed them and grieved for my ma, da and sister and was so grateful for Mrs Tucker's care and love. One day we were chatting away and, like me, she was worried about Bill's health. I was teary at what was not said but hung in the air. She held my hand looked into my eyes and soothed me with the words, 'No matter what fate has in store I will be here for you and your children.'

The weeks passed and their doctor delivered Frederick Leslie Tucker on March 20th in what had been Bill's bedroom with his school photographs on the wall. It was not all a pleasant experience but when the doctor gave the baby to me, I again remembered nothing bad. Again, God was in his heaven and baby in my arms –that was all that mattered. Ten days rest and being waited on hand and foot by Mrs Tucker and her daughters was heaven on earth and together we managed feeding with relative ease. Later when I was allowed up and about, I was sitting in a lovely arbour with climbing roses filtering the sun, feeding Frederick and thinking how happy I was when it got even better. Bill appeared with a huge bunch of roses. It was like a dream.

With the rest I settled easily into feeding and caring for Fred despite constant demands from May for attention and even trying to pinch Fred's milk but we managed. Bill played with her and that usually fixed things. After my lying-in period, as I found out it was called, Mrs Tucker invited their family and friends for an afternoon tea of beautiful, delicate sandwiches and sweet meats. They were lovely people and generous to a fault with gifts for Fred. Mrs Tucker was smiling like a Cheshire cat she was so proud of Bill and his children. I had a sherry or two, yes another new thing I enjoyed and felt I was floating. It was all perfect. So, so different to Birdsville. In everything. Just when I thought the day could get no better, I was wrong. Jimmy and Nonnie, very obviously pregnant, appeared. That was just so good and words cannot explain the emotion I felt. Utter joy will do.

Bill was tired but was looking better every day. We were walking in the garden one day and something came up about Fred's birth. With a straight face I told him that, 'I found the birth easy because I laughed so much about having a baby with you and your mates watching everything.' I then pointed out some ducks and their babies on the pond and some other things.

Bill looked puzzled. It reminded me of the jasmine night in Warwick when he proposed to me.

Here I was teasing him again. He was even more confused this time the dear love, but eventually he understood and smiled.

Ballarat was a beautiful place with gold being the driving force for wonderful buildings, churches, nice houses and hotels, parks and wide avenues. We walked and drove a sulky all around the town and surrounding areas, had picnics, visited my in-laws and most importantly Nonnie and Jimmy. That was an absolute delight. She was so poised, glowing as only a woman can in the middle months before the lumpiness sets in. I shook my head in wonder and thanked God every time I saw her. It was nice to see that she was so confident in handling Frederick, a good sign for the future.

Oh yes there was something else. Easter Sunday was a huge event with about 20-30 people coming and going during the day at lunch and afternoon tea time. Frederick was the centre of attention and we were so proud. Nonnie and Jimmy came a close second and we had a wonderful time talking about the days in Warwick. Late in the morning I had a weird and unpleasant feeling and felt faint for the first time in my life. Bill sat me down. I then realised what was wrong. I was disorientated because every year, since I had been in Australia, I worked at Easter. This year all I had to do was get to Melbourne from Birdsville, have a baby, relax and enjoy myself. I stood up held Bill's hand and re-joined the party. But all things come to an end. We had planned a few days in Adelaide and caught the train from Ballarat. It was lovely with my husband and babies. As much as I loved the Mullers, knowing I had the Tucker family in Australia who cared for me, our children as well as their son was a feeling I never forgot. That went into a very special box.

Adelaide was lovely. We stayed at the South Australian Hotel on North Terrace where Bill had met with Mr Field and Mr Dittmar and they and their wives had an evening meal with us. They both gave us some lovely baby clothes and some very valuable advice about not swaddling the baby in the heat. I knew that but politely thanked them. For the next few days we went to the Adelaide Oval and watched a game of cricket. It was a Test match between England and Australia, apparently the first test to be played after Englands cricket had been turned to Ashes the year before. I had no idea what the game was about but I was happy to see Bill enjoy himself with friends from Melbourne.

Unexpectedly for us, after the last day's play there was a huge corroboree with hundreds of Aboriginal people, dancing, and playing booming, throbbing instruments and clacking sticks together. The music, feet stamping and the hollow log drums they beat was mesmerising. We had heard little of this culture of Aboriginals. It was usually treated with contempt by white people. A typical comment might be 'Can't find the bastards must of gone orf on walkabout or havin 'a bloody corroboree or sumbthink.' Frederick woke once but settled quickly with the rhythmic beat. It was irresistible and May was enthralled. We were both very quiet walking back to the hotel, deep in thought. Next day we went home.

# 32

# Reflections

I drifted off at times in the train but in between dozes thought of my three years in Birdsville. I had married, run a hotel and had two children. I can't say I was surprised but the isolation was almost paralysing for the first few months. There were about 100 whites and eight Chinese in the town and only 1000 in the vast district. Everyone knew everyone's business and being in a hotel we were the centre of gossip. It was similar in a way to Warwick but there were places to go and things to do there away from the hotel. The weather was lovely when I arrived in autumn, much like summer in Warwick but later in July there were night time temperatures below freezing and it became fiercely hot by September and October. The opening hours of the hotel were from 8 am to 10 pm but with cleaning, normal meals, late suppers and early breakfasts , ordering and unpacking goods and office work it was more like 16 hour working days or more. The work at Warwick had prepared me well for Birdsville but the isolation and distance added a new element.

On the bright side I loved, with every ounce of my being, living with Bill day and night, at work and play and when the babies came, I felt complete. He was kind, patient, strong but gentle and we worked well together as a couple. He appreciated my way of seeing things through a woman's eyes. We had more women customers than the other hotels and that was not by accident as I had learned much from the Mullers. We were a good team and it showed on our bank balance.

On the subject of bright things, Nonnie and Jimmy had a little girl she called Susana Clare, named after me and my home. She asked and I agreed to be her godmother.

We were blessed with Eadie and Eddie, the Aboriginal couple, who Murray and Pat had known for some time and now worked for us. I renamed Eddie, Jack, as they never understood who I was calling with my accent. We had quarters for them and they cooked, cleaned and did what we asked, inside and out, always cheerfully. I certainly had things to learn. They did not get wages. Somewhere to live and tucker was their pay and that was the same on the stations. We changed that in a small way and opened a disguised account for them and deposited a regular amount to be kept for the future. We certainly made sure they had excellent food, blankets and clothes. Jack, Eadie and I often took a billy and had tea and hot buttered scones, kept warm in a tea towel, on the banks of the Diamantina in the shade of a gum tree.

They were very shy but enjoyed showing me things I either didn't see or didn't understand like animal tracks, little holes in the bank where a yabby might live and could be hooked out with a piece of wire. They also caught and cooked mussels, perch and other fish and birds that lived in or around the Diamantina River. They also showed us how to wash and prepare nardoo so it was safe to eat and explained to us in their way that if Burkre and Wills had eaten the nadoo prepared for them they likely wuld have surviced but they were too proud.

They both had excellent hearing and an ear for the sounds of animals and birds, people, and musical instruments and they could mimic many. One day I was talking to some men in the bar and Jack sneaked up behind me and made a noise like a dingo. I dropped what I was doing and swung around to see Jack looking up at the sky whistling. After everyone laughed a man told me that Aboriginals had many skills to identify danger, find their way to the different parts of their tribal land and to go at the right time to find food. To communicate by making the cry of a bird meaning 'I can see a kangaroo' would not frighten the animal like a human voice would. They also had an 'ear' for shades of meaning when meeting strangers from tribes who spoke different languages this skill could be a matter of life or death. The man also said that Aboriginals never seemed to forget sounds they had heard. He had worked in the Northern Territory and in Arnhem Land where the natives called white people 'Balanda' a name that came from Malayan interpretation of Hollander for the Dutch people who had visited those shores centuries before. I was fascinated with this conversation and it helped explain why they understood me far more easily than some non-Irish people in town.

After we returned from Ballarat we had a little get-together on the river bank and I took some special cakes and biscuits they liked and cordial I had made. When we were ready to go Jack gently put a two feet long piece of wood about an inch and a half in diameter with a knob on one end he had been smoothing with ash and sand into my hand said, 'Wadi stick, for you.' I thanked him. Later I showed it to Bill who said it wa from a Wadi tree that only grew near Birdsville and one or two other places. Because it was so hard, Wadi wood was prized as a weapon and was also used to carry fire from one place to another as once alight, it stayed that way for a long time. Often some twigs of dead finish, a hot burning wood, were taken with it to relight if necessary.

It was very valuable as trade goods and a weapon. I laughed at the thought of the second use. Why would I need a weapon?

# 33

# Fate

Things were good for us in 1889. Bill, me and the children were well and we had recovered from but still basked in the joys of our trip to Ballarat. The effects of the 1886 deluge were still obvious. Plenty of feed for the large mobs of cattle travelling through Birdsville to the railhead at Hergott and then by rail to the southern markets. The drovers were always thirsty when they returned from these trips. Some wanted a bed for themselves and a stable for their horses, so we were earning a 'good shillin' as they say here. We also had a bonus with a very busy New Year's Eve or Hogmanay as our Scottish guests insisted was the correct name.

After we had welcomed 1890, I went outside late at night as it was still very hot. I walked a few hundred yards and sat on a tree stump and gazed at this sky the like I had not seen in Ireland, not only because there was often cloud or fog at night but, as the navigator on the *Gauntlet* had explained, there were more stars visible in this part of the world. I thought of home, as I so often did, but was comfortable in this new land, with my children and lovely, loving husband and was close to God under his heavens. I felt that I could pick a star just by reaching up. I had something else to thank God for because pregnant I probably was. When Auld Lang Syne rang out, although it wasn't Irish, it might as well have been as it made my heart sing. I am not sure how long I sat there but the sky in the east was lighter when I went inside and found my bed.

But life has a way of turning comfort into pain. On February 23rd Robert Frew died suddenly. We were terribly upset. He had inspired us to come to Birdsville and helped us every inch of the way. It was a huge funeral and Bill presided over the wake and made a wonderful speech. The next morning Bill complained of a headache that was clearly due to too many drinks the night before. Or so I thought, but then I realised that he has been a picture of respect and sobriety. I gave him some medicine made from willow tree bark, a cup of tea and water and put him to bed but his headache got worse, his temperature rose and he complained of bad aches and pains all over. He tossed and turned and moaned all that day and most of the night. I was terrified. Wet cloths and drinks helped but he took no food and slept poorly. Next morning Mary, our Aboriginal kitchen maid, gave him some bush medicine her mother used for fevers and later he was able to have some breakfast and a cup of tea. Dr Milne was worried about him and also gave him some medicine and told me to give him boiled water only, no food.

For the next few days he was unwell but slowly recovered and after about a week he managed to do a few odd jobs around the hotel in the shade. I thought he was getting better but soon he became unwell again with fever, stomach pains, bloating and constipation, headache, chills and a bad cough. He also had many little pink spots on his body I thought may be bites of fleas or lice but they did not itch. It was like someone had walked over my grave when the doctor said that they were signs of typhoid fever.

He settled down again after a few days but then became worse again. His pain was more severe, he was feverish, his nose and bowel bled and he couldn't think straight or talk sense at times. He was so weak he could not get out of bed even though he had both constipation and diarrhoea that happened with typhoid fever. Then his belly swelled until it was as tight as a drum. Dr Milne tried morphine, laudanum and other things but to no avail. He became worse and worse, the fever increased and he slowly lost any sense of where he was and of me. On March 24th he had a huge vomit and died. I laid him out with the help of a friend and the next day he was buried under a tree he had always liked in the Birdsville cemetery. Later his grave was marked with a fitting tombstone.

I remember the funeral with everyone in town and nearby attending. His mate, Johann Groth gave the eulogy and reminisced about their time together as original settlers nearly ten years before. After that we went to our hotel but I collapsed and remember nothing for a week. I was told it had been a wonderful wake. My friends had put me to bed and I lay unmoving, not speaking and staring into space for seven days, kept alive in the heat by the sips of water they gave me every few minutes and wet towels put on my body. There was someone with me at all times. I was washed and my personal needs met and I just knew the children were also cared for. When I did return to this earth from wherever I had been I remembered what had happened to poor Bill. What I did not know was what would happen to me and our, now my, children including the baby I knew was in me.

There was no choice. My friends particularly Mrs MacDonald the recently arrived wife of police Sergeant Arthur MacDonald had done all that could be expected caring for me and my children and previously helping me with Bill when ill and after his death. They could do no more. Eadie and Jack were irreplaceable. They had been in the background over these horrible few weeks making sure we had water, the cooking fire was alight, the children were fed, the stables cleaned and endless cups of tea and scones were produced. I can never thank them enough.

I had an obligation to run the hotel until the end of 1890. There was no Bill to share the job. It was now all up to me. I made myself see that as the blessing in disguise. I was often teased in the bar being a woman and an Irish one at that but I did enjoy mixing with our customers and if any one got out of line our regulars would not put up with that for long. A few weeks after Bill died was the first time anyone caused me any real concern. I was on my own tidying up in front of the bar when a drover, who had been leering at me the night before, when in his cups, came into the hotel. He walked over to me and asked if I was looking for a real man for my bed now Bill had gone. Before I could do or say anything he had me by both wrists, told me how pretty I was, pulled me towards him and tried to kiss me. I kneed him very hard where it hurts. He swore and yelled awful things about what he was going to do to me and then appeared to calm down and smiled an awful smile at me. He then slowly but strongly took hold of my shirt and a fair bit of me as well with his left hand. He smiled again with the coldest eyes I have ever seen and slowly pulled back his right fist. I was paralysed with fear.

The next thing that happened was a blur. I heard a scuffling noise and a yell and sensed something flying past my head and then a crunching noise as the drover collapsed from a blow in the head. Gentle Jack had been in the cellar and heard the man's threats. He had insisted that I keep my Wadi stick in the bar and knew where. He threw it with good effect, jumped the bar and grabbed the drover by the neck but he was unconscious so he let him drop. Jack gave me such a big smile. I knew it meant 'I thought something bad would happen, I must keep close to her and the stick.' Well it seemed reasonable to me and thank God he did!

Later when I had stopped shaking, I said something like. 'You could have killed him.' He shook his head and said, 'Na, hit in head he fall down and get up, hit in neck he die.' Well that was a good job. I wondered where kind gentle Jack learned to make such a weapon, use it so well and know within inches whether it would kill someone or not. I definitely put that in my 'forget about it box' after Jack's actions. He took a considerable risk striking a white man, but he was well thought of and it was in a good cause.

The man's yelling had also attracted Sergeant MacDonald, who had been walking past the hotel, and he praised Jack for sorting things out. When the drover woke up, he handcuffed him none too gently and frogmarched him to the police station cell and let him think about things for a few days. Sergeant MacDonald made it quite clear that he was not to come to Birdsville again - ever. Most men would not tolerate anyone mistreating women and those who did were given short shrift or worse. I later heard that some other men made sure he understood the Sergeant's message very clearly indeed.

I did think more about Jack and Eadie after this. He and Eadie had few friends and only casual contact with the local Aboriginals and others passing through with cattle or helping the cameleers. They were devoted to each other but had no children. One day they were caring for May and Fred while I was busy. They were kind and patient with them, like grandparents. I asked about their children. They both just shook their heads, looked sad, said goodbye, and left. I made a mental note to ask Murray and Pat about this when I had a chance.

In contrast to many, Murray and Pat had a genuine liking and respect for Aborigines or 'black fellas', as he called them in a friendly and good-humoured way, but when he knew someone or worked with them it was always by their name. The nature of his job meant that he was away from home moving cattle from one place to another on a station, mustering for sale, weaning calves, branding or droving often for weeks or months on end always many miles from other people with three or four men.

This meant sleeping on the ground in a swag, a blanket rolled in a piece of canvas that held a few spare clothes. Food was sometimes fresh meat, but otherwise salt beef and damper made every day in the ashes of the previous night's fire. Often, they had to ride tiring night watches as well. It was hard, dirty and dangerous work for white and black men. Murray told us that he always made sure a black fella went with him because they knew so much more about the weather, where water might be and could find their way back to where they had come from if there was trouble. They would stick it out no matter what if they had been treated with respect.

Bill and I took a lot of notice of what Murray had said. It was in our natures to be polite and kind to others. It was not hard to like and be grateful to Jack and Eadie because they had certainly helped us and we probably could not have managed without them. I certainly saw living proof of Murray's advice when Jack saved me from being punched in the face or likely worse. Soon after that Murray and Pat were back in town and called in as they had heard about my adventure. I praised Jack and Eadie and asked about their lack of children. Pat nodded at Murray; 'She needs to know.'

Murray drained his tea, had a puff or two of his pipe and put it on the table. The man who laughed and joked at anything and everything had disappeared. Murray's face was expressionless and he began to talk.

*When the white men came to Australia, they treated the Aboriginals little better than animals. They took their land, their women, infected them with measles, tuberculosis and venereal disease and introduced them to alcohol, a poison. The Aboriginals fought back but most times lost any conflicts because guns and horses will always beat spears and clubs.*

*White men trying to make a life for their families were threatened and understandably afraid. There were places where there were two or three hundred Aboriginals and only two or three men or one family trying to gain a foothold in this huge land. And there was killing of white settlers to be sure and just as sure the reprisals by the whites were far out of proportion to the deeds they were avenging.*

*Murray said how blatant and public the punishment handed out to blacks was. He described an incident he had read about and later gave me the cutting that I am now copying. It was written by William Carr-Boyd, an explorer, gold prospector and prolific writer after who the Carr-Boyd Ranges, in Western Australia, were named. He wrote under the name of 'Potjostler' that I assumed was the Australian equivalent of our Irish 'pot stirrer.'*

*He wrote from Amaroo near Boulia, north of Birdsville, on the 17th July 1878 about a man called Greensmith who was missing, presumably killed by Aboriginals, as they found a blanket that had belonged to him with group of Aboriginals. He went on to write that some weeks before another group had raided his hut at Amaroo when he was away and 'taken all they could carry' so they followed their tracks the next day and recovered his possessions. 'And then had satisfaction.'*

*Murray went on to describe an incident at Lake Hope, again I read the newspaper cutting later. 'Henry Dean, the manager, wielded severe measures against local Diyari Aboriginals who tried to resist stock encroachment on precious natural water supplies during a bad drought period.'*

*'Trooper Poynter was sent to protect the Europeans against attack he expected after the 'affray' when four were killed and several wounded. He asked for 100 cartridges as he had no doubt he*

*would soon need them.'*

*These episodes were violent enough but there were other much larger attacks on Aboriginal people and hundreds were killed in western Queensland.*

*Susana, white people thought that Aboriginals lived in a great open land so they could move somewhere else if white men wanted their land. But they could not. The borders of their tribal lands were every bit as real as the borders in Europe.*

*A particular tribe may have had five or six neighbours joining their borders. They would occasionally have skirmishes, often broken up by the women of both tribes, and they would have dances and other celebrations at certain times.*

*Tribes further away were a different matter, the more borders crossed the more dangerous it was and trespassers were killed unless they had permission for ceremonial reasons or trade. This was well known to the tribes and soon learned by the white authorities, particularly in Queensland, where a native police organisation was established. These troopers essentially had no feeling other than hatred for tribes far away. They had guns, horses, uniforms and the authority to kill others of their kind and they did, usually led by police.*

*There had been some trouble around Birdsville with a few whites and cattle killed putting the fear of God into the settlers in these lonely places. There was a determination to stop that and there were several places where many Aboriginals were killed for the most trivial reasons or simply because they were there.*

*One of these expeditions about 20 years ago killed one or two hundred people simply enjoying a celebration. There were only two survivors and my dear Susana they were Jack and Eadie. They were 12 -13 years old at the time, too young to be at ceremonies, so they went to catch a dingo pup from a litter they had tracked.*

*Jack was on one side of a sandhill and Eadie on the other looking for tracks when Jack heard some horses on the opposite side of the hill. Terrified he crawled up the side of the sand hill being very careful not to be seen against the skyline and peeped over the top.*

*He had heard the horses slow down and stop and he saw why. They had Eadie. Jack never told me what happened exactly but it doesn't take much imagination. He waited until he could no longer hear the horses and crawled down the sandhill very carefully to Eadie who was lying, badly bruised, in blood-soaked sand, barely conscious and no doubt would have died had Jack not been there.*

*Somehow, he dragged and carried her into a gully where there was water and plants that had bulbs and the odd snake they could eat and they stayed there until she was fit enough to travel. Fortunately, it was spring, so it was not too hot or cold and they managed to reach a station where some of the old people from a different group of their tribe had camped.*

*And Susana that is where we met Eadie and Eddie, as we knew him, because we had just been appointed to manage that property. We had learned before how to live with our cattle and with local Aboriginals.*

When I wrote all this down in my journal sometime later it read like I was calm and logical, but I wasn't. I was shocked to my soul, hurt and disbelieving. I had heard stories before and I knew someone who was killed by Aboriginals and it had hardened my heart but when I heard of wholesale murder on this scale it turned my mind to mush.

On the 22nd January 1889 about eighteen months before, when we ran Tattersalls hotel, Sub Inspector Sharpe shot and killed himself on the verandah of the Police Station and was brought to the hotel. This was the custom and indeed the law, as it was in Ireland, if there was no undertaker around. I did what I could for him. He looked at peace. I couldn't help but think that maybe he was riven with guilt and could not go on doing such an unpleasant, difficult, dangerous and thankless job.

I did not ever get to understand the whole situation but it made me sad. Perhaps if Bill had lived, we could have made some sense out of this brutality and cruelty. Sadly, that was not to be and now the only thing on my mind was the survival of me, my two living children and my unborn child. That was the world I had to save not the big scary one outside.

It was a struggle to keep going in the first part of 1890 but I managed to see it through. My children exhausted me but kept me alive at times I believe. Bill's death affected me badly. I could manage during the day but at night the sight, sounds and smell of his death would envelope me until I fell asleep exhausted.

One night I sat down on the tree stump as I had, seemingly an age ago on New Year's Eve, but it was only six months or so before. I had to plan the foreseeable future. A baby expected in August and then Christmas and finishing my time at Tattersalls.

Seamus was with me and we talked for hours. I came away sad, hurting but strangely comforted.

I knew what I had to do for the coming months for myself and the children, all three of them. I would and did do what I had to.

*Bill's grave at Birdsville*

# 34

# Life After Bill

After Bill died, I walked in my sleep and slept when I walked for months. Dr Milne agreed I was with child, expected in August 1890. With help from friends and dear Jack and Eadie somehow I managed to look after May and Fred and share the love of them with the one inside me; the last 'piece' of Bill I would ever have. I had to look after him or her with all my strength. I gained great solace from the Lord and, as always thankfully, from my beloved Seamus. With the help of Dr Milne my precious, precious baby girl, Alberta Jessamine was born on August 14th 1890. She was named after her father and the Persian word for the lovely smelling jasmine, that Bill and I so loved in Warwick.

I was pleased but bore a crushing sadness that Bill would never see her and she was so much like him. I swallowed enough food and water to feed her but vomited, lost weight and was bed ridden for three weeks. The instinct to live and care for my children could not break through my pain, I wanted to die. One night Seamus was by my side and he was on fire with anger. He screamed at me for deserting my children and Bill and told me to do what God intended and walked away without another word. It worked and, helped by a blood and bone guardian angel, Clara Haylock, I recovered from probably a fatal decline.

Clara Haylock, who was about to have a baby, her husband William and their five boys arrived in Birdsville in early

September from Tiboorburra, north of Broken Hill, on their way to take up land at Charleville. They settled into the hotel and next day she saw Dr Milne who said the baby was not lying properly, birth was imminent, and she should stay in Birdsville. She was a midwife and worried about the 500 mile journey to Charleville and was delighted with Dr Milne's advice.

A few days later with some difficulty she had a baby girl, Alice. The bad news was that Mr Haylock could not get to Charleville in time, so missed his land allocation, but he and his boys went to see a relative in Bedourie. Selfishly I was delighted that Clara did not go. My emotions were raw. I was not eating well, my milk was drying up and I was getting worse every day. I needed her.

Clara was a charming, witty, lively woman and said that the wee baby left her with nothing much to do, so she cared for me physically, mentally and professionally and did the cooking and cleaning. Last, but not least, one morning when I was struggling, she fed Alberta. I was gob smacked and protested but Alberta was clearly getting what she needed. It only happened twice and then I was fine and fed her like the others. It is hard to imagine a greater bond between two women and we became great friends. I could talk to her about Bill. The Australian way was to deny the sadness of people. 'She'll be right' was the code for men and women. But I wasn't right. I was hurting. I explained my sadness and anger about the loss of Bill and she listened, sitting quietly. After a pause, she smiled and took my hands in hers and gently offered the words, 'Look for the light from the past shining over your shoulder; you bathed in it in the past and you can bathe in it in the future.' It was hard but I always had a good imagination and it helped, especially if I rubbed my wedding ring on my cheek.

Mr Haylock decided to use his horses and cart to start a carrying business and to expand as necessary. He could not compete with the camels on cost or carrying capacity, but he could make more frequent runs to surrounding stations and Bedourie. He did well and soon had a team of 20 horses and relief drivers. Clara worked as a mid-wife in Birdsville but going to a station, unless nearby, meant leaving three weeks before a baby was due and staying three weeks after to ensure baby and mother were well. She settled well into our little community. I did the right thing and looked after the hotel until the end of 1890 and then managed the billiard business and my children.

On New Year's Eve 1890 I again visited my tree stump. I was sad but something good had happened. Certainly I could recall the horror of Bill's dying days if I tried but I had to make an effort. When I thought and dreamt about him he was the fit and lovely man I loved. Sad but pleasant memories. Clara's words were working.

The years 1891 to 1894 were all about me being a mother. May went from three to seven, Fred one to five and Alberta a babe to four and me from 33 to 37 and Clara's children two to nine plus the wee one. I lost Ma from a long sickness but Da was still hale and hearty. That was another loss that hurt me terribly, but I had to shake off my grief and keep going. Long periods of happiness and peace in Birdsville were rare, it was a hard place. Dr Milne left in the middle of 1893, a blow to us all but we were pleased to know that a Dr Hoche, who had trained in Germany and worked in Port Pirie and Farina, was replacing him in December.

Dr Hoche, his wife Nellie and three children aged four, three and seven months made the six day coach trip after the short train ride from Farina to Hergott. There were now 20 cattle stations on The Track. Nellie was most positive about the trip and described much better accommodation than I experienced seven years before. I was delighted that they had lunch on the way at Cowarie as the Hellings had returned to their home.

Unfortunately, they arrived at Birdsville in the middle of a typhoid epidemic. Dr Hoche treated patients who he isolated in Burt's store, at nearby stations and, in the midst of this, Nellie got the disease and he cared for her at their home. Clara, Jane Ward, the postmistress, and I tried to help but to no avail. Nellie had periods of feeling well, relapsed and like Bill, did not survive and died on February 24th, 1894, only a half an hour after she had said good bye to her two older children. Doctor Hoche had sent an aboriginal runner to Beetoota more than 100 miles away to get champagne he thought might help his wife but he returned, too late, with the two bottles. We drank them at her wake. He tried so hard to save her and understandably was distraught. He told me in a quiet moment when she had not long to live that, although he liked her, 'I married her because there was a prejudice in Port Pirie against unmarried doctors particularly from Europe. I could not get a certificate to practice so moved to Farina and the drought brought us here. I was notified last week that my papers will be recognised in Queensland. She has paid a dreadful price for that to happen.'

Jane Ward took the Hoche children to Hergott. At Hergott she met Nellie's sister-in law Lena who collected her nephew and namesake Len and took him back to her home at Caltowie. Jane continued her journey to Port Pirie with the other two children. On the way to Hergott Jane had narrowly avoided the flooded Diamantina River but when she reached Port Pirie she found out that her brother-in-law, the father of three children the same age as the Hoche children, had been drowned in that very flood. It took three weeks before she returned home, utterly exhausted physically and mentally. She grieved for a long time over her brother-in- law. Fortunately, she had a governess to look after her children.

Dr Hoche stayed around until May for babies and patients with typhoid, once at Monkira 130 miles away for three weeks. He then returned to Port Pirie. Seven people died of typhoid in Birdsville and perhaps the same in the surrounding district and 104 in Queensland, far less than the 530 in the 1884 epidemic. I was told that he was so distressed and distracted with his work that he could not look after his children and boarded in a hotel. He drank heavily and used morphine for a medical condition and died by his own hand accidentally taking too much of these dangerous substances. Nellie's sister wrote to Jane thanking her for what she, Clara and I had done and mentioned that Dr Hoche had studied epidemics. After he passed his exams, he worked on a United States ship where there was an epidemic of an infectious disease amongst passengers. He was praised for his skill and they lost no patients. We did not know how lucky we were. Cometh the hour, cometh the man. It was a sad end for a dedicated doctor.

Gloom overcame me. It took me a long time to find the sunshine coming over my shoulder again.

# 35

# Time Heals, And Hurts

Our life was comfortable. When Alberta was born I was given a pet shorthorn house cow, a wonderful milker. We had goats to eat and milk, to sell or serve in the hotel, a few chickens and vegetables from the Chinese gardens and staples from the stores brought by the Afghan camel strings. As mentioned before Jack or Eadie often caught fish, yabbies and other shellfish in the river and trapped or speared a variety of ducks and other birds. These treats were most welcome and no doubt good for me and the children.

Clara had three more children between 1891 and 1895 and with my three there was never a dull moment. I had been close to my mother, sister, Nonnie, Sarah and Mrs Muller. Apart from Mrs Muller in Australia I was the leader, the strong one and happy to be so. Clara though, was the one I could go to, pour my heart out and be treated uncritically, with courtesy and kindness no matter what was happening in her life. I often thought Alberta and I owed our survival to her. With Clara's help I regained my usual sparkle and energy and accepted an offer by Tom Merrifield to take over the licence of his Tattersalls Hotel in 1895-96 as he had some business venture to pursue elsewhere. I was happy that the children were receiving some schooling, even if it was only being provided by parents. I could usually help in the morning when the hotel was quiet.

A George Dennett had worked in the pub for a year or two and

I had met him often. He was a fine looking, powerful man, most affable and helpful. One night I had a second look at a drover in the bar who reminded me of the man who attacked me, but it wasn't him. Later we had a drink after cleaning up and George asked if I had recognised the drover. I looked puzzled and he told me. 'He is the brother of the man who attacked you but a decent cove who would never hurt a woman.' He added, 'No one will ever harm you while I am here' and gently patted my hand. I was sad, lonely and still in my thirties with the normal feelings of a woman my age and he was a kind and gentle man. Things happened between us and in mid-1896 I happily accepted his proposal of marriage. This duly happened at the Police Station and a great party followed at the hotel. I already had wedding rings on both ring fingers and needed no more. George was fine with that, it saved him money as he told someone.

Next day George asked Tom to put the hotel licence in his name as we were now married and that was the way he wanted things to be. Tom didn't want to go to the trouble and expense and told him so. George got really cranky and told Tom he was not going to have a woman for a boss. Tom dug his heels in because he was running behind in his project. I had trusted the two men I had loved so why not George? I told Tom I would sort it out with the court at Windorah and he was relieved to hear that, as was George.

Tom was canny though. He explained to George that I had experience in managing the finances in his hotel and would continue to do so and every month I would send financial statements to him. If they were not showing that the hotel was going along alright then our employment would end. He spent an hour or more with me later explaining what information he wanted and to let him know if there were problems and repeated those last few words. He then showed me a contract of employment for the three of us to sign covering the things we had discussed. He needed a witness so Jack fetched Sergeant MacDonald. Tom asked George to come in from the bar and explained the contract and in particular the monthly reports he required. George was ashen then red as he read the contracts but was cunning enough to know that he was still on a good thing, signed the contract and with poor grace stormed back to the bar. I signed, as did Tom, and Sergeant MacDonald witnessed our signatures. The sergeant suggested I leave my copy of the contract with him because things like that do go missing. I thanked him and gave him the paper.

After Tom left I spoke to George, pleased that we had sorted things out. He held my hand and thanked me for being a good wife, but there was no smile or warmth in his eyes and his grip was painful. He then pulled me to my feet and took me to the bed and hurt me. The kind and gentle man had gone and never returned. He was not the man I thought and made my life a misery, but I hid it well. I was afraid to say anything to anyone as he had made it plain my children would suffer if I did. It was a constant battle between us. I knew there were rules to follow about handling and recording money, wages, goods and services. He just saw a lake of grog and money he could dip into when he wished. Somehow, I manage to rescue enough cash coming in, to pay for goods and wages but he managed to flaunt every nice thing I had encouraged to gain and keep customers. It was an uneasy truce, but we managed, and on rare occasions he was even nice to me physically. I acted the part in return but with a heart of ice.

He was a charming man when it suited him but he was rude and aggressive to our drinkers for little or no reason and over the coming months he had several fights but always arranged it so the customer threw the first punch and he threw the last. He also stole from the drinkers by the oldest trick in pubs. When a group was having a session, each man would leave his money in front of him so the barman could take from the man whose shout it was. As the session wore on beer was spilt on the bar and George was there to wipe the bar with his ever present towel collecting a few coins each time. He had no conscience about doing anything to get money. When a ringer wanted to drink his cheque out George would oblige and get him so drunk that he wouldn't know where he was and then, George with some of his cronies, would play cards with the 'victim'. Sometimes ringers and shearers would stretch their cheques out for a week or more but with George, his cards and crooked mates it was only a day or perhaps two. I hated this more than most of his tricks and tried to give them food and water and a bed, sometimes successfully. Another scheme he had was to buy cheap whisky and rum from smugglers who crossed the border from South Australia and sell it out of the back door of the pub. The pub lost, the customs lost and so did I. I was generally able to keep some sort of financial order with difficulty. I was able to put in some information that Tom was bound to identify as 'dodgy' and I hoped he would realise what was happening. George was nice to the children and gave them sweets and other treats but there was always a message to me, ' You must be careful you don't get lost and fall down a hole', 'Watch when you go near the river, sometimes there are bunyips and they will pull you in,' and one day when May was ten my blood ran cold when he tickled her under the arms and when she tried to get away, he smiled and said, 'You will like that in a few years.' Our bed was no joy for me and I just surrendered and did what he wanted. Sometimes it wasn't much he was so drunk. I was desperately worried I might be with child as my courses had become shorter and less frequent.

I was reassured when Clara told me it was likely early change of life. I threw myself into the school and gained some peace and pleasure doing that, but it was a long and horrible time for me. Clara knew that there was something wrong. I was grumpy, sad, anxious, thin and over- protective of the children but I could not tell her I was so afraid of this man I had married.

Birdsville was a very small place with fewer than 100 people and no one could miss behaviour like George's. Soon the only people at the hotel were his mates or at least the people who would put up with him to get free grog. It was nearly a year since we were married and the pub was in terrible shape. Clara's husband William had been very busy with his carting business and if he had a drink it was at the Birdsville Hotel where he had become good mates with the owner. Clara asked him to visit Tattersalls and see what was going on and he came home with some interesting information that Clara passed to me. She and William were from Broken Hill and had only been in Tiboorburra a few years before Birdsville. William had recognised George from Broken Hill days, but by another name and heard he left Broken Hill under a cloud two or three years before. William's brother in Bedourie had visited and said that he was not a man to be trusted.

And then a fairy tale happened. Tom had identified the fear and message in my letters and returned to Birdsville. He walked into the pub and stared at George, unblinking and spat, 'You bastard.' George threw a punch that missed by miles as he was so worn out from grog. Tom hit him twice and he fell down. He got onto his knees crying and begging not to be hit again. Tom was disgusted with this craven blubbering coward and turned away just as Sergeant MacDonald, as arranged, walked into the bar. George saw him and pleaded that Tom had attacked him. Tom shrugged and said, 'George fell over,' as did the barman and as did I.

Sergeant MacDonald put George in handcuffs and informed him, 'I am arresting you for a series of offences in three states and the customs want a piece of you as well. I will provide you with the paperwork in our nice comfortable gaol for you to study at your leisure.' Later he was to be tried in Roma for embezzlement but the trial did not go ahead for some reason and he was released. I have no knowledge of any other trials or punishment except banishment from the close world of Birdsville. He had broken all the rules. I never saw him again and took back the hotel licence and stayed there until the end of 1898. This creature took away my self-respect, my pride in being a woman and mother and left me shattered. I had always been friendly to men and enjoyed their company, strength, way of looking at the world and sense of humour. But no longer. I always thought I was a nice and good person and the men who I had loved cherished that, but that swine tore the guts out of me, not to mention my soul and he had even stripped Seamus and Bill from my dreams.

May was nine, Fred eight and Alberta six when we married. May vaguely remembered Bill and Fred perhaps. They had no real knowledge of men apart from the blokes in the pub and their godfather, Murray O'Brien, a fine man. From the time they could begin to understand, they knew my friend Seamus and their da were fine, gentle, courageous men who loved me. This Dennet bastard gave them all the wrong ideas. I tried to hide the ugliness but May knew something was very wrong. I had no doubt that the vague idea she had expressed on occasions of being a nun took root at this time. Living in a safe environment protected from men and doing good deeds must have seemed an attractive way to live her life. My anger and pain were unremitting for years but life went on.

In 1898, when Clara's daughter Alice was eight, someone stole her father's twenty horses and, while trying to find them, William either drowned in the flooded Diamantina or died of thirst in the pitiless desert. His body was never found. By the time Alice was ten her five older brothers had disappeared working on stations or other jobs where being able to read and write was an option not a requirement. Clara had to work and that meant weeks away on stations leaving ten year old Alice to look after her three siblings and to provide the town with fresh milk by milking twenty goats. She walked them to and from the town common every day and put them away at night to protect them from dingo attacks. Nights were horrid for Alice at times, with sick little ones or drunken abuse and fighting at the hotels scaring them all. She always felt safe when she could see the glow of the light at the police residence across the paddock and that would lull her to sleep.

# 36

# Weather, Rabbits...
# and a Friend Pulls the Pin

The late 1880s and early 1890s were good seasons. The South Australian Government had drilled artesian wells on the Birdsville Track at Lake Harry, Kopperamanna and Dulkaninna from 1890-1898 and planned to drill wells the rest of the way from 1903-1916, making the Track safer for man and beast. The cattle industry had grasped the easier access to markets, in Australia and the UK, with both hands. Sidney Kidman bought August Helling's mail run in 1892 and then, knowing the permanent water in Derwent Creek, bought Cowarie from him in 1895 the first station on the way to owning the biggest cattle operation in the world. Rather than buying a station in one area and run the gamut from bankruptcy to fabulous wealth totally at the whim of nature, he had a dream. That was to develop a chain of stations from the Gulf of Carpentaria to the Channel Country and connect with the southern markets via the Birdsville Track and the railway at Hergott Springs. Somewhere on his land there would not be a drought. By 1898 he had added Owen Springs in Central Australia, Roseberth, Pandie Pandie and Haddon Springs and by 1900 five other stations in the Channel Country. Including a property near Broken Hill, he and his brother Sackville owned 41,000 cattle, 23,000 horses and 22000 sheep and they had only just started. I met him many times. Not tall, but broad chested with a curly black beard and hair. He drove a buggy and always wore a suit and hat. He was a quiet man and while he did not drink alcohol, many times we talked in the lounge of the pub.

And there were rabbits. In 1859 James Austin from Glastonbury in Somerset sent 24 wild grey rabbits to his brother Thomas in Barwon Park near Geelong in Victoria. They multiplied so rapidly that they were in Southern Queensland by the mid1880s. I remembered seeing them in Warwick but took little notice until Tom caught some and we had roasts and stews. In Ireland rabbits belonged to the landed gentry and if caught pinching one it was a one way trip to Australia or worse. I felt quite special eating them. They turned up in Birdsville in the 1890s. Jack caught one and he and Eadie liked it so we ate rabbit once a week or more, but few of our customers would try them.

Rabbits caused unimaginable damage and cost to Australian farmers and pastoralists. Some people made livings selling the meat and skins. Others were contracted to reduce rabbit numbers by simply killing them. A rabbit proof fence was built near Birdsville and was patrolled by boundary riders. They had to patrol sections from 30-40 miles to inspect and repair. They were provided with paddocking, water, horses and a hut. Practicality was paramount. Married men were placed at cross roads so their wives could open the gates when they were on patrol.

By 1899 there were 294 miles patrolled but construction had halted due to the drought causing insoluble trouble with transport of materials. Like others in Australia these fences were of limited effect. I felt guilty. While the stations were spending incomprehensible amounts of money to get rid of rabbits, I was doing well buying skins and reselling them to the Akubra hat makers in Hobart and providing the odd drink for the fencers and trappers.

One night in late 1899, Murray and Pat came for dinner and, as usual, we had some nice food including wonderful cool rabbit from our Coolgardie safe and lots of drinks. Unfortunately, Murray gave us some disappointing news. He reminded me of the conversation he had with Bill about droughts 10 years before. 'There were some you just know are real and Susana I know this one is a right bastard so that has made up my mind. My job will be over for years, I am thinking, so there is not much point in hanging around as I will be 60 soon. We are moving to the Clare Valley to grow grapes and make wine'. They were the godparents of our three children and I doubt anyone could have done more in that job as they did before and after Bill died. We became quite maudlin after that when the kids had gone to bed. They left two or three weeks later and there we were on the top of the slippery slope, ending this century and staring at the next.

# 37

# Education

After the disaster of my marriage, I again agreed to continue at the Tattersall's Hotel in 1897-98. It was difficult to bring back the standard of service I had taken pride in but slowly it happened. Birdsville was a tight community and we looked after our own. They knew what George was like and, once we were shot of him, they came back in droves.

I was financially comfortable but the other dream of parents for their children, education, was missing. Australia had adopted the Irish system of education where the Government provided free primary schooling for children aged five to twelve to produce children who could, read, write, understand arithmetic and get jobs in the post-Industrial Revolution world. Politeness, cleanliness and tidy schoolwork were expected and taught as necessary, but the provision of government schooling would not happen in Birdsville until 1900. In the meantime, there was no school, just occasional wanderers passing through, like hedge teachers in Ireland. They had board, beer and bed supplied in return for teaching our children.

I was talking to Pat O'Brien and Clara one day about this and what we could do. Pat laughed and clapped her hands like a little girl and said, 'I would love to help you. I spent 10 years teaching our three girls on a sheep station and did some studying to be teacher but the distance and Murray's job made it all too hard. My youngest daughter K-K, for short, still has her books and I will ask her to send them to you.

We begged and borrowed slates, easels, chalk, pencils, paper and text books from neighbours, family, offices in Birdsville and even the new Education Department. One of the station hands even made a very heavy slate black board from local stone and with help from two mates hung it on a wall in our little school room that we had set up behind the hotel. Somehow with some other mothers we organised ourselves and ran what was an amateur school for about 10 children so they would have the basics to take to the proper school planned to start in 1900. I proudly wrote to my da, sister and some friends that I was now a teacher in a school I had started. Well it was true to a point and they loved it.

May had started in our non-government school when she was five in 1892 and finished what we could offer, aged 12, in 1899. Fred was 11 and a year behind May. Alberta also started aged five in 1895 and was about half way through our program aged eight. I was 40 but as fit and happy as I had been for some time. May had expressed an interest in being a nun in the last year or so. Clara's sister was a nun and they had spoken about the good things nuns do, such as teaching. I remembered playing nuns but never to the point of it being a calling, but May was thinking about this life and I would do what I could to help her. I contacted the St Joseph's convent at Kensington in Adelaide, founded by Mary McKillop and her group of sisters. They were most helpful and suggested that May return to school in 1900 for two years to see how she managed formal schooling because becoming a nun and a teacher certainly needed a good grounding in reading, writing and arithmetic. In a prosperous country with a growing population those subjects were vital for girls to get above the drudgery of cleaning, washing and the like. So I enrolled May in the new school with the idea of going to St Josephs as a boarder when she would be 14 or 15.

In 1899 Miss Ferry, the governess at Wards, was appointed as teacher to the Birdsville Provisional School to organise it for the formal opening in 1900. Two months later she resigned because she was refused three months sick leave she had requested. She died later, likely from consumption and was buried in the local cemetery. Soon after she resigned, a new teacher, the girls always knew as 'strict Mr Duggan' arrived. Alberta, Alice and their friends enjoyed the learning and the contact with others. Alberta and Alice were inseparable and loved checking supplies that arrived on camels, making lists, counting money and making more lists. They made few mistakes and asked intelligent questions. They also looked after Clara's little ones and had great fun playing teachers with them.

Alberta told me Alice was sleepless with excitement before the school picnic. No doubt in her life there was never time for fun. It was all about work and survival. That thought also haunted me a few years later when Clara found her a job at the Mulka Store half way between Hergott and Birdsville. Alice wrote a letter to Alberta and it read in part, '*The store managers have some cattle and are often away looking after them. I sometimes spend days by myself, seeing nobody and nothing but the Strzelecki Desert (I had to copy that big word Alberta.) Something good happened yesterday, I found a whole box of books by Charles Dickens and I plan to read them. Love from Alice.*

I read that with a mix of emotions; deep and utter sadness that she never had a girlhood, but with admiration and joy for her courage and ability to cope. Perhaps we all had to pass these tests to make a mark in this new land for ourselves, our children and their children to follow. It was a land that devoured the weak in heart or sinew.

It must have been the fairies who reminded me that Charles Dickens, the man who encouraged Caroline Chisholm in her work for women, was helping a brave, resourceful little girl in one of the loneliest and harshest places on earth, where there were still many men passing who were 'wanted or not wanted.' I could only thank God for her luck and the decency of the passing men. I found out later that she spent two years there and was 14 when her mother and her four children moved to Adelaide in 1904. She had read and reread all of the Dickens' books in the shed. A truly amazing girl.

Fred was in the first class in the new school. He wanted to work on or around stations and had enough common sense, just like his da, to know he needed to stay at school until he had mastered what we called the 'Three Rs: Reading, Riting and Rithmetic' to know how to work out right angles when building, care of land, volume of tanks, to count stock quickly, estimate weight of cattle, understand profits and losses and to put all this into meaningful English verbally and on paper.

I completed my agreement with the Tattersalls pub on January 1st 1899 after a big New Year once again but it was just a job these days. Sadly my friend, 35 year old Mrs Adams, the cook at The Royal died of heat apoplexy as did boundary rider Edwin Callick soon after. The drought heat was a killer.

1899 was nice. The billiards business was still doing well and I enjoyed giving the place and the spare rooms a good going over with brush, brooms, rags and mops, whatever was needed. I had bought a Singer peddle sewing machine that duly arrived on a camel in bits before Christmas, so I was delighted to put it together with the children's help. I had a wonderful time with my new toy, making clothes for me and my children and my other one Alice, who was feeling the loss of her father very much and the poverty of her mother. Everything I made her was always followed by a note or a bunch of wild flowers. I spent hours planning clothes to make. Nonnie was happy to get what materials I wanted from Ballarat where there was a woolen mill and a wonderful range of fabrics I had seen and bought when I had Fred. My parcel from Nonnie eventually arrived and, while putting the materials away, I found a parcel wrapped in brown paper addressed to Bill. My hands trembled when I opened it. It was the three leather bound volumes of *Robbery under Arms* and a card that read;

*Dear Bill*

*Please find the complete works of my book you ordered for Susana that has finally become available in Australia. I am sorry I could not get it to you, for Susana, before Christmas. I tore up your cheque as I have much pleasure in giving this to your lovely wife as a small token of my appreciation for the care she bestowed on us at the hotel. Yours 'ROLF B'!!*

I remembered Bill promising he would get it for me and had tears in my eyes but sunshine all around me. I promised myself I would read a chapter a week and I did with joy for the necessary 52 weeks until it was finished. It was as though Bill was at my side. I was reading it one evening as it was getting dark and thinking that I would be able to read by the light shining over my shoulder. I laughed at what Bill would have said about such a ridiculous idea. And I smiled and smiled as I drifted off to sleep, happy, as the darkness came.

# 38

# A Century Ends

I had developed the habit of reflecting at the end of each year but this time it was the end of the century and as I had been alive for almost half of it and for much of the industrial revolution there was much to think about. Foremost in my mind was the oath I made soon after Bill's death now almost ten years ago. I could not fix the world outside, but I would strive mightily to look after myself and my children. That is what I had done and would continue to do every day on earth God will grant me. My da had two sayings I remember so well, *'To thine own self be true'* and *'Do unto others as you would them do unto you.'* Add the Ten Commandments and that was the code I did my best to follow. We were all fit and healthy and the children were doing well at school. A plan had been made for their future schooling and we were secure in our lives having received a handsome amount from Bill's Mother's will as she had inferred so long ago in Ballarat.

Birdsville was a tough and rough place with men and women of all sorts. I remember a cartload of prostitutes camped on the river bank near the rabbit fence builders' camp. Some big money changed hands that night for sure and certain. The sergeant found out what the 'owner' did to keep them working and they left, going where I did not know. Many publicans cheated customers particularly when they had a cheque to cut out and sometimes allowed them to drink rot gut rum with little or no food until they got DTs, somehow survived, died or their money ran out. Mr Muller showed me that being proud of what you provided, not cheat and be polite to customers was a lot easier in the long run as reputations spread and no one likes to pay for fights and unfortunately I had experience of that conduct, although I had never treated anyone like that. If someone did want to drink out a cheque I would care for them and make sure they ate and had money left to go on their way. Whether it was north, south, east or west, it was a long hazardous journey from Birdsville to any other place of refuge and I wanted no one's death on my conscience and I was now even more fixed in that behaviour.

The men who brought rabbit skins to me were usually filthy dirty and covered in blood much like the kangaroo shooters in Queensland. I offered them a wash before they had anything to drink and most took up my invitation. When they came back, I bought them a drink and offered them a meal that they usually accepted and they drank some more so I got most of money back I had paid for the skins. If not me, someone else would have got their money but I like to think I treated them like someone would treat my children. Perhaps I succeeded.

There were customs officers on both side of all Australian colonial boundaries to collect taxes on the goods carried by camels, pack horses, teamsters, bullock carts or mobs of cattle or sheep that entered their state. There were several posts in the general area under the jurisdiction of the Birdsville customs. These barriers were to be removed under the new Constitution of Australia. Yes, we would lose money from the customs staff and miss wonderful people like the Wards, the customs officer and post mistress, but the cost of maintaining the outposts must have been considerable. And a lot of revenue was missed anyway. The main tracks were watched but it beggars belief to think that people moving cattle or camels about over thousands of square miles would follow the main tracks unless they wanted to. All they had to do was move over an imaginary line and sell anything to whoever they wished.

Cattle duffing, or stealing someone's cattle is a crime and was not to be tolerated. It was the province of bushrangers and their like who could be shot in the act or hanged if convicted. Cattle were life. August Helling went to no end of trouble to get a man, who had killed one of his cattle and left the area, into court. That is straight forward. But there was a related practice, in the million square miles of Australia's outback, called *poddy dodging.* Like having sex and drinking beer, everyone did it. Poddy calves are new born, orphaned calves and on dairy farms are often fed from a bottle and get a swollen tummy, called poddy, from all the milk they drink. It did however come to mean an *unbranded* calf. In other words there are no markings indicating ownership although usually these calves have a protective mother with a brand. Calves in the outback might not be rounded up until they were six to twelve months old or more. Most stations had no boundary fences. So at a given time the ringers/stockmen from adjoining stations might meet somewhere near their boundary, likely at a fenced yard with a bronco panel where they would count, sort and brand the calves whose mothers they could identify.

On the other hand, ringers of no fixed abode could find these cattle, hide them somewhere and brand them with a registered brand or alter the brand they had. When the animal had no brand, a cleanskin, sometimes cattle duffers would brand them with a cooler branding iron so anyone checking it would think it was an old brand that had healed. A running iron also was used, a straight piece of iron with a handle used to alter other brands such as an o to an 8 or v to a w. Not a good bit of kit to have in your saddle bag if the coppers, or worse, the owners of the cattle, found you with what they reckon were their cattle.

One of the moral dilemmas I had was the 'Jack's as good as his master' attitude of the Australian bushman. Ned Kelly was revered by many and Harry Readford raised the same emotions when he blazed the Strzelecki Track with 1100 stolen cattle and showed a way for Queenslanders to get to the southern markets. I had mixed feelings. To steal from the rich to some was alright but when I saw how much pain and money August Heeling spent on one cow it did distress me. These men cared passionately about their animals. There were some funny stories on the same subject. A man from a nearby station used to bring the hotel a side of beef every race day, Christmas and Easter when we were flat out. His price was a bottle of Scotch and one of rum. He did the same for the police, every two weeks with roasts and steaks. One of them tried not to accept this and was told, 'Well get your meat in Adelaide son.' Immediate change of opinion.

This man died during the typhoid epidemic that took Nellie. One of the customers, when he heard, took off his hat and said, 'Poor bastard' paused and added "e must 'ave 'et his own bloody beef for the first bloody time and 'e gort so wild 'is guts blew up and killed 'im stone bloody dead.' Everyone laughed and toasted the departed. I was puzzled and asked what he meant. He explained. 'One day the ringer bought a few cattle into 'is ' omestead yard. The boss asked who owned them and the reply was, 'Six of ours and four from next door.' The answer, 'Well done son, four killers, just what we need.' That answered my question. It was the first time for many years I had heard the fairies whisper in my ear 'You Irish eejit'.

Another time in the bar a retired ringer was talking about days gone by and said, 'I sort of found enough cattle to give a well-known fella a start on his station, but I can't tell ya who or I would be in trouble.' And winked. He was a nice man, a good customer and taught Fred the leather work, such as making green hide ropes, to be a good ringer. I remember him saying how important hygiene was in a cattle camp and he showed me a leather set of pouches he had made to hold his plates, pannican and cutlery to ensure cleanliness. The stitching was recessed so it would not rub on anything. A dress maker would be proud of it. He wasn't in the best of health but helped us with odd jobs. I often called around to his place with a meal or cakes. One day I commented on a lovely, beautifully kept dining room table. He smiled as he tapped his index finger on the side of his nose, winked and said, 'A present from Mr Kidman.'

A contemporary of his, described him as ,'A lovely man, who never let the truth get in the way of a good story.'

Time had flown since I left Warwick and I had done my best to keep in contact with my parents and Bill's. Sadly, of the four only my da was still alive. My sister, her husband and children were well but I heard little from them. I think where I was and what I did was all too much for them.

Sarah and Thomas had moved to Brisbane and he had risen to a senior position in charge of the other seafarers and spent more time at home. I did not know if they ever married but Sarah's letters were full of excitement and love and I was sure it was all true. There was no mention of children. Nonnie had two boys she called Bill and Jimmy, not William and James. I was very emotional about that. Somehow, I understood. They were our loves and it was another thing that locked Nonnie and me together. Mrs Muller had passed away a few years ago after she had sold the hotel for almost the same amount as we had sold The Royal Hotel. Bill did well to copy the design. Biddy, Betty and Tom Jackson, as always were different and wrote me a lovely letter.

*Good morning Susana. our deer frend I do hope you are good. We got your letter about the mug Fecker you married and we was all sad and pleased for you in a way.*

*We have good news. The three of us had good jobs at the flash new hotel on Quay Street, The Criterion that opened in 1890. We looked after catering and cleaning and Tom became a real star entertaining in the dining room and the main hall. And if that was not enough we now have five children three boys and two girls. We love them all and sometimes forget who had who.*

*We have given up the hotel and have a lovely house with a big yard backing on to the place we built as a café. Sometime we serve the evening meal but mostly it is for lunches. Tom is really good at what he does (I seem to remember telling you that before!!!!!) and has developed some acts with the children, singing and dancing and some sketches. They have even done some acts at their school.*

*We are blessed.*

*Love Biddy, Betty, Tom and children*

*PS*

*I had to learn to write better and I am very pleased!*

What a wonderful story. I answered it and later found out that their café was very successful.

Last, but not least, Pat and Murray O'Brien had found their dream, a manageable vineyard south of Clare they had called *Fools Folly.*

# 39

# Federation and Beyond

Federation was a huge subject in the newspapers when we could get them. Many Queenslanders were indifferent to the concept of an Australian nation. A common saying was, 'I am a Queenslander not an Australian.' I am sure it will be a good thing to have one country instead of six colonies and one territory but the only thing that affected us was that borders would now be open to man and beast. There would be no more customs fees, registering stock, lining up and so on. We would now have politicians representing us in a central government and every one of the new electorates to elect the Commonwealth Parliament had Irish voters. That made me feel good because I had been told at home that anywhere I went in Australia I would be finding someone Irish. A better situation than in the USA where immigrants tended to stay in the same areas for generations and many became ghettoes.

Unfortunately, the political changes were forever remembered in the words Federation Drought. Birdsville had good rains in 1895-96 but from 1898 to 1902 there was a terrible drought. Waterholes became clay pans, the Diamantina and Cooper Creek were dry. Supplies were so short we ate weevily biscuits and lived on rabbits, kangaroos and saltbush if we could find any and that wasn't easy. Desperate for supplies, all ears strained to hear the tinkling bells of the Camel Strings. For a few years camels had been banned from the town except for loading and unloading and clear support given to the more expensive teamsters and their horses because they needed saddles and horse shoes. Not a good way to treat the cameleers who had kept us going for decades.

The drought was bad but in 1902 it became a true disaster throughout Australia. Inland areas were devastated and the safety net of feed for agistment on the coast was gone. Some papers said half the sheep in Australia had perished and unknown thousands of cattle met the same fate. And indeed millions of rabbits died but not before they dug up roots and ate them.

Sidney Kidman was reported to have lost 70,000 cattle but another big mob survived and was big enough to breed his way back into business. This proved his whole point I reckon.

The population of Birdsville was over 100 when I arrived. In the drought it dropped to about 80.

At the end of 1902 and in 1903 the rains came.

The children started asking me a lot about my childhood and parents, perhaps a reaction to the awful and frightening times they had witnessed. I promised them that I would write them a story of growing up life in Ireland, the journey to Australia and my life in this country. This became a monumental task, but it has been successful.

With the drought so bad and shortage of billiards players, travellers and indeed staff for pubs I thought it was right to go back to work and did so for 1902-3 and then had a nice break and worked again in 1905 and continued in 1906 with another extended break in 1907. My sewing, talking to the children about my book, my life, the business and the search for happiness and sanity were all progressing.

Without a doubt the most wonderful thing that happened to our family since Bill died was on Wednesday morning January

23rd, 1907. Fred, Alberta and I, in the loving presence of Hester, her late grandmother that I could sense, stood at the St Joseph Convent Kensington in Adelaide and witnessed May being professed as a St Joseph Nun. My life now made sense. My da was still alive and he sent a little bible with a message for her in his own hand. Monsignor Byrne presented it at the end of the service. We had a wonderful time in Adelaide at the zoo, Art Gallery and museum where we saw a fossil of a Diprotodon, a giant wombat the size of a hippopotamus found not all that far from Birdsville at Lake Callabonna, 75 miles south-west of Cameron's corner. I had made and sold some clothes for children with funny little Diprotodons embroidered on them so it was exciting to see the real thing. Last, but not least, we caught the amazing, comfortable electric Bay Tram to the beautiful beach at Glenelg with its wonderful jetty. I even bought the children a fishing line each and they caught enough Tommy Ruff fish for tea that we cooked over a drift wood fire. We also attended mass in the lovely Catholic Church at Glenelg.

We caught the tram back to Victoria Square and walked to the Terminus Hotel on North Terrace where I had stayed in 1886, 21 years ago. We wandered around Adelaide on the Friday and saw a race meeting advertised at Victoria Park on the Saturday. Next day we caught a tram and walked to this magnificent racecourse that had two sections, the grandstand and outer, with a green space in the middle of the track where many people were having picnics. We were wearing our best clothes and were invited into the Members' enclosure as we had come so far. It was a glorious day and a wonderful experience. The people were friendly and there were tea, cakes, alcohol if desired and glamour. Fred was a good judge of horses in the mounting yard and picked four horses for us to bet on. They all came first and we won 35 pounds.

On our way out to catch the tram we noticed a magnificent brand new stone building opposite the racecourse called 'The Queen's Home.' I told Alberta, with a champagne fuelled giggle, it was where Queen Victoria stayed when she came to Adelaide. A lady next to me said 'No, it is a maternity home and only five years old' I looked blankly and she added, 'A hospital where women go to have babies.' 'Why?' was on my lips but I kept quiet. I noticed Alberta looked at it intensely.

We caught the tram on the corner of Dequetteville Terrace and Alexander Avenue with a plantation of trees dividing it. The tram then passed a nice looking hotel and Alberta piped up, 'I am going to live here one day. A race course to ride my horse and make money, near the city shops, a corner pub a short walk away and a hospital to have babies.' We changed at our hotel and walked to the South Australian Hotel to treat ourselves and who should be there but Mr Dittmar and Mr Field and their wives. Probably the best food I had ever had in the best company without Bill. That night I started to heal.

*May Tucker became Sister Dolorosa*

# 40

# Light Returns

I was strangely settled and calm once we boarded the train home and took our seats. The hustle and bustle of the city passing by was exciting as always as were the fields of grain, sheep and cattle on the agricultural land we passed through. The trip was a cleansing experience. My children were growing up and becoming my friends and caring for me as much as the other way around.

Even before I left Ireland I helped Da with the hotel money and business. This had become a greater interest in recent years of necessity. As the train rattled along I saw a pattern. The assets I had were 20 years with a loving family, learning about love and finding that for 10 years with Seamus and Bill. Spending less than a year with another man was definitely a liability but he no longer exists. Expenses: yes, he was an expense in money, love, dreams and pain. Profits: money, love and dreams in amounts a thousand times more than the cost and no limit to how much more I can achieve. I came to realise that the months of pain were a minor hiccup in my life and in time I will get over it. And I did.

Seamus and Bill visited me, smiled and shook hands with each other. And that was another first day of the rest of my life and the children knew. I returned to work full of enthusiasm about life, love of my family and the future. Fred was doing well with his mail run and someone wanted to buy it and he was keen to sell, but being nobody's fool, he wanted to secure a job before selling.

Alberta was keen to learn the hotel business and I wanted to teach her. I also wanted to turn my notes into a book for my children and their children to read. My ancestry, Seamus, their father and our love must not be allowed to die.

Alberta had always been interested in counting our stores, keeping records and working with money so we worked out a system where she would be responsible for the books at the hotel.

She would do most of that work at home where she had peace and quiet. Things were going well and in 1908 she turned eighteen. We were very close. May had gone from our lives, apart from letters, and Fred was working out of Windorah about 100 miles the other side of Mount Leonard Station that the Sinclair and Scott men looked at a few years ago and stayed at Tattersalls. I did not have the licence at that time, but I was helping out and remembered them well. Somewhere around the traps I heard that they were likely to buy the place.

Alberta was a great help to me. She had lost her dad, her sister, Alice her best friend and rarely saw her brother with whom she was very close. Surprisingly perhaps, Alberta was a kind, patient and loving young woman. I desperately wanted her to have the happiness and love I had experienced from my grandparents and parents and her dad, short though it was. I think it was Clara who told me that a woman needed a man to be her father, lover, brother and friend. I pondered that for some time. When I thought about it I realised that Bill was exactly that to me. He really was, even in such a short time. That gave me a sad but wonderful feeling and I was able to tell Alberta. She was quiet and thoughtful, asked some very important questions and looked at me with a knowing look and said, 'Ma, I understand. That was you and Da. 'We held each other and cried for our loss. That day she went from a girl to a young woman.

About a year later Jack Scott wrote to Tattersalls where I had the licence and booked rooms for himself and Allan and Stanley Sinclair who planned to take up Mount Leonard in March 1909 and they duly did stay with us en route.. They were keen to meet people in the bar, talk to me, stock agents and anyone else who could give them information about the local area. I noticed that Jack remembered Alberta and said, 'G'day Alberta, nice to see you again' and doffed his hat. The men spent a few days talking to all and sundry and I noticed Jack looked worn out one afternoon and walked down to the river to have a spell, as did Alberta later, by chance or intentionally. They sat together looking at the river and talking for some time before coming in for tea. The men headed east in the morning.

The race meeting soon followed. It had become more popular since the end of the drought. Among the 200 people camped there were Jack and his work mates who could be spared from the station. It was a rite of passage for a new man, ringer, manager or owner to attend this event.

Alberta was busy at the hotel and only saw Jack for a short time after the races when the bets were settled at Tucker's pub. They were very friendly in the short time they spent with each other and I mentioned that to her when we were cleaning up. She told me that Jack would not be in on Sunday night as he as his blokes were heading off early Monday morning and added 'Jack would make a nice brother.'

Jack did not return to Birdsville again until just before the 1910 races and he came with two ringers and 200 cattle for sale. Jack was fortunate and sold his cattle, cash in hand, to Edgar May, a Kidman manager and good bloke. Jack and Alberta chatted away about the station and his dreams. They were so natural talking and communicating without words. It was lovely to watch. She was me with Seamus and Bill. Alberta was in a similar fix as Jack because the hotel was busy all the time particularly when the bets were settled after the races at Tucker's pub so they saw very little of each other. They spoke of course but that was all. Jack had to leave at sparrow's on the Monday and left a note for Alberta apologising that he saw so little of her. She read it and muttered, 'Doesn't matter. You are old enough to be my bloody father' and screwed up the note and tossed it in the fire. Alberta was not her cheerful and happy self and I knew why but when I asked if she was alright, she would snap, 'Yes I am.' It is so sad when your child is hurting and you cannot do a damn thing to make the pain go away.

Time moved on, Christmas came and went. I had agreed to run Tattersalls from 1906 to 1912 and it was now 1911. The reality was that the last two or three years had caught up with me and I was no longer able to work the long hours that were required. There was method in my madness in accepting the position for six years. Alberta could not hold a publican's licence until she was 21 in 1911. I held the licence and Alberta ran the place. It worked out well for us both. I could help when necessary but mostly I lived with my dreams and my nice new typewriter writing this, my story from the diaries, notebooks, journals, memories and pieces of paper I had accumulated over the decades. Central to everything was to help Alberta in the world she was to face. I had never forgotten my teacher Jane Moloney's words about women having to look after themselves and sadly she had foretold my future. I hoped Alberta would marry a good kind man and I did have a feeling that would be Jack Scott. But until that happened, I would teach Alberta all I could about running a business and building a nest egg for what the future might hold.

Everything rotated around the races in Birdsville and in 1912

Jack did appear a few days earlier than usual, without a mob of cattle and drovers. He stayed at the hotel. He and Alberta were like lovesick puppies and excused themselves to go for a walk along the river. I was not surprised that when they returned Jack spoke to me privately and asked for Alberta's hand in marriage. It was my happiest day in 22 years.

They will be married on March 2nd, 1913 at Currawilla station about 80 miles north east of Mount Leonard. This is the residence of the officiating registrar, William Henry Watson. Like with Bill and me, there were irreconcilable religious conflicts, so they also chose a civil ceremony.

My life will also change. Jack had a little sleep-out built for me attached to the homestead so I will move to Mount Leonard with my papers and typewriter and finish my story. I am proud of my origins, life, work and children. Bill and Seamus often come to see me, usually holding hands with their spare hands reaching out to me, I believe. I have run my race and will be at peace in the bosom of Alberta and Jack. I know one day, in the land that knows no parting, I will walk hand in hand again with the young men I had loved and lost. I let the light from that day shine over my shoulder many times in the years to come.

# BOOK 4

# A NEW CENTURY
# AND A NEW GENERATION

# 41

# A Different Perspective

While Susana, her children and friends were celebrating the coming of a new century, they were fearful that the drought would persist and that cast deep shadows on their celebration.

Seven hundred miles away other people were enjoying themselves and were confident that when the drought broke, a venture they had planned would succeed. They were the descendants of Angus and Morven Scott and their small boy James, aged five who had immigrated to South Australia and settled at Kersbrook, 22 miles from Adelaide in the late 1850s. Copper had been found at Kapunda and Burra in the 1840s but the rush had petered and the economy was flat. The Scotts were able to buy good land cheaply and Angus soon understood the different ways of farming in Australia and as soon as he could, bought a South Australian made Ridley Stripper for harvesting grain.

Their Scottish brethren Elder, Barr-Smith, Waite, Angus and others had founded dynasties of wool and sometimes cattle and new arrivals studied their words with Biblical reverence. As the years passed Angus Scott understood and practised four things. Drought will come and so will rain, do not be greedy and always be planning for the next drought. Despite some bad seasons, his cautious approach worked and the family prospered. In 1859-61 other copper deposits were found at Moonta and Wallaroo. The Moonta mine was huge and was the first company, in Australia, to pay a million pounds to its shareholders. Angus Scott bought their shares and with the dividends improved his land or bought more from those who rushed to work in the mines. The family's wheat harvests and wool clips increased in amount and quality. In 1870 James started formally working on the farm although like all boys on farms he had been working almost as long as he could walk. James learnt to wool class and he could always find work at the neighbours to earn some spending money. On the grain side they contributed to those harvests that were the biggest of the Australian Colonies and wool was also selling well.

James eventually took over from his father and in due course married Skye Sinclair the daughter of fellow farmers and friends they had met soon after they arrived in Australia. Undoubtedly the friendship was nurtured by the identical beliefs they had about farming principles and practices. Skye and James had a son, John James in1882. Farmers growing crops did well in the 1880s pastoralists did did not. Land degradation, confusing rules about leases, the cost of operating such large properties and a drought had devastated many pastoralists who lost up to ninety percent of their stock. In the long run it turned out to be the catalyst for better management of the land. Peter Waite trialled reduced stocking rates, dug damns, sunk wells, introduced fencing and spelled paddocks on Paratoo Station. With these measures and improved control of rabbits and dingoes, Waite accumulated 250,000 sheep after fifteen years in South Australia. Profitability returned to the pastoral sector.

The Sinclairs and Scotts had watched the cycles of the pastoral country where they knew many people. When they heard of Kidman's plans and the reasons to take up land in the Channel Country their ears certainly pricked up. They understood the importance of permanent waters and fall back positions for feed and water at other stations in this drought plagued land. The positive factor was when droughts broke the Channel Country had an incredible ability to fatten cattle. The railway reaching Hergott Springs, in 1884, would make it easier to send cattle to market. Sinclair and Scott knew about the risks and danger to man, animals and fortunes but they developed a keen interest in this part of Australia and it became a passion as intense as that of their fathers to move to Australia. Parallel to their normal lives the Sinclairs and Scotts were quietly reading, talking, asking and finding out all they could about the Channel Country and its properties, water, rivers, soil types, breeds of cattle, and sheep and anything else that came to mind. They were not to be rushed.

# 42

# The Next Generation

John Scott went to the Kersbrook School and then boarded at Prince Alfred College, a Methodist private school in Adelaide. He became friendly with boys from stations and visited their homes where he grew to like their horse work and the wide open spaces of the pastoral country.

After school he attended Roseworthy Agricultural College, the first institute of its kind in Australia. He enthusiastically passed on to his father the importance of using phosphate for crops, a discovery made there by Professor Custance. After Roseworthy he worked as a jackerooo in 1898, aged sixteen, at a small sheep station the family owned at Orroroo in the southern Flinders Ranges, 150 miles from Adelaide. Later he worked at Wilpena Pound station during the infamous Federation drought that lasted from 1896 to 1902. They were hard times on the land. Money was short and animals were dying. He learned to manage stock, what bushes and trees they could cut down for feed and sadly to kill calves and lambs and perhaps the most important lesson, when to sell stock.

After he moved to Wilpena Pound he and his parents met once or twice a year at Wilpena or Kersbrook via The Ghan and buggy rides to and from the Hawker and Gawler Railway Stations. Like all parents they were surprised how he had grown and matured. He was determined, purposeful and strong with a special way of looking at the horizon, the outback people called, 'The thousand yard stare.' On one of their trips his parents met his boss, August Helling, who showed them around and complimented them on their son. Later he mentioned Birdsville, The Track, the Channel Country and Cowarie. This was his property that he had to leave because of the drought. He knew more than most about that land and they talked and drank until midnight. They came away with a deep understanding and insight as to why, as Methodists, they were raised to not drink alcohol and had sworn off it. They did so again the next morning.

John was made Head Stockman at Wilpena Station in 1902, when 20, just before the Federation drought broke. The rains came in early summer so the grass was soon up to the sheep's bellies and wet their wool. This attracted flies and they became flyblown with maggots eating their very flesh. The men had to work from dawn to dark to clean this stinking mess with shears and fly oil. The sheep were weak and many died. They also lost cattle who were bogged and found too late with their eyes picked by the crows. Their son, now Jack, nevermore to be John, wrote that he was proud that they had kept enough stock alive to ensure the survival of the station. He added that he cried himself to sleep each night for a week when the crows and the maggots were at their worst. When his mother and father read that they had tears in their eyes. His mother nodded, 'He is tough and strong, but he is kind and cares. A real man. I am proud of him.' His dad nodded with her. They held hands for a long time.

# 43

# To The Channel Country

The improved country after the rains were the conditions Sinclair and Scott had been expecting for a decade. They talked many times to August Helling, visited Murray O'Brien in Clare at his *Fools Folly* vineyard, met with Dalgety's and many other people who knew the country. There was one station that suited them and that was Mount Leonard 100 miles east of Birdsville, in Queensland, near Haddon's Corner. It was settled in the 1870s and owned by a number of people since then including the legendary John Costello of Kimberley fame. At the time of their interest it had been owned by Theodore Foot and his sons for many years. Just before Theodore's death in 1893, more than a dozen runs were consolidated under one name, Mount Leonard. It then covered 777 square miles and in 1898 carried 200 horses and nearly 10,000 cattle second only to Sandringham with 365 horses and 15000 cattle in the Diamantina district and this was in a time that was considered to be the start of the Federation drought. Teeta was a permanent water hole adjacent to the main track between Birdsville and Windorah and the homestead. Another advantage was access due west to Birdsville, south west through Haddon to the Birdsville Track south of where the Diamantina crossed it and south east to Innamincka. A good situation in flood prone areas.

The die was cast. They had formed a company Sinclair, Scott

and Co. and inspected the property in 1904 and found it in excellent heart. The Foots had been good managers. They had sold about half their stock before the drought really took hold and various mobs since. The cattle were in reasonable condition as was the country. They expressed an interest in the property, but raising the finance and getting all the paper work done was difficult. The drought was the worst in Australia's history and, with other factors, had led to a Depression in the 1890s and early 1900s from which the country was only just recovering. Money was short and, if that was not enough, Federation had been the biggest change ever in Australian politics. Some business had to be done in South Australia, some in Queensland and some in the Commonwealth Government offices in Melbourne. And all of these departments had to know who did what.

It was a nightmare but finally after years everything was in place and then the worst possible thing happened. The Foots sold Mount Leonard to Frederick Bowman. They were devastated and contacted Dalgety's, because they believed they had a valid contract. It took a year or more of legal action, nail biting anxiety and poor sleeping. Dalgety's eventually told them Bowman had transferred his leases of Mount Leonard to them. They were invited to Dalgety's office and signed the transfers on December 16th, 1908. The signatories were, Allan Sinclair, his son Stanley Sinclair, John James Scott, who had managed Wilpena since 1904, and his Uncle Elliot Scott. They had taken on the property on a walk in walk out basis, meaning that everything was left as it was when the purchasers inspected the property. Livestock, equipment, harness, saddles, harness, carts, tools and household goods unless included as personal belongings of the sellers. When they were inspecting the property Allan Sinclair was very fussy about writing everything down in a notebook, number of bulls, saddles etc. On the way back to Birdsville Stanley and Jack asked him why he did that. His answer; 'I have bought a number of properties and it is amazing how a black stallion with a white blaze or a cart with one spoke missing has disappeared, or there were a few sheep less when I have taken possession. Since I started taking notes that has never happened.' Then he smiled and opened the notebook. There was nothing written down. The Scotts and Scots are canny.

In the middle of March 1909, when the Foots had everything organised and the weather was less hot, Allan and Stanley Sinclair and Jack Scott caught The Ghan to Hergott Springs, then the coach to Birdsville with their swags, some clothes and little else. Their other gear was long gone on camels and had arrived at Mount Leonard. They had to wait a few days at Birdsville and stayed at Tattersalls as they had done in 1904 and renewed their acquaintances with Susana and other people who they had met on their previous trip. They did their best to catch up with the local news, how cattle prices were, what rain had they had and the like. After the frenetic rushing and tearing about to get this far they enjoyed a few days of rest, particularly Jack. He had met Susana's daughter Alberta in 1904 when she was 14 and politely said 'G'day, Alberta' when he saw her in the pub and went about his business.

The next day he wandered down to the banks of the Diamantina and was lost in thought at this river, having never seen the Murray in South Australia. The Diamantina was not in flood but irresistible as it swirled and noisily rushed towards Lake Eyre. After a time, he knew that he was not alone. Alberta had wandered down to the river as well. They said little but were comfortable together and Jack, now 27, suddenly realised that Alberta was no longer a girl of fourteen, but a comely, sensible, young woman of nineteen. They parted company next day when Jack and the others headed into the dawn in the now regular weekly coach to Windorah. This would be the greatest test of their mettle in their lives. Jack and Alberta both hoped they would meet at the Birdsville races in the first weekend of September. Jack was never a chatty sort of person, but he was quieter than usual on the coach. He would be the manager of Mount Leonard, a far tougher job than Wilpena.  He was excited rather than afraid of that challenge.

*Teeta waterhole with publican from Beetoota Hotel rowing, his daughter, Jack Scott and Stan Sinclair (partners in Mount Leonard). The gabled homestead in the background was built in 1918 and Jack died in 1920.*

# 44

# Mount Leonard

Mount Leonard's stone homestead was comfortable with four rooms with a separate stone kitchen. There was also a men's room, store, buggy and harness shed and a set of branding and drafting yards. Since they had inspected the property an area near the homestead had been fenced into three horse paddocks and there was a new windmill on the well. The first thing any new manager or owner of a place does is to have look around. That means all over the property. Jack like Murray O'Brien knew the value of Aboriginal stockmen in their country. When Jack first visited he met two strangely named Aboriginal brothers, Hermann and Fritz. They were about his age and very pleasant and capable men. He had also met a ringer, Jackson Croswell, who had been on the place for years and Jack asked him to stay on as head stockman for a trial period. The four of them, with two pack horses for their supplies and swags, rode out at dawn on 1st April 1909.

They were away for six weeks. Available water is everything on a station. That is where they started. Teeta waterhole was next to the homestead so that took care of itself. Next was Pierikoola and Wyerie and Dippery holes in the north and finally to Kulpie on the southern boundary. Jack showed his surprise at how dry, rocky and sandy the country was but the cattle looked in fine fettle. Jackson mumbled 'They find a bit of a pick in the gullies, somehow.' Jack climbed every hill and looked in each gully and at every fence and gate and made notes of it all.

The races in Birdsville were soon upon them. There was nothing more important for Jack to do. Any new man to Birdsville, particularly a manager and owner, had to meet the tight group of local men and fit in. If he did not his life would be even tougher than it was already. He went to the races and camped with his men and the others at the course. He enjoyed himself, had a lot to eat and drink, laughed at jokes and told a few himself. He saw Alberta briefly at 'Tucker's Pub' after the races but she was too busy to do more than say g'day. Next morning, as he had intended, Jack went to Tattersalls for breakfast. Alberta and Susana were surprised to see him and Alberta asked her mother if she could join Jack for breakfast. Jack was about to ask Susana to join them when he caught a glint in Alberta's eye so he swallowed that idea. Susana welcomed Jack and served them both their breakfast on the verandah, in the early morning light. They had a good yarn but it was all too short. She had to go to work and in a sense so did he at the races. He explained that he would be leaving next morning at sparrow's, before she would be out of bed. As he rose from the table and put on his hat, he gave her a little two fingered salute and said, 'Good bye. See you soon.'

After the races there was the long trip home and Jack thought about his work and life. He and the stockmen spent much of their lives out on the run. Cattle work seemed endless and the distances likewise. Mustering, drafting and branding were done yearly with each mob. If there were big mobs of cattle they would use the homestead yards. If it was counting and branding calves from small mobs, remote places with bronco panels were used. Even when there were no specific tasks the ringers rode around the cattle, hence the name, just being with them. Jack allowed no rough and ready 'cowboy' stunts with cattle. With enough patience, treating the cattle gently and just being with them they would be far easier to handle than a mob that no one had seen for a year or two. The cattle looked better, were worth more, did not knock themselves or each other around so much and were less dangerous. A win-win situation. When hungry the men would kill a steer, half skin it and leave the other half on to keep it clean and take the good cuts for grilling, roasting, stewing or salting. Sometimes they had onions, potatoes and dried beans, sometimes not, but they always had flour to make damper and tea. It was a tough life but those who lived it wouldn't have it any other way.

Jackson Croswell was doing well as head stockman and after about nine months, in mid-1910, Jack told him he had done enough and would he like to make it permanent and he accepted. Jack needed the advice of a head stockman on day to day matters and also in planning for the future. Croswell was a thinker and Jack encouraged him. He had a brilliant idea about Miranda station in South Australia about half way to Birdsville. He told Jack that it was not managed well and explained, 'They run sheep. No one else does now because of the wild dogs. Many horses went to the Boer War or to other armies, so now there is a shortage of horses. Jack, Miranda ran 'em before they can do it again.' He added that if they were thinking of getting a lease they would need another stockman or two because managing a property 50 miles away would not be possible. Jack asked him if he knew anyone who would fit the bill. He said, 'Yes I do. A young fellow Fred someone has the mail run and knows horses. He gets more out of them gently than most people being hard. He is twenty one or two and has won the two Birdsville Cups he has been in. Not only can he ride he understands how to look after horses.' Jack was keen. 'Ask him if he is interested but I will need to check with my partners in Adelaide and that will take a while.' I like the idea.

Jackson Croswell spoke to the mail man and asked him to call in next time he dropped the mail at the Beetoota Hotel. He had the 'Thousand yard stare' like Jack and was tall, slim, fair and handsome. Jackson introduced him to Jack as 'Fred the mailman.' Jack asked him his second name and was told, 'Tucker, Alberta's brother.' Fred, with a lovely, gentle smile said, 'I wondered when you would realise. My mother and sister think a lot of you.' Jack shook hands and told him they needed an extra ringer as one had left but there may be a job later as manager of a property they had their eye on to run a few cattle but mainly horses. Fred was interested, as he had always wanted to be a ringer, but needed to sell his mail business and, after all, they were not sure about the new venture. They had a laugh and agreed to keep in touch. By the time Jack and Jackson had nutted out a formal plan and sent it to Adelaide it was time for the 1910 Birdsville Cup. It was a golden opportunity to kill two birds with one stone. They rounded up a mob of cattle on the Teeta waterhole and drafted off 200 steers to sell and help the cash flow.

Jack had contacted an agent in Birdsville who Murray O'Brien had recommended and two weeks later got a reply that there were experienced drovers available to take the cattle to Hergott and he had the organisation to see them safely to Adelaide. Jack had decided to drive the cattle himself to Birdsville with Herman and Jackson as he wanted to familiarise himself with the landscape, feed and watering places and how the calves, in the mob, now about 10 months old, travelled. And he just might see Alberta.

The trip was uneventful and took eleven days to cover the 100 miles as they were not in a hurry. When they reached Birdsville, they yarded the cattle, made sure they had a drink and headed to the Tattersall's Hotel for a wash, beer and a feed. He had written to Alberta and she was helping behind the bar and served him and his mates their dinner. When they had finished their meal a man they had seen at the yards with another mob of cattle introduced himself as Edgar May and told them he was manager of one of Kidman's stations. He asked Jack if he was interested in selling the mob he had brought in. May explained that they had plenty of feed at the station now.

He offered Jack a pound a head. Jack had that amount in mind in Adelaide. Expenses were about five shillings a head and cattle being knocked around was also a cost. He had heard that Kidman men were smart and hard but the price sounded good to him so he accepted the offer with a handshake and was paid there and then. The next morning he handed the cattle over to Edgar May.

He then went back to the hotel for a late breakfast that he shared with Alberta and again he enjoyed being with her, sharing his dreams about the station and hearing about her mother, brother and sister and people who had passed through town. He went to the races and made new friends and rekindled those from the previous year and even backed a few winners. He hoped to have breakfast with Alberta but had to break camp too early so he wrote her a note apologising and put it under the hotel door.

# 45

# Moving Along

By the spring of 1911 the deals had been done. Fred's mail business was sold and the lease taken up on Miranda station with Fred as manager. Jack had not heard from Alberta since he had left the apology note in the previous September except an informal exchange of Christmas cards now eight months ago. He had been extremely busy understanding how the station worked. How the climate, seasons, feed patterns, stocking rates, waters, economic situation relate to each other and now Miranda was in the mix. It took many years, not a few months, to understand. He sat down after dinner on the 19th of August and wrote what he knew to be the most important letter of his life.

*Dear Alberta*

*I am sorry that things did not turn out so well for us on the cup weekend.*

*It is a new world I have moved into and people need to get to know and trust me. If not, my job will be very hard to do. Part of this is mixing with men at functions like the races. Station life is lonely and opportunities for socialising with other station or townspeople rare. That may be only once or twice a year selling cattle, the races, a wedding or a funeral.*

*You have learned how to run a pub and a big part of that is getting on with your customers and staff and you do it well. I am sure you have had to make personal sacrifices to do that. Look what your mother and father had to go through to get where you are.*

*I enjoy a drink and some fun and games with men at the races or similar places but I am not a drunk or a womaniser. I shall go to the next races and if you wish will find a way for us to spend more time together.*

*Your brother enjoys his job with us and I look forward to working with him on the new venture we are starting.*

*Please give my regards to your dear ma.*

*I really like and admire you Alberta.*

*John J. Scott*

Jack struggled with the letter and it took two hours to write. He should not have worried. Two weeks later he received a letter from Alberta.

*Dear Jack*

*Thank you for your lovely letter. I was thoughtless and selfish.*

*I look forward to seeing you on the races weekend and perhaps longer.*

*Love Alberta.*

It smelled nice and went under his pillow. Every night he opened it, read the word 'love,' smelled it and put back under the pillow and slept well. He managed to again organise cattle to take to Birdsville for Hergott. Fred being the new man had to stay home. He understood the rules.

Jack camped with his men again and met the regulars and some new folks at the races and was more relaxed than he had been. These men had taken the measure of him and he could tell he had passed and that made him feel good about himself. Once again, he could not spend as much time with Alberta as he would have liked but there was something different. The looks, smiles and touches between them had all changed and it was a wonderful feeling. As always, the station called but Susana, Alberta and Jack shared a very pleasant farewell breakfast. Susana cleared the table and excused herself. Jack stood up ready to leave as did Alberta and shyly gave him a parcel that held a large, about eighteen inches square, chambray neckerchief with Mount Leonard embroidered on one corner in black. 'I noticed when you were here before your old one was much worn. So I made this with my mother's super Singer sewing machine for you to match your work shirts. I hope you like it. Stand up please and I will tie it around your neck.' As she did, she gave him a chaste kiss on his cheek and added, 'It looks nice.' Jack had never received a nice gift from a female other than relatives and was stuck for words but managed to get out a very sincere, 'Thank you Alberta that is very special. I will wear it every day.' And he did. All the way back to the station he thought of her nice gesture and kiss. He finally admitted to himself he loved her and did not want to bear the loneliness of station life any longer. He wanted her to share his life.

# 46

# Jack and Fred – 1912

Jack and Fred had decided to breed Waler horses at Miranda origionally bred in New South Wales in the early years of the colony from Arabs, Cape horses from South Africa, Timor ponies and a touch of Clydesdales or Percheron draught horses. Jackson knew the breed well and had ridden a few as had Jack. They were the most outstanding cavalry breed in the world and had been ridden by stockmen, explorers, bushrangers, drovers, police, mounted infantry and cavalry. Thousands had been sent to India as British Army remounts since the 1830s and they were used in the Boer War. They were 15-16 hands and when used by the army had to carry 224-288 pounds of rider and equipment. It had not registered with Jack that their fast walk and moving into a canter without trotting was an advantage for cavalry horses. With the load they carried a trot could hurt their backs, the rider and damage or lose some of the equipment they carried.

Jackson, Fred and Joe Thompson, an Aboriginal stockman and mate of Jack's, scoured southern Queensland and north western New South Wales for these animals and managed to buy 250. They were in one mob at Thargominda and had been handled so were easy on the track. Jack and Jackson headed straight back to Mount Leonard 400 miles away. Fred and Joe brought the mob behind them. They yarded them at Mount Leonard and looked over them again very thoroughly. They were all supposed to be in foal. And it seemed that way to Jackson and Fred. None of them were branded so that had to be done. A hectic and unpleasant job. After a few days of rest, food and drink for man and beast, Fred and Joe took them the next 100 miles to Miranda.

It was a very busy time once again. They had bought cattle as well as the horses for Mount Leonard and Miranda, so this all needed to be organised. Branding, castrating calves, repairing what fences they had and building more, checking the waters and so on. They usually ran shorthorn cattle but decided to try Herefords at Miranda with the horses. All this took time and manpower. They had some ringers leave but replaced them and employed another man to fence, check the waters and make any major repairs as necessary at the two places.

On the rare night Jack had the luxury of his bed he would look at and smell Alberta's letter and usually and understandably fell fast asleep. One night he could not sleep. He desperately wanted to be with Alberta. He was lonely and rapidly nearing thirty. He dreamed of having a family but all he seemed to do was work. He did not object to the sleeping in a swag watching or managing cattle. Those things had to be done.

He did remember, when a young man, how nice it was when he and his dad came in from the paddocks in winter. There was a fire, hot water for a wash, a meal and his mum for a yarn. He said to himself, 'You soft bastard. Stop it.' But then replied to himself. 'No I want to marry Alberta and I will.' He wondered whether the lack of physical intimacy was a hurdle to jump. She certainly liked being with him and the few physical things they had done were nice. His mind went round and round until he went off to sleep exhausted. Next evening he wrote to Alberta and asked her if he could meet her on the Thursday of the races, before the mob arrived, as he had something important to ask her. He also asked if her mother would be around the place. He received a reply in about ten days. It read. 'Dear Jack, Yes, we can meet. Yes, Ma will be about and Jack --------Yes! Love A. Jessamine. He puzzled over the letter. Was she saying yes? Why Jessamine?

She seemed to be happy to see him so that was good. There was no point in worrying. He would go as planned. One night in his swag, head pillowed on a saddle bag, he was dozing off under a blanket of stars and woke up like a shot. He had asked Alberta about her second name and she told him that it was the scent in the air when her da proposed to her ma. She had also told him she thought the proposal was the other way around! Jack felt a gush of pleasure, heat, love and excitement course through every fibre of his body. He knew she meant YES.

In due course he went to Birdsville, sneaked into his room, cleaned up, put on his best clothes, found Alberta and they went for a walk, once again, to the river bank. They found a sheltered spot and sat on a fallen tree. He took her in his arms and proposed marriage in his way. She answered yes in hers. After an hour or so of pure bliss being together they walked back to the hotel. Jack found Susana in her office and asked for Alberta's hand. Susana was so excited. She kissed Jack on the cheek, held both his hands and said, 'You will be the father, brother, friend and lover she needs. This is the happiest day I have had for 22 years. Thank you Jack and God bless you both.' That year the races were really wonderful. She was on Jack's arm all the time and wore a new dress that her mother finished the week before and was radiant, lovely and everything else a girl in love is. Jack remembered a line from a poem at school about springtime being when a young man's thoughts likely turn to love. He said that to a mate who replied, 'Jesus Jack you look like the cat that swallowed the bloody cream. Never mind that bloody poetry bullshit. You are a lucky man.'

After the races there were toasts galore. Alberta was loved in Birdsville and Jack had earned the respect of those who knew him. When the party ended Jack went to his room and Alberta to hers but on the way she woke her mother and sat on her bed and asked, 'I have seen the evening and morning star tonight and they were beautiful. It was as though they spoke to me about something important. It was such a strange feeling but nice in a way I do not undertstand!'

She added, 'Thank you for somehow teaching me, or allowing me to learn who the right man for me would be. I know he will be my father, brother, friend and lover. I am so, so happy.' Her mother held her close. They both watched the morning star until they fell asleep in each other's arms. The last thing in Susana's mind as she went to sleep was, 'I have never told her about the morning and evening stars.' In the morning she asked Alberta that question. Alberta answered 'You mentioned Venus once or twice and pointed out how different it was to Mars. Why?' Susana gave her a hug, kissed her cheek and got up to face the day.

# 47

# Another Wedding

The glow from their engagement lasted a long time for Alberta and Jack but the reality of life got in the way. There was the festive season for the hotel and then the matter of their wedding on March 2nd, 1913. Immediately after the races Susana ordered material through Nonnie at Ballarat. Although she had lost touch with Sarah she wrote and Sarah answered promptly. She was delighted at the news and offered to make Alberta some under things like she made Susana before her wedding. Susana shivered at that but she wished her daughter a happy marriage in all respects and Sarah's suggestion was certainly a good start. She already had Alberta's measurements as she was making her wedding gown from silk Nonnie had given Alberta. When Alberta tried on her wedding gown she was overcome. It showed off her tiny waist, a matter of great pride to her. She promised her mother to keep her gown forever she loved it so much.

The couple were fortunate that the wedding would be at Currawilla because it was one of the few places with sheep and that meant a functioning shearing shed they could use for the service and formalities. There were shearers' quarters with a kitchen separate from the main house. Thirty people were expected and like the races and Susana's wedding the celebration was not for one day.

This was when neighbours needed neighbours. William Watson the owner and officiating resident helped. His stockmen killed and hung a beast in the fly proof meat house and broke it up before the wedding. Several sheep were also killed. The costs would all be sorted out later maybe at a sale. Jack would provide beer, rum, whisky and wine Susana bought from the same place as Mr Muller did all those years ago. Susana and Alberta caught the coach to Mount Leonard and conveniently arrived the Tuesday before the wedding. They unpacked their luggage in the spare bedroom, had a wash from the bowl Jack had put there, combed their hair and went into the sitting room. Their chins dropped, mouths opened and their eyes popped. Sitting in front of them were Alice and Clara Haylcok. Tears, laughter, sobbing, more laughter from the four of them and even Jack had to blow his nose every now and then.

They all settled down with a nice cup of tea. Alice was now a nurse and had become interested in the Australian Inland Mission established a year before by the Reverend John Flynn to make life particularly childbirth safer in outback Australia. Alice was friendly with an Alfred Traeger, an 18 year old neighbour, whose father was part of Flynn's organisation. Alfred was planning to work with the telegraph and had heard about a radio transmission by Professor Bragg in 1905 in Adelaide. He told Alice this exciting discovery would play a big part in such a sparsely populated and vast land. Alice was most interested because she had just finished nursing studies and planned on working in the bush like her mum and that meant delivering babies. Traeger Senior knew of Clara's and Alice's vast experience of the outback and Alfred asked if they would visit Lyndhurst and Innamincka, the patch Flynn had allocated to his father and have a look around. Clara and Alice had been invited to the wedding and were at Innamincka at the time and fluked a ride with a stock agent through Haddon to Mount Leonard and had only been there a few hours.

The day's surprises were not yet over. After they finished their tea and fresh damper, Fred Tucker came in, said a happy hello with hugs and kisses to everyone and rushed out. Alberta saw him wink at Jack on the way. Jack said, 'Ladies, please line up behind Alberta, hold hands, shut your eyes and follow my lead' as he took Alberta's hand. He led them onto the verandah and halted, still holding Alberta's hand and said, 'Alberta, the very first day we met I felt I had known you forever, a lovely feeling.' He added 'Open your eyes.' Fred pulled at a large tarpaulin that slowly revealed a big square thing that flummoxed everyone until Alice yelled, 'It's a T model Ford' and ran around patting it like a horse.

That broke the ice and everyone was yelling and carrying on. Jackson Croswell handed around bottles of beer from the car to everyone. As Alberta took hers he directed her to 'Launch her like a ship.' She took him literally and chucked the full bottle of beer at the car. Fortunately, Fred was between her and the car and took his best catch ever in all the years he had played cricket. He gave her the bottle and implored her to pour the beer on the car, not hit it with the bloody bottle. And she did, just like a queen. When things had settled down a man in a grey dust coat introduced himself to Alberta. He was a mechanic from Charleville and had delivered the car and given Jack and Fred driving lessons over the last two weeks. He would return after the wedding at a convenient time to teach her to drive. Fred left for Currawilla in the two horse buggy soon after, packed to the gunwales with food, drink, clothes and swags and would camp on the way there. At dawn on the Thursday before the wedding Alberta, Jack, Clara and Alice mounted the new chariot with minimal clothing, food and water but a mass of spare parts, tools and a large instruction book on how to fix things in the Ford. They travelled the 100 miles to Currawilla by mid-afternoon.

Not only was Alberta's and Jack's personal life to change forever the T–model Ford would forever change travel in the outback and everywhere else. They all managed to find a place for their swags, unpacked and settled down with cups of tea. Jack wasted no time in taking Alberta to meet the Watsons. They had some formalities to deal with and when that was done Mrs Watson showed Alberta the bedroom where she and Jack would sleep. It was a beautiful room with a place to wash, a standing full-length cheval mirror, lounge chairs, a small table with two chairs and double doors and windows opening onto the verandah on the southern side of the house. Last, but not least, was a double bed covered by a quilt embroidered with roses with four large feather pillows. Mrs Watson gestured with an open hand, 'Your marriage bed Alberta, and may it be as nice as when it was mine.' Alberta was nervous as she and Jack had had little physical contact but what they did have was certainly nice. Her mother had told her more than once how wonderful her wedding night was and now this lovely lady was saying the same. Alberta began to feel a strange but nice excitement.

After seeing the bedroom Mr and Mrs Watson took Alberta, Jack and Susana to the shearing shed. They gasped with amazement. There were set tables with chairs with one table for the bridal party set aside from the others. The floor had been scrubbed and shearing gear put away and even a canvas screen put around one of the pens defining the ladies' lavatory. The mens' was outside somewhere. The next two days passed quickly with the car a centre of attraction for all and sundry. There were about thirty people there. A crow flying over would think it was chaos but by Saturday at three o'clock everyone was in their best clothes. The food and drink were organised and the blokes had done their bit by keeping out of the way and talking about everything other than the wedding. Even though it was only a hundred yards from the woolshed they took the highly polished and dust free Ford T from its hiding place with its V of white ribbons from the radiator to the windscreen pillars. Jack and Fred walked to the shearing shed and waited. The man who had delivered the car from Charleville, Doug Watkins, drove Alberta, Susana and Alice, the bridesmaid, to the front of the shearing shed.

Jack and Fred were waiting in 2w23front of Mr Watson and turned as they heard an in-drawing of breath from the crowd as Alberta, on Susana's arm, entered the shed. Her silk dress was beautiful by any standards. It had a high neck collar with a bodice that emphasised her tiny waist and a white layered skirt. The whole outfit was embroidered with silk threads. She was a princess. 'Here comes the bride' was played on what had been a covered piano no one had noticed. A fiddler followed and someone in the crowd played a harmonica. It was spectacular and applauded by everyone.

Fred was best man, Alice the bridesmaid and Susana out shone them all. She was so proud. Despite everything she was happily giving her lovely daughter away to a kind and decent man of courage and substance. Her son was part of it all as well. She thought she would burst with pride as she left Alberta next to Jack and sat down aglow.

The ceremony and formalities proceeded as expected with speeches and toasts from Mr and Mrs Watson, Fred, Jack and Susana. After that it was on for young and old. Eating, drinking, dancing, singing and just simply having fun because for most of these people this was a rare occasion.

The night wore on and Jack and Alberta slipped out to the shearers' quarters with Alice and Fred to help them into their going away outfits as protocol demanded. Jack was easy, he took off his suit and dress shirt and put on a chambray shirt and sparkling white moleskins and his washed and ironed neckerchief Alberta had made. Then they waited and waited. Fortunately, Fred had the foresight to have flask of OP rum in his suit pocket in case of snake bite so that was put to good use.

Alberta's dress did take time to remove and to be folded up into a neat bundle, wrapped and put in the bag with her going away clothes. She also wanted to have a wash, put on some perfume and Sarah's gift. Alice was busy getting clothes out of Alberta's bag and putting the wedding dress back in and had not noticed Sarah's present. It was not only the daring garments, but the confident way Alberta wore them. She was in every sense a beautiful, seductive, confident woman. If she was nervous it did not show. When everything was how she wanted it, Alice helped her put on her mushroom pink suit and cloche and both joined the waiting men and the party. Alice could see how Jack adored her. She couldn't help herself think, with a little shiver, 'Jack, you would never have dreamed of what is in store for m'lad; not in a million years.' Alberta joined Jack and they held hands as the crowd made a circle around them and sung 'For they are jolly good fellows,' gave three cheers and moved in and out around the happy couple. The crowd then formed two lines leading to the door. Women threw confetti and the men did their bit making a tunnel touching stock whip handles or rifles with their mates opposite. The song 'Auld Lang Syne' was unforgettable.

They walked out the door. Fred was standing to attention by the car, swept his hat off and gave his hand to Alberta to help her step on the wooden box he had put in place to help her into the car and Jack followed. Fred shut her door, put on his hat, sat in the driver's seat and drove the car ain a slow circle with Jack and Alberta waving and departed into the darkness. He escorted them to the homestead where their life together would start. After he put the car away he walked back to kick on in the shearing shed and chuckled to himself, 'In a week there will not be a single person between Birdsville and Windorah that hasn't heard about this shindig, not a darn one'. He actually said 'Not a darn one' out loud as he looked at the sky and noticed that the evening star, or perhaps it was the morning star, looked unusually bright.

*Alberta Jessamine Tucker*
*Born: 14 August 1894, Birdsville, SA*
*Died: 20 March 1956, Glen Osmond, SA*
*Married Jack Scott: 2 March 1915, Windorah, Qld*

*John James (Jack) Scott*
*Born: 24 March 1882, Kersbrook, SA*
*Died: 26 December 1920 – Diamantina River, Qld*

# 48

# A New Day Dawning

By Monday afternoon the place had been cleaned and the guests had departed. Jack, Alberta. Susana, Clara and Alice spent a pleasant evening with the Watsons and left early the next morning for Mount Leonard after checking the car and filling it with petrol that Fred had brought in the buggy. They stopped at a shady spot for a lunch of salt beef, damper, wedding cake and tea. They soon were on their way again and reached Mount Leonard late in the afternoon. They all went to bed early. Susana and Alberta were alone at one point and Susana couldn't resist telling her, 'It is the first day of the rest of your life my dear daughter.' Alberta hugged her and replied with a smile brighter than the sun, 'If those days and nights to come are half as nice as the last three I will have a glorious life.' Susana shed tears of joy.

The days, weeks and months to follow were difficult sometimes because Alberta had no real idea of how a station worked. There was Old Polly, a lovely Aboriginal lady, who was the cook and looked after the kitchen and cleaned in the house. She knew what to do and when to do it. Life in the hotel had been busy and tough at times but was relatively ordered. They had to think ahead for supplies but if they had forgotten something there were two or three stores in Birdsville and the other pubs who helped each other out. On a station everything had to be ordered six months ahead, never forgetting the high probability of floods.

Alberta had common sense and experience from the hotel and had to keep financial records and manage the budget that Jack and the other partners had worked out the previous year. It was a company and more complicated than the hotels were, apart from the early days when her ma and da owned The Royal. Since then, they were only licensees and had kept simpler records. She was fortunate in having her mother there and benefited from her foresight and the experience in the hotels. She had the ideal preparation for station life.

She had always liked and been good at ordering and checking things and it was not long before she had increased the variety of food. Most of the goods still came from Adelaide via Birdsville but the mail came from Windorah so they could get supplies, by coach, from there as well. When the men were out with the cattle, and that was much of the time, they ate fresh and salt beef and damper with some spuds and onions.

She knew that was not a healthy diet so did her best to provide variations in the meals they ate at home. She had accumulated the usual salt, sugar and flour but added bicarbonate of soda and tartaric acid to make damper, ordered sago, rice and barley and dried legumes, dried fruit, nuts and dried cake mix. There was jam, molasses, honey and treacle, pepper and curry powder. For flavourings she used caraway, sesame and poppy seed, nutmeg, cinnamon, cloves, cardamom, mace, allspice and mixed herbs.

They had kerosene lamps and candles and the new safety matches made by Redheads. Like the hotel, or perhaps even more so, she had to deal with injuries and illnesses in black or white people of all ages. She had built up supplies of such things as aspirin, laudanum, quinine, Senna leaves, methylated spirits, needles and thread for sewing cuts, rum of course, poultices, bandages, powders of various sorts, zinc cream and Vaseline. Passing tinkers kept her cooking gear in tip-top condition and often her medical supplies. It was amazing what they kept in their carts.

She was enjoying the challenge and loved Jack to distraction. She was so happy. She had harboured doubt deep down because Dennett was nice initially but as the weeks and months passed, she relaxed and often hugged herself with joy. After a few months she realised one day that she was with child. Jack and Susana were thrilled to bits at the news. Unfortunately there were no midwives available and the next few months would be insanely busy and Jack could be far away, even on Mount Leonard, let alone Miranda. There was nothing more to be said in Jack's opinion, first babies were dangerous and Alberta needed to be in a safe place before, during and after child birth and that would be with his parents who had retired and lived in the Kent Town area of Adelaide.

Alberta wrote to Clara who suggested that she leave home about three months before her baby was due. Alberta was delighted about the pregnancy and felt strong and well. She understood the risks and she would graciously do what her mother, husband and expert friend suggested.

Alberta and her mother made clothes for her and the baby who would need a shawl, nappies, cot sheets, bonnets, nightgowns and she would need personal things and clothes as well.

Somehow everything came together and was packed in the Ford with their swags, tucker and other camping gear ask Jack would take her to Hergott. As they were about to leave Old Polly's daughter, Young Polly came to her, averting her eyes, with a coolamon in her hands and passed it to Alberta, smiled and said, 'For baby' and ran away before Alberta could thank her. It was a bowl about the length of her forearm with fingers extended but wider. Very similar to a cupped hand only bigger with a curve like a banana. A coolamon has many uses but this was definitely for holding a baby. It was made from reeds held together by plaited grass and resin. Old Polly was still there and Alberta gave her a big hug and asked her to pass on the hug to Young Polly.

And then they were off to another date with destiny.

*The dependence on Aboriginal ringers at Mt Leonard*
*and other stations is made obvious in this photograph.*

# 49

# One and One Makes Three

Jack and Alberta decided to take a week to get to Hergott over 400 miles away. They stopped in Birdsville and it was strange for Alberta to be a paying customer in the hotel where she grew up. There was a reason. She had contacted Jack and Eadie and asked if they could meet. The Shire council had built a cottage on the Tattersall land, where they had lived for years with the hotel paying the rent. Alberta's ma and pa had been paying an assurance policy since they had employed Jack and Eadie and it had matured about two months before. Susana had approached the Shire and after much argy-bargy bought the house in the names of Jack and Eadie.

There was sleight of hand somewhere as Aboriginals could not hold land but Susana had done it. Jack and Eadie had little understanding of ownership but understood that they could live in this nice place forever. They were quiet and soon went to bed. Next morning they realised what had happened and had smiles a mile wide. Alberta and Jack both hugged and thanked them for all they had done for Bill, Susana and the children. They had no children or relatives so when they died the house would go to Fred.

That night Jack and Alberta camped at Goyder's Lagoon. Although it was cold at night the days were warm and they had their first swim together. They had never been away on their own before so this was their honeymoon and they made the most of it. All good things end and this was no exception. Hergott and the train soon appeared and Alberta had gone. It was a long journey and Alberta was calm and relaxed with the thought of the little one inside her and the memory of the wonderful last few days. The train journey was not as bad as she thought and soon she was in Adelaide.

Alberta had seen a picture of Jack's mother and father so she recognised them at the station. They were met by their groom and carriage and after about half an hour were at their property, *Penindi,* a beautiful home. She was shown her room and unpacked, had a lovely bath, brushed her shiny hair made shinier by the baby, dressed and went downstairs to the parlour for an informal evening meal. Things were a little stilted as they hadn't met before but Mr Scott was friendly enough and they had some soup, tea and toast and an early night.

Next morning a Doctor Scott, no relation, visited with a midwife to meet her. They fiddled and poked around with her and that was not pleasant. Then they sat down with Mrs Scott and had a cup of tea and scones. The doctor and midwife were pleased with her and said they anticipated no trouble, but the midwife would call to see her and check her blood pressure that doctors now thought was involved with the nasty and dangerous toxaemia of pregnancy. They told her to exercise, drink lots of water and milk and try not to put on too much weight. They planned for her to have the baby in the house as she expected. She wrote to Jack, her ma, Clara and Alice and met the latter two several times.

Mrs Scott was polite but a quiet lady and her friends she met were the same. They were not jolly like her family. Alberta did enjoy where the Scotts lived and had fond memories of the

Victoria Park Racecourse and the Queen's Home where she had imagined having babies and perhaps she still might. She walked past Prince Alfred College and once looked through the iron fence and swore Jack was one of the boys running around chasing a football. She could not help a few tears.

One Sunday Mrs Scott suggested, well insisted, Alberta join them for the Sunday service at Kent Town Methodist Church. Jack had warned her about this and they decided that she should be grateful and join them. She held her rosary beads firmly and actually enjoyed the service in the massive church, bigger than any she had attended. Far from being sad and moving she thought the hymns were uplifting. Her heavy heart lifted.

The time of the birth soon came and, as expected of a fit strong young woman, Alberta had a normal delivery of a boy and with him in her arms soon forgot the physical discomfort. Like all parents they had discussed the name for a boy or girl. John Leonard it was. Soon mother and baby were getting on well. John did have a lump in his belly button that Mrs Scott put a penny and tape over and tickled him. Motherhood never goes away.

Jack was very good at writing letters and although devilishly busy, kept her up to date with goings on at the station. In one letter he wrote lovingly about the joy of their trip alone to Hergott and how much comfort it was to him on the long trip home. He added that since she went to Adelaide the company had been interested in buying Dulkaninna Station about 50 miles north of Birdsville. It seemed to him that they had learned from Sidney Kidman and had bought Miranda about a week's droving time from Mount Leonard and looking at Dulkaninna a week further and then another week to get cattle to Hergott. He had called in on the way home and spent a few days looking around and thought it was a good idea and passed that onto the company. They bought it a few weeks later. The doctor visited her about six weeks after John was born and pronounced mother and baby fit enough to go home. After suitable gifts of chocolates, flowers and a thank you note to the Scotts they went home.

*Quiet cattle and relaxed drovers.*
*Mount Leonard circa 1914-15.*

# 50

# One Life Ends and Another Begins – 1915

Alberta was pleased to be home with her little bundle. Jack met her at Hergott and they had a slow trip home getting used to being a family. Jack said 'I am John and they call me Jack. Let's call the little bloke Leonard, be good for business!' So it was for a very short time until Leonard inevitably became Len. They stopped at Birdsville and were greeted royally with their baby, particularly by Jack and Eadie who looked ten years younger. They had a secure place to live with a nice vegetable garden. 'No more pay money to Chinaman' said Jack with a broad beaming smile. They stopped at Miranda where Fred could not help chortling at and tickling the baby. The men talked business while Alberta fed Len and all slept well.

Next stop Mount Leonard where Alberta soon got back into the swing of things and it was wonderful to have her ma to help and care for Len but it was obvious over the coming weeks that Susana was deteriorating mentally and physically. One day Alberta reread a letter she had written to them when she had moved to the station and was perfectly lucid. 'Thank you for taking me into your home and your hearts. I hope for three things. To be a help not a nuisance. To see and hold a grandchild. The third is that when my time comes, I would like to be with the Saint Joseph nuns in Jamestown. I have arranged that and they will welcome me. I am sure May's spirit will be there if she cannot.' At the time Jack and

Alberta both had tears in their eyes and held Susana's hands. Jack had softly answered. 'We love you being here and proud to give you a grandchild and will take you to Jamestown when the time comes.'

The Dulkaninna purchase went through and Jack and Fred had to employ a manager and stockmen. There were cattle and sheep, as well as horses on this 2000 square mile property so there was a lot happening. World War 1 had started and was of concern to everyone in Australia. The stations provided the troops with meat, leather, tallow and wool. Most people thought that Britain would give these jumped up bloody Huns a bloody good thrashing but that was not happening. There was a 'head in the sand' mentality. The news from Europe was horrifying with tens of thousands of troops killed on both sides, sometimes in one day. Jack's job became harder. Stockmen, drovers, shed hands, shop keepers, bank tellers and many others enlisted. He also had his family to care for. In early November 1914 Alberta realised she was with child again. Clara had told her the formula to work out when babies were due so she knew baby was expected on about the fourth of June. Alberta would need to be in Adelaide mid-April to be safe. Susana was deteriorating. Jack and Alberta talked for hours about what they could do. Eventually they left at the end of March and took Susana to Jamestown. Alberta was able to settle her ma as the nuns also found a room for Alberta to stay with Len. Jack returned to Mount Leonard as soon as possible.

Alberta was in Jamestown on 25th April when the Gallipoli landing happened. She felt someone had walked on her grave. The carnage in Europe was too awful to take in but it got worse. From February 1915 to January 1916 was the Gallipoli campaign. 60,000 Australian soldiers fought. There were 26,000 casualties and 8,000 deaths. Australia was never the same again. Some say it was Australia's coming of age. Susana had been anxious about Fred who wanted to join the army but Jack had reassured her he would not because he was an essential food producer. Alberta caught the train to Adelaide thinking that she would never see her mother again and she was right. There was a telegram waiting for her at *Penindi* saying Susana had a stroke and was unconscious. A later telegram informed her that her ma had passed away on the 26th May 1915.

Alberta was distraught at her mother's death. She, Fred and their ma had been so close. She was truly a good person and Alberta's heart ached. Tides and babies, however, wait for no one, and on June 4th Mary Josephine was born.

The birth was uncomfortable and Alberta felt flat rather than elated when Mary was born. This did not go away. Clara and Alice knew she was in Adelaide and visited her. They were so worried that one of them sat with Alberta several hours a day for a week or so. She just lay there rarely talking. Her milk was not coming in as well as it should. Clara remembered Susana like this and here was Alberta, the baby, whose life she had likely saved, also distressed. Clara always had an answer and next day introduced Alberta to a smiling, happy woman who was a wet nurse she knew. This angel visited for a few days and with baby feeding better and Alberta's milk coming in things slowly improved. Alberta was still tired and afraid of something. She had always known her ma was fey and sometimes she wondered about herself.

There were other things to worry about. Mrs Scott was polite and generous but Alberta felt no warmth from her. Mr Scott was different but he was away most of the day. The weather was cold but Alberta enjoyed walking up and down Norwood Parade and Hindley Street and picturing Jack playing football at PAC. She loved playing with Len who often wanted to hug Mary but that did not work out so well, but it was all good fun. She often went to the Kent Town Methodist Church on Sundays but on her walks visited Catholic churches as well. Mrs Scott did raise the idea of the children being raised as Methodists as that would be better for them. Alberta did not agree.

Before she went home she was having tea in the parlour with Mrs Scott and two of her neighbours when Mary cried so Alberta went to soothe her. When she returned and neared the parlour, the door was ajar. She heard one of the ladies who was hard of hearing yell. 'Well you know what Rachel Henning said about the Irish?' and they all laughed. It so happened that Alberta did know what she said about the Irish. It was something like, 'The Irish are dirty, keep them in the kitchen don't let them in the dining room.' Alberta was too quick for these genteel ladies and as she walked in said, 'I heard you mention Rachel Hemming. I have read her book and I often use her recipes when we are having guests at the station. I must return to my baby. Thank you for your company and best wishes.' Next day she left. Mrs Scott, with a smile that would curdle milk bid her farewell. A cheerful Mr Scott loaded her luggage into the buggy and took her to the station where he organised a porter to take care of her belongings. He carried Len and Mary to the train and firmly shook Alberta's hand and thanked her for using their home to bring her babies into the world. He added 'Please tell Jack we love him and he has a bonnie lassie and if ever she needs me I will be here.' Alberta gave him a big hug and kissed him on the cheek and added 'I will and thank you' and boarded the train, a babe on each arm.

She returned to Hergott where Jack was waiting. They stayed at that lovely pub and headed home with stops at Dulkaninna, Birdsville and Miranda.

# 51
## 1916-1918

The stations were working well. World War 1 was still raging and Alberta was with child again. She had no problems with her previous babies and explained to Jack that having to take two babies with her to Adelaide and bring three back would be difficult. Most important was that she did not feel comfortable in Jack's mother's house and certainly would be less welcome after her comments about Rachel Hemming. She and Jack decided to have the baby at Mount Leonard and made the arrangements for a midwife to come in early December for the baby expected in late December. Alberta carried on with her babies, chores and accounting for the business. She was more relaxed than when she had to go to a strange place and be away from home for so long. She literally whistled while she worked.

In late November they received a letter from the midwife to tell them she had to look after a mother with unexpected twins and damage from their birth and would not be able to attend Alberta at Mount Leonard. In theory Jack could have driven her to Hergott to catch the train but the headwaters of the Diamantina had rain so the Track could be a problem. Also there had been summer rains in South Australia and the Ghan was often derailed. They chose to stay at the station.

When she came into labour he rode as fast as he could to get the neighbour's wife. On his return he found Alberta sitting on their bed tying the cord and Old Polly holding Jean Marie. So all ended well. It was 29th December 1916.

*Jean Marie, aged 3.*

Soon after Jean was born Fred Tucker enlisted in the 50th Battalion of the Australian Army in Adelaide on January 8th, 1917. He joined in South Australia because Jack's family came from there and his, Jack's and the stations' business dealings were done in Adelaide. It was also easier to get to Adelaide than Brisbane. Jack had tried to stop him as his work was producing food. Alberta was devastated as she was close to him and had only just lost her mother. He was adamant and eventually was sent to fight in Europe.

In 1918 Alberta was with child again and went to Adelaide and stayed in a house owned by a Mr Maddern in the eastern suburbs of Adelaide. Clare Delores was born in Adelaide on March 7th, 1918. Jack wrote to her on June 13th in a jocular tone, 'You are taking the house for another two months. You will be getting to be quite a townie. Ah, how you would like to live down there in Adelaide.' On July 9th Jack wrote and was confused about her wanting to stay longer and suggested it would be good for her to do so. She would miss the heat of summer and the additions to the homestead and 'That it would not be nice for you and the kiddies.' He went on to write, 'By your letter you seem to be little annoyed & say that you could live without me. Jess dear, don't be silly as I don't want to live without you.' There were more of the same caring words. He appeared to use Jess short for Jessamine as an endearment. On 19th August he wrote again pleading for a wire to let him know if and when she would be coming home.

On September 13th, 1918 Fred, her beloved brother, was killed in the Battle of The Hague on the Hindenburg Line. 'Shot in the face with an exploding bullet.' Alberta was still tense and sad from her mother's death, depressed and worn out with the extra baby and afraid of what trouble Dennett, who she had seen near her house with a woman, might do to her or her children. The thought of what an 'explosive bullet' would do to Fred's beautiful face would not leave Alberta day or night. She was at the end of her tether physically and mentally and alone in Adelaide with four children. She sought solace in her church and her mother's memory. She had lost her brother but still had a husband whose love and care for her was blatantly obvious. She had him to share her problems and grief. Her ma had no one to share hers so long ago.

*Frederick Leslie Tucker*
*Born: 20 March 1889, Ballarat, Vic*
*Died: 13 Sept 1918, France*
*Buried: Villers-Bretonneux Memorial, Picardie, France*

She was depressed at the thought of returning to the station and living in a dirt floored four roomed old stone building. It was hard enough with three children and now she had four. She wondered if she had not grizzled so much would anything have been done about the house at all. As it was, Jack had to make a fuss to get four rooms added to the new house rather than the three the firm had suggested. The additions to be done by a man from Charleville, would cost more than 700 pounds. That was something to look forward to but she found it hard to get enthusiastic about anything.

One day on a walk with her brood around the racecourse, a thought popped into her head and she sat on a bench to muse. She had accepted her role at the station but it had grown with the new properties and development of Mount Leonard. There was more income for sure, but it also meant more men, more rations and more work for her as did a fourth child. The ringers and any other workers, black or white got rations every week of flour, sugar, tea, tobacco and salt to go with meat. Everyone could buy other things from the store such as jams and pickles. The Aboriginals usually had wives and children so more rations and work for her when children or adults got ill or were injured. She had been struggling with her bookwork, running the house and looking after babies. Now it would be so much harder.

This depressed her more but now she at least knew what her problem was; a large straw had broken a small camel's back! About a week later she wrote a long letter to Jack saying that she would not be home for Christmas and would not do so at all until the house was finished. Nor would she return unless she had a girl and a bloke to help with the huge amount of stores and rations that they would have to handle. Jack replied as soon as he could, agreeing to everything.

Alberta used her new energy to order furniture and fittings for the new house from Harris Scarfe in Adelaide and then, with the children, spent a sombre Christmas with her in laws at *Penindi,* as was their custom. It was obvious that Mr Scott had put his foot down and Mrs Scott was much friendlier to Alberta and the children. There was no more talk of raising the children as Protestants. The hatchet really was buried when Mr and Mrs Scott took the older children out at least two days a week while Alberta was making up her mind what to do. They gave her the space to think.

Time is a healer and by March she was healing. She had dreams, not nightmares, Clare was nearly one, the summer was nearly over, the new house finished and above all she missed Jack. It was time to go home.

# 52

# The Last Lap – 1919-1920

Alberta left Adelaide for Mount Leonard in early March 1919. Mr Scott happily helped her with the large task of getting the belongings and clothing of the four children and herself together with the detritus of living in Adelaide for a year to the train station and onto the train. It was a long, hard, dreary, hectic, hot and uncomfortable trip. She was physically tired beyond belief but when the train rattled into the Flinders Ranges their beauty had a soothing effect on her. Though tired, she was pleased to be heading home. When the train reached Hergott, or Marree as it was now called because Hergott was a German name, her tiredness was of little consequence when she saw her Jack. He had a huge smile and was hopping from one foot to another like a frisky colt. She knew he loved and treasured her as his letters had always shown. The little ones were all over Jack and Alberta joined them. As always Jack was well organised and had their third T Model Ford all ready to go. He loaded it with essentials and decanted the rest from the train to the storage shed to follow by camel.

Alberta had written to Jack a few weeks before about Fred's death and as the miles passed she laid her head on his shoulder and talked about Fred's and her mother's death. She was hurting more than anyone Jack had ever seen. She showed him the communication from the Army giving him the merciless details of Fred's death. 'Shot in the face with an explosive bullet. Body not recovered'. He was Alberta's brother and Jack's best friend and business partner. The thought of that happening to such a handsome, gentle person chilled them to the bone, even in the heat. Neither of them would ever forget that day. They made the usual stops and duly arrived at Mount Leonard. Jack was never a big drinker, and neither was Alberta, but on the way they sipped and finished the bottle of Scotch Jack had in case of snakebite.

Alberta was thrilled to see Old Polly, her son Wally and Young Polly and pleased to find out the latter two would be her offsiders. There was a tangible lifting of hearts, hers and the station folks, now she was home. Jack's letters were loving and positive but at the station, Jackson Croswell told her, 'Jack was like 'e had a ferret up 'is moleskins. Jumpin' 'here and there physically and mentally. Drove everyone up the bloody wall Alberta. Now he is like a little puppy dog lyin'on his back, with his tongue hangin'out waitin 'for a bloody tickle. Good to see you, I gotta say.'

The added rooms were wonderful as was the effort Jack and Jackson had made with paint brushes, brooms and arranging the furniture, ornaments, pictures, crockery glassware and other things she had ordered in Adelaide. She knew she would have to reorganise it but that could wait. What they had done was a strong message. Jack loved her and understood the bad time she had experienced in the last year and he showed he cared. Straight away she made one room the office and another a store room both opening onto the verandah the other two for bedrooms. With the nightmare of 1918 receding and the memory of how patient and kind Jack had been and what he had done to welcome her home, she realised how lucky she was to be loved so much and it was mutual. Alberta threw herself into her work and thrived on the happy atmosphere and the financial success that she had helped create. She soon had the books and all the other things she had to do sorted out and running smoothly. Jack was the same, everything and he were 'tickety-boo.'

A year later Jack's parents wrote to them and said that the house where Alberta had stayed so long in Rose Park was for sale. Jack and Alberta thought very seriously about this. Alberta had benefitted from her mother's, Fred's and Bill's mother's wills and Jack was earning good money and had some savings so they decided to go ahead and buy 14 Alexandra Avenue, Rose Park.

They had planned on going to Adelaide in June for the end of the financial year station business so that worked out well. They could kill two birds with one stone. Alberta had enquired about Fred's effects and contacted the Victoria Barracks in Melbourne and arranged for them to be sent to her new address in Adelaide where they arrived on the 7th July 1920. They left for home a few days later with sad hearts as it reinforced the reality of Fred's death.

Alberta was with child again and not surprisingly chose to have her baby in Longreach, 270 miles away, rather than in Adelaide or to rely on a midwife again. Alberta was busy getting her things ready for Longreach and found an unopened parcel in the office addressed to her. It was the journal her mother had written and finished somehow in her misty world at Jamestown and the dear nuns had it bound and had posted it. There was a note on the frontispiece of the book in her mother's hand.

*To dearest May, Fred and Alberta.*

*'I hope this somehow conveys the love and pride I have in my Irishness, my parents, my husband, you and my grandchildren to come. Your ma.'*

In another hand was.

*'To you Alberta. You are the one to carry on. Love May'*

Alberta sat in a chair and held the book without opening it further. She made the decision to read the book when she was alone, before or after her baby came, who, if a girl, she would be Susana.

Jack drove Alberta and the children to Longreach where they stayed at the convent and the older children went to school. She and Jack wrote to each other almost every day but the postage was unreliable. She had one letter from Jack where he wrote, 'Jessie you say you have no letters from me but you know I write every day if I can. I have four letters from you all in the same post. It is a d--- nuisance. I am glad you and the kiddies are well. Love Jack'

Alberta knew Jack was worried because the firm had bought 1100 cattle from Walga Station near Urandangi on the Northern Territory border, 116 miles southwest of Mount Isa and he had not heard what had happened to them. Alberta received a letter from Jack on 13th November. There had been rains in November and Jack wrote, 'It is still raining like old Harry. Will have a big flood' and further, 'Total rain in one fall six inches thirty points. The biggest flood I have ever seen.'

In the same letter he wrote that 'Perce Hudd is going to Townsville. He might call and see you in Longreach.'

On 9th of December Frederick Albert Scott was born.

On 19th December in another letter Jack described 'Good rains right down to Marree' and confirmed that the Hudds would visit her.

Alberta was lying in at the convent waiting to go home and becoming increasingly anxious. The bush telegraph knew the Channel Country was in flood and Jack was waiting for cattle from the other side of the flooded Diamantina and undoubtedly worried about the cattle. Alberta and the children were guests at the convent for Christmas and the children had a wonderful time with lollies, presents and Father,(Mother actually) Christmas.

Next day Alberta was struck with a desperate foreboding. 'Mother of God please make it too much Christmas dinner, don't let it be me Irishness knowing something bad has happened.' Late on the night of the 27th December the Hudds visited very late and gave her a letter, dated 26th December from Jack that she opened after they had feft. It was chatty, and loving with ten 'kisses,' more than he had sent before.

The letter was long and had much tosh and small talk but there were lines that froze her very soul.

*Got a wire from Sinclair last night*

*Am advised Easdon (a drover) left Walgra steers Cluny (a station near Bedourie 100 miles away) no explanation send men enquire immediately.*

*So, Alberta I am starting with Joe Thompson for Cluny today. Easdon must be blocked by flood waters.'*

Alberta fainted and knocked over a chair. A young nun came to help. Alberta woke from the faint and sat cross legged on the floor with her head bowed and when she looked up the nun noticed her dead expressionless eyes as she said 'My husband is dead' and started making a repeated high pitched wailing noise.

The young nun ran trembling and fetched the Mother Superior who knelt next to Alberta and held her as the heart-rending wailing continued. The nun, frightened asked 'What is it Mother?' Her reply was, 'It is keening my child, the lament for the dead by us Irish. 'But Mother how does she know?' asked the nun. The older woman looked at the young one, crossed herself and

314

whispered. 'Because she is fey, now let us have no more of this. We need to look after our grieving sister.'

Alberta keened for an hour or more and then collapsed and slept for most of the night, only being responsive when Fred was put to her breast. She slept until lunch time and in the afternoon a policeman came to the convent. He showed her his notebook where he had written. 'On the Dec 26th Jack Scott and Joe Thompson had ridden into the fast flowing 60 yard wide first tributary of the Diamantina River. Joe said that Jack's horse reared and fell backwards. Jack fell off and despite Joe's efforts he was swept downstream. Being a non-swimmer, he would not have survived. After an exhausting and unsuccessful search for Jack's body Joe had a day's ride to Beetoota police station and raised the alarm.' He added that the police and Mount Leonard hands were looking for Jack's body.

The Mother Superior insisted that she stay until she was well enough to face the physical and mental blows ahead. 'Let me put it this way Alberta, you need rest until Jack is found and at home you will not rest. Please stay here, we can help when others cannot'.

Alberta agreed. Jack was found six days later at Monkira Station and buried there in the presence of police who reported to the coroner. This place is known as Scott's Grave. Next day Jackson Croswell, with heavy heart drove to Longreach picked up Alberta and the five children and drove them home with an overnight stay at the Windorah pub. All the way Alberta clutched Susana's re-wrapped and still unread journal to her breast.

It was all a blur to her but the day before Alberta left Jackson Crosswell spoke to her privately and gave her a small package. It held Jack's faded, torn, frayed and stained embroided neckerchief she had made for him so long ago. Jackson had washed, folded and ironed it and wrote a card with the words. *Alberta, he did wear it every day, I know. He truly loved you. Jackson*

Alberta took the precious cloth in both hands and held it to her bosom. Tears welled as she looked at Jackson and whispered, 'It must have been very hard for you. Thank you so, so much Jackson' and for the first time since that dreadful day, tiny though it was, she smiled through her tears. Jackson gently touched her cheek at the doorway and said, 'It has been a privilege to have known such special people. I will never forget you. May God bless you' opened the door and walked out of Alberta's life but not her heart.

Sinclairs and Scotts did everything they could to help Alberta's return to Adelaide. It was a tiring, sad and desperate period and took six weeks or more for Alberta, the children and possessions to be settled at *Penindi* in Adelaide and then her new home. She had got her wish to live near the Adelaide city shops, the Victoria Park Racecourse, The Queen's Home and the Britannia Pub.

She raised her family in that home and died nearby at the home of her daughter Jean in 1956.

Leonore, Alberta's granddaughter, remembers hearing her rasping breathing that stopped for many seconds and then started again, seemingly going on forever. She also remembers saying to her father, 'Please do not tell me Nana is dead. Please say she has died.' The inevitable happened and Nana was at peace.

Later that night Leonore saw Venus and a new moon through a gap in the canopy of a gum tree. Venus was cuddled into the moon's curvature as if the moon was holding her close. The message was clear. Leonore's Irish genes spoke and she heard them, 'The battle is over Alberta. You be comin' home now.'

*Alberta's 50th Birthday*
*Standing: Len, Mary, Jean, Clare and Fred.*
*Alberta seated with Clare's dog, Shep.*

*Leonore's family (the Sullivans) enjoying a picnic in the 1950s.*

*From Left: Susan, Tim, Leonore, Michael Jnr, Jean holding Simon,*
*Jacqueline, Michael Snr holding John.*

*Leonore and our two daughters at a 'Fashion through the Ages'
function to celebrate South Australia's Sesquicentenary in 1986.
From left: Sarah, wearing Alberta's wedding gown; Kirstin
wearing Jean's gown; Leonore wearing her own wedding gown –
and she did again at our Golden Wedding Anniversary in 2019.*

# FROM THE AUTHOR

Leonore's mother, Jean, bought us a magnificent sideboard almost 50 years ago. On it are two china urns from the Mount Leonard sideboard and head and shoulders portraits of Alberta and Jack. Alberta has a mass of beautiful hair that I understand was auburn, like her mother's. She is pretty and looks into the camera. She has a knowing, mysterious and quizzical look hiding a smile.

Jack, on the other hand is more obvious. He looks past the camera with that 1000-yard stare. He seems a determined, confident and fearless looking bloke who would bristle easily and not suffer fools gladly. There is much in his letters to Alberta about what was happening at the station when she was in Adelaide and one gave me a real measure of the man. 'Tom Kidman is here. He is going to put up a wire yard at Moola. I will be jolly pleased when he has gone. He wastes too much of my time talking, can't get away from him, he is one perpetual talk all day.'

This book describes many events. The salient facts about Susana, Alberta and their families are known and take place on a realistic background of history and geography in Ireland and Australia. Most, if not all, of the stories are true but some happened at other times and in other places to other people. Lastly there are many things that could have happened.

We have more than 20 letters from Jack and Fred to Alberta

that her children Mary and Clare kept and their niece Jacqueline typed from the originals. They are a treasure trove. It is crystal clear that Fred, Jack and Alberta were close and loving kin. I find that comforting as there were many brutal men in those places and times. In the 1930s, at a neighbouring property, a woman shot and killed her husband for unspeakable cruelty to herself and her children. A jury took just 10 minutes to find her not guilty of murder.

Alberta's first child was *Len Scott* an RAAF pilot who crashed in Ambon during World War 2 and, along with his crew, was beheaded as a spy by the Japanese.

Mary, the second and Clare the fourth child never married. They served in that war on the home front and cared for their mother until she died in 1956. They both reached their seventies.

Jean, the third child married Michael Sullivan, who was sent overseas with the army soon after. Jean also served with the Red Cross in Australia. She reached her 80th year and Michael 102nd. They had seven children including my wife Leonore. Mary and Clare were devoted to Jean's family.

The last child was Fred who worked in the north of South Australia at a number of jobs. He had health problems and died relatively young leaving a wife and four children.

On a happier note, Susana's first child, May, became a Saint Joseph nun, Sister Dolorosa, and taught at St. Josephs School in Port Lincoln. Len flew Jean in his Tiger Moth to visit her before World War 2. As children Leonore and her siblings had to write letters to Aunty May. She was a feared and brutal marker. Decades later our four children went to that very school.

Alice Haylock was true. She was the mother of Ray Whitrod, Australia's and I believe the British Commonwealth's most decorated police officer. Alice's mother Clara lived in the south west corner of the City of Adelaide where Ray was born, presumably delivered by Clara. That house was about two miles from Alberta's home in Rose Park so it was likely they met. The source for Clara's and Alice's stories is Ray Whitrod's autobiography, *Before I Sleep,* my friend and writer Rory 33Barnes helped him complete and win that race. I was privileged to learn so much from him about the extraordinary lives of Clara Haylock, her daughter Alice and grandson Ray.

Some other odd and sods on this journey were:

Jackeroo/Jackaroo is used interchangeably and definitions vary from 'An impoverished colonist' to 'sons of pastoralists learning their trade.'

*Robbery under Arms* was a monthly serial and first printed as a single volume in1889. It has never gone out of print!

Charles Dickens did not care for Caroline Chisholm. In *The Dickens Boy* by Tom Keneally he has Dickens son, Alfred, say to his brother Edward at Mombar station, in New South Wales, 'Anyhow the guvnor parodied this Chisholm woman in *Bleak House* calling her Mrs Jellby, and though he gives her great cause, and she also has a slovenly home, uncared for children and a beaten-down husband. He didn't even like her you see, but he *believed* her.'

The Clipper ship *Molly Woodside* is permanently dry docked in Melbourne and is almost identical to the *Gauntlet,* the ship that carried Susana to these shores.

*Red Haired Mary* is an Irish song par excellence. I have only mentioned the chorus. The words are wonderful. Grace O'Hea, a nurse with who I worked, sung it many times in our home in Port Hedland

I came to know the Jolly family well who lived next door to number 14 Alexandra Ave four years after Alberta died when I was 16. I am unsure whether Alberta's daughters Mary and Clare were still at number 14 but some of their stories about cars roaring up and down in the back lane and party noises suggests that they may have been.

I have been privileged to learn and describe the achingly sad history of Leonore's family. They and many other people past and present whose paths I have crossed on this journey were special. I will remember them. We shall not see their like again.

# ACKNOWLEDGEMENTS

Firstly, thank you Leonore, my wife, now of 52 years, for her loyalty and patience. Her ability to detect what I wrote, rather than what I meant to write, was a great help.

To Jacqueline Kinloch, her sister, thanks are due for transposing 30-40 pages from letters and collecting all the family history details and memorabilia right up to the day before I wrote this. They really were the impetus for this book. Jacqueline and Michael Sullivan, their brother, joined Leonore and me on a trip to Mount Leonard two years ago. Due to work commitments it was far too rushed but better than not going at all.

I have had dedicated friends sharing my journey helping with plot selection, proof reading and grammar, some censoring and above all encouragement. In alphabetical order!!!

John Granger. A friend of many years has spent hours late at night checking and suggesting changes. He is not in a good place at the moment and taking the time he did is much appreciated.

Mary Gudzenovs. A bright cheerful enthusiastic scholar and writer and immediate past president of the Eyre Writers. Always helpful and encouraging. She put the book together

Brian Mills, the pedant's pedant. Unbelievable knowledge and attention to minute detail.

Aileen Pluker. A teacher still, once of our children, now of me! The youngest 90 year old I know and a brilliant writer. So clear and to the point. Leonore suggested some of the narrative should be censored or culled. I appealed to Mrs P. Verdict Not guilty. Publish and be dammed.

I am fortunate that many other people also helped me describe the lives of station people. They were 'Chook' and Lorraine Kath, the managers of Mount Leonard, Jane Benson the daughter of Bob Wilson from Wertaloona, David Brook in Birdsville, the late John Bryson, aka 'Salt Water Jack', ex Channel Country station manager Bill Napier and my longtime friend Dick Bagshaw. A particular thanks to writer Bill Marsh, who in half an hour, set me on the path to writing books when I had been procrastinating for years. I am proud to say we have become good friends.

Brian and Pam Murray have been close friends of ours for almost 50 years. Most of what I know about station life is largely due to them and they contributed much before and during the writing of this book.

I was fortunate to contact Peter Beirne at the library in County Clare Ireland. He laid the foundation for the story.

Jonno Coffs from the tourist centre and Bernie from the National Trust's Pringle Cottage in Warwick had a major effect on the Warwick section. Paul Munson contributed mightily telling us about and showing us Mullers' Oddfellows Home Hotel. It was wonderful to literally touch it, still in remarkable shape. The shepherd's hut at Pringle Cottage is also worth going a long way to see.

My special insider mate Michelle Dillon at the Diamantina Shire Office in Bedourie sniffed out all sorts of bits and pieces. Thank you Michelle.

Louise Mrdjen and her staff at the Port Lincoln Library were unfailingly kind, interested and courteous with my many requests for books and other information. Please accept a blanket thank you as I doubt I would remember everyone's name and that would be unfair!

www.ingramcontent.com/pod-product-compliance
Lightning Source LLC
Chambersburg PA
CBHW070055120726
47909CB00002B/393